DROPKICKS AND DANDELIONS

TITAN WRESTLING

VAL SIMONS

AUTHOR'S NOTE

This book deals with the emotional fallout of grief and features the on-page death of a side character.

∼

While I was writing Headlocks and Heartbreak, my father was sick. I was hopeful about his prognosis at first, but unfortunately, he died ten days before the book was released. He never got to read it.

I was in the process of writing Niall and Amit's book when he died, and I lost all motivation to tell their story. It was too light and needed too much banter for me to do a good job, so I abandoned that project, shifting instead to Kenji and Gordon's story.

To say writing this book has been therapeutic for me would be a massive understatement. It has, quite literally, kept me from falling apart. Finishing their story has been bittersweet, because it feels like I'm losing something all over again. As you read this book, I hope you can feel the love I have for my dad. If you have lost someone close to you, I hope you find yourself here. Grief is lonely, but you're not alone.

Thanks for giving this book a shot, and thanks for all the kindness you've showed me over the months since H&H's release.

Love,
   Val

PS: On a less serious note, this book does *not* accurately portray the realities of any current professional wrestling promotions as far as I know, and any accuracies are coincidental. I have taken many liberties about the industry so I could tell the story I wanted to tell and create a universe where my ideas can work.

To anyone living in a world that has become permanently darker.

CHAPTER 1

"YES, SIR. I HAVE HEARD OF URINE BEING USED TO AID IN THE decomposition of compost, but I don't know if urinating directly on your plants poses the same benefit," Kenji said. He waited impatiently while the man on the other end of the phone yelled at him, frustrated that the fern he'd purchased from Kenji's aunt's shop had steadily lost its foliage for weeks until it finally died.

He glanced at the ferns he had hanging from the ceiling and felt a pang of sadness knowing the one belonging to this customer had met a harsh, drawn out, kind of gross death.

"I understand you're upset. You can compost it with the city as part of your trash pickup, included in your monthly fee. Please come in, and we can discuss a discount on another plant. ...No, please don't bring the fern. Thank you." He hung up the shop phone and put some antiseptic foam on his hands for good measure, the sharp scent of it replacing the phantom urine he smelled.

Golden light streamed in through the front window of the shop, illuminating the motes of dust swirling in the sunbeams. They would have been pretty, except their existence was a constant reminder of his inability to keep up with the dust and dirt that came along with caring for hundreds of plants. He grumbled, grabbing a feather duster to clean the leaves of a plant in the front window.

The shop, Kiko's, had been owned by his aunt for decades. Her wish was for him to inherit it someday, but he wanted to pay off the outstanding loan she had before he took it on so his aunt could retire and live out her golden years with some amount of financial security.

It had all felt impossibly distant, the loan being an amount far beyond anything he could manage on his past income. But he'd managed to land a developmental contract with Titan Wrestling, a professional wrestling promotion based in Portland, Oregon, and was finally earning enough that he was able to tuck some money away each month, slowly inching towards his goal. All it would take was a lot of time, a surprising amount of food, and a willingness to abuse his body, and in a few years, he'd have enough saved.

It would happen even faster if he could land a contract with CWA, the country's largest wrestling promotion, but those were hard to come by. He was going to try, though, because the thought of competing at the highest level *and* retiring his aunt was too tempting to ignore.

Until recently, he'd often pictured himself quitting wrestling permanently to spend his days watering, pruning, and potting—and running a business, of course, but spreadsheets and insurance quotes weren't exciting daydream fodder. But in the last year, he'd been landing more matches thanks to his boss, Mike, who formed Titan after a lengthy, successful wrestling career with CWA. The level of attention he was getting from the public was exhilarating, and his skills in the ring had improved enough that Mike was beginning to pour serious money into Kenji's growth.

The thought of a quiet life, one where he sat peacefully at a plant shop, tending to customers and scanning spreadsheets, was harder to imagine now. Not when the alternative was an even better version of what he was already experiencing.

He was bending over to pick at a spot of something sticky on the wide paddle leaf of a banana plant when he heard the door chime. Kiko's was closing in a few minutes, and he had a televised match starting just a few hours later. He'd been hoping to get a quick workout in before he went on, so when he saw the man who'd stepped into the shop holding a paper list, he sighed. It wasn't common for customers to come in with a list of plants, and the ones who did tended to be... difficult.

"Hello!" he said, smiling as looked up to greet the customer. Kenji's breath caught when he saw the man who stood before him. He was unbelievably gorgeous, wearing a t-shirt, *with a plant on it,* and shorts that showed a generous amount of thigh. The man's eyes literally sparkled from the grow lights Kenji had placed strategically around the room, and it may have been the dust Kenji couldn't keep up with, but he swore he saw him wink. "Can I help you find anything?"

"Hi there," he said. "I am looking for a few plants. I'm new to the city and my neighbor said your shop is the best, so I'm hoping you can help me." He held up the list.

"Of course. Let's see what you've got there." Kenji moved closer, holding the man's gaze and trying to rein in his intensity. He took the list from the man's hands—hands that were gorgeous, with neatly trimmed nails, smooth skin, and a distinct lack of a wedding band. "Wow, you have some rare stuff on here. What is it you're doing with these guys?"

"I wish I had a cooler answer, but the truth is that I just love plants. I lost a few in the move. I put a star next to those.

I'll be taking them myself next time, you just can't trust moving companies with anything like that."

"I totally get it. I'd be devastated if I lost some of the plants I have at home," he said, smiling. "I'm Kenji, by the way."

"Rob," he said, his voice warm as he extended his hand to Kenji's. He held Kenji's hand with an unexpected gentleness, but firm enough to send a tingle up Kenji's arm.

"It's very nice to meet you."

Rob leaned his elbow on the desk and grinned down at Kenji, who was a head below him, seated on a stool. "Likewise."

Kenji was sweating, and strands of his black hair plastered themselves to his forehead. Was it warm? It was summer, so probably. But Kenji didn't react this way to men, ever. He'd been a happy bachelor for his entire adult life, save for a few attempted relationships here and there, none of which lasted more than a few months. And he was fine with that. But something about this guy made him feel all tingly.

Ignoring his body's reaction as best he could, Kenji focused his eyes on the computer screen in front of him and grabbed a tissue to dab at his forehead, hoping Rob didn't mind the sheen covering his face. He typed away, making a list of plants, identifying which ones were in stock and which would have to be special ordered.

"I have a few of these, but I'll have to order a bunch of others. But do you want to see the propagules I have going? I can probably find some fun stuff there you might be interested in."

"Do you have time? I know it's past closing now." Rob glanced at his phone to check the time.

"I can make time."

Near the store's back room, Kenji had set up a small nursery and propagation area for baby plants. It was bright and warm, and when he and Rob stood by the bench Kenji used to grow the plants, they were forced to stand close together.

He showed Rob the plants he'd grown himself and the special babies he was attempting to propagate with mixed success. He used words and phrasing he knew a fellow plant enthusiast would understand, and it was weirdly stimulating. Not just talking to an absurdly handsome man about something he was passionate about, but to be sharing this side of him, bonding with someone over something he didn't let most people see. Moments like that made knowing what he really wanted even more difficult. He really did love the plant store.

His coworkers knew he worked at a plant store part time, but they had no idea the current plan was for him to quit wrestling and do it full time. The only people who knew that were his aunt, Akiko, and his best friend Gordon, who loved the store as much as Kenji, and was happy to cover for him when he went out of town for work.

"So, um. Thanks for humoring me. I can really nerd out about this stuff. I've bored everyone in my life so much they run when they see me coming."

"I love it. I loved hearing about your plants. I can feel the passion," he said, rapping his knuckles on the bench next to a row of recently planted corms. "And when these guys are ready to go, I want like six of them."

Kenji couldn't help but grin as he led Rob back up to the front to complete his special order. He packed up the plants Rob had picked out, threw in a few freebies, and slid an order form across the desk.

"I just need you to fill out your name and number. I'll call or text you when they come in, and you can come pick them up."

"Perfect. It was really good to meet you, Kenji. I look forward to hearing from you."

"It was my pleasure!"

Rob winked at Kenji, a real one that time, then smiled before he stepped into the warm, summer evening.

Kenji stood still for a moment, basking in the excitement of the last few minutes, before he remembered he had things to do.

He glanced at his phone and saw that he had two hours before his match began, which meant if he hurried, he could still fit in a workout. He'd be rushed, but it was worth it to have spent half an hour with a man who not only knew what an epiphyte was, but had a favorite species.

"ANT," Kenji said, sticking his head out from behind his locker door. "I met a guy."

Anthony, Kenji's tag team partner, sat on the bench facing away from him. He didn't react, which Kenji assumed was because of the noise of the other wrestlers chatting away before the matches started. Kenji and Anthony were up second, so most of the guys were still getting ready.

"Ant!"

"Oh, sorry. What's up, man?"

"I met a guy," he repeated. "At the store, before I got here."

"Okay? You meet a guy like every day," Anthony said.

Kenji glared at him, though that wasn't really fair. Kenji did "meet" his share of guys, but he wanted Anthony to be excited about *this* one.

"No! Not that kind of meet. He came into the shop, and he said he liked my propagules and complimented my mosses. He did a special order, and we hung out for like half an hour, and we didn't discuss wrestling at all. I don't even know if he knows who I am."

Anthony's eyebrows raised slightly. "Oh."

Kenji grumbled and slammed his locker shut. He pulled on his leggings and scoffed at Anthony. "Be excited for me, asshole!"

"I'm sorry. I'm just so tired. I didn't mean to not be excited enough."

Kenji's face softened, though he still wanted Anthony to care more. But Anthony was a dad to two kids, one of which was a tiny baby, and Kenji imagined he was getting very little sleep.

"How's the family?" Kenji asked.

"Uh," Anthony said, staring off into space.

"Are you going to make it, man?"

"I don't know, to be honest." Anthony laughed. "God, this sucks. What time do we need to be out there?"

"In about thirty minutes. We go in after Will and Dicky."

"Wake me in fifteen."

THIRTY MINUTES LATER, Kenji was standing on the middle rope, climbing his way to the top turnbuckle, steadying himself when he got there. The crowd was vibrating, and he felt it flow through his body, the excitement feeding him. He took a deep breath before leaping from the ropes, landing a moonsault on his opponent before folding their leg and pinning them for the full three seconds. He launched to his feet, the official raised his arm in victory before Anthony joined him in the ring.

For just a fleeting moment, everything else melted away. The shop, his doubts, his uncertainty about the future. This was where he belonged, and he just had to figure out how to hold onto it.

CHAPTER 2

GORDON WAS ON HIS HANDS AND KNEES IN HIS KITCHEN, USING A long serving spoon to dig dry pasta out from under his stove, grumbling questions about how difficult it could possibly be to carry a box of pasta from the cabinet to the stove.

Kenji was leaning against the counter with his arms crossed, grumbling his own questions about why it was so necessary to find every individual dry noodle he'd kicked to the back of the stove when a perfectly good bug would probably come along at some point to carry it off somewhere else.

"Because I don't want bugs in my house, Kenji, that shouldn't be a difficult concept," Gordon said.

"If you think there aren't already bugs living here, you're dumber than I am."

"You know, you could help. It would be done in half the time, and you're the one who dropped the box."

"You're doing such a good job, though. And look, you're like a little seat," Kenji said. He walked over and sat down on Gordon's butt and gave it a quick pat, the touch sending a spark of electricity through Gordon's veins, which he forced himself to ignore.

"Why are you like this?" Gordon feigned annoyance, but he would die happy if Kenji just gave him a gentle tap on the ass once a day for the rest of his life.

"I'm bored. Can we go do something?"

"I am doing something. Right now. I'm cleaning up your mess."

Kenji groaned dramatically, rising to his feet before walking into the living room to stare out the window. "What if we go for a hike?"

Gordon looked into the living room and saw Kenji watching a squirrel seated on the rock wall in front of his house. He had a tiny, dreamy smile on his face and Gordon wanted to use the dry pasta in his hands to poke his own eyes out.

"Okay, we can do that. I'll go get changed as soon as I'm done."

Pasta cleaned up, Gordon walked through the living room towards his bedroom. He caught a glimpse of Kenji, still at the window, looking like a cruel joke the universe played on the rest of humanity.

He took a mental snapshot and kept moving, ignoring the way the sun reflected off Kenji's long, shiny, black hair and the way the blue color of the walls complemented his dark brown eyes. He refused to dwell on the way Kenji leaned against the armchair and how it accentuated the curve of his butt, or whether the shorts Kenji was wearing—weirdly short and obscenely snug—would stretch against it on their hike.

One would think that after ten years, the unrequited feelings Gordon had for his best friend would have grown stale, freeing him from the very hot, very sweet prison Kenji unknowingly kept him locked in. But they hadn't. If anything, the last year or two of their lives had caused his feelings to grow and settle into permanence.

Kenji had moved out of his apartment when Mike decided to send him out of town more often because he'd wanted to be able to care for his ailing aunt when he could. Now he split his time between Gordon's house and his aunt's house, which meant more time eating meals together, more chances they'd pass each other in the morning as they got ready, more days Gordon would come home and find Kenji asleep in his bed— because Kenji preferred the softer sheets.

The two of them usually hiked the trails in Forest Park, but this time, they decided to venture a little farther out of town to a more challenging trail. Kenji entertained himself on the drive by guessing what crops were growing in all the fields they passed. It was a lot of fields, and Kenji was almost always wrong, which was weird, considering how much he knew about plants.

"Indoor plants and agricultural crops are worlds apart, Gordon," he'd said.

When they finally arrived at their destination, Gordon stood and stretched his arms back, his shirt lifting slightly, temporarily exposing his round, fuzzy belly. Kenji did the same, and Gordon couldn't help but laugh at the difference in their bodies. But Kenji didn't notice. He just seemed happy to be there.

"What's funny?"

"Nothing. Just thinking about how out of shape you are."

Kenji laughed. "Totally. Speaking of which, if I break an ankle up there, can you get me back down?"

"Do you ask all your hiking buddies that question, or just the fat ones?"

"Believe it or not, I do ask all of them. Asshole." Kenji kicked at Gordon, who was bending down to tie his shoe.

Gordon grinned at him from his crouched position. "Well,

sadly, I can't carry you down a mountain. I'll have to leave you to the coyotes. I think they hunt in pairs or small groups, though. It'll be a swift death."

"I don't think two coyotes would be swift at all, Gordon." He looked a little worried.

"I'm not going to leave you up there. Plus, isn't this hike like six miles? I think we'll be fine."

Kenji gave him a relieved smile. "I trust you." He glanced up at the trail and Gordon saw his eyes scan the horizon where the sun was already on its way down.

Yes, they probably should have left earlier, but Kenji asked to stop by the store before they left, and then he asked if they could stop by the rock museum they passed on the highway. As much as he tried, Gordon just couldn't say no to Kenji.

Gordon stood up after tying his shoe and stretched his legs, readying himself for the hike. He was fat, yes, but he was also strong. He enjoyed hiking and being out in the sun, and Kenji was a great hiking partner for a variety of reasons.

For example, he was very fit, so he kept Gordon motivated. He was also very strong, so if Gordon broke *his* ankle, Kenji could help him down the mountain. And, as a bonus, he looked really good in those weirdly small shorts that Gordon was happily following to the top of the trail.

On the way up the mountain, Kenji, not at all breathless and excited about nature, pointed out his favorite native plants. Gordon, very breathless and could not care less about plants, pretended to be interested.

It wasn't hard, though. Kenji made everything more interesting.

They reached the summit within an hour or so, right after the sun started to set. A wooden bench had been placed just off the trail, allowing hikers to sit and appreciate the view. The two of them sat and ate snacks while they watched the sun continue its descent behind the hills and mountains to the west, and Gordon wished, like he did most days, he could just turn his feelings off.

CHAPTER 3

THE KIKO'S STOREFRONT CAME INTO VIEW AS KENJI CROSSED THE street after his workout at the arena. Akiko was putting a sandwich board outside offering a BOGO sale on four-inch potted plants—something he'd suggested weeks ago when his nursery started overflowing with young seedlings. The sight of the sign eased his nerves somewhat. His aunt's confidence in this small suggestion made him feel more assured in the future of running the shop.

"Obachan!"

"Kenji-kun, what do you think of my sign?" She beamed at him, her slightly wrinkled cheeks pulled up into a smile.

"I think it's great! I can't wait to watch all those little guys get new homes today."

He held the door for her and after they entered the shop, and Kenji spotted a whole pile of plants behind the desk.

"Is that the special order for Rob?"

"Yes, it just came in today. I tried calling but didn't get an answer. I have to run some errands before the bank closes. Can you reach out to the customer?"

She dug through her purse, looking for her keys. Kenji

noticed the age spots on her hands and watched her soft, thin skin rub against the zipper, which left white marks on her skin from the teeth.

Akiko was sick, and as much as he tried to stay optimistic, he sensed she hadn't been completely honest with him about her prognosis. She'd always been strong and independent, almost to the point that it was frustrating to him and Gordon. She refused to let them go with her to doctor appointments and stayed quiet about any details.

As time passed, Kenji began to notice little things that worried him. Her feet shuffled a little more slowly through the shop, her voice was weaker when she spoke to customers. Every reminder of her fragility settled like a rock in his stomach because he had to deal with watching her slow down while his interest in taking over the shop faded. It wasn't just the mounting pressure he struggled with, it was the realization that he might not reach those goals in time before... Well, before it didn't matter if he did or not.

Akiko never complained about how long it was taking. Occasionally, he tried to tell her to sell to someone else, someone who could afford to buy it this year. But every time he suggested it, she snapped at him, saying nobody could love the store more than him, and that she didn't mind waiting until he was ready. And that was the worst part of all—she wanted him to take over so badly, he felt like he couldn't be honest about what he really wanted.

"What are you staring at me like that for? Never seen an old lady look in a purse?"

Kenji jumped at her interruption. "Sorry. Long day. I'll text the customer now. You take the day off. I've got it handled here."

She nodded at him and shuffled to the back room for a

moment before returning with a feather duster and Kenji sighed. So much for running errands.

A ray of sunlight poured in through the window, illuminating Rob's tray of ordered plants, like a sign from the heavens. He thought about taking a photo to commemorate this moment, because *what a memory for the photo album*, but then he realized some of the plants could burn from even the smallest amount of direct sunlight, so he rushed over and moved them.

After sending a quick text to Rob letting him know the plants had arrived and to head on in, he busied himself so he'd stop waiting for a response. He snipped a tiny, brown, uncurling frond from a Boston fern hanging in the corner and frowned, thinking about the poor fern that met its untimely death. He shuddered, but was interrupted by the door chime.

Kenji's thoughts went directly to Rob. It would have been ridiculous for him to have arrived four minutes after Kenji sent the text, but whatever. He was excited! And he'd been successful in an initial propagation of a new plant and wanted to share his progress with someone who could appreciate his efforts.

He tried to calm his nerves and turned around, expecting, or just hoping, to see Rob. Instead, Gordon's smiling face was there behind the giant fern he'd just been pruning.

"Oh, hey! I wasn't expecting you," he said.

"Well, I hadn't seen you since you got back from your road trip. And I missed this lady," Gordon said, taking Akiko's hand and giving it a gentle squeeze.

Kenji grinned at them. Sometimes he suspected they loved each other more than either of them loved Kenji. He didn't mind that. In fact, it gave him a lot of peace knowing Gordon was always around when Kenji had road trips and work overnights, especially now, with Akiko's fragile health.

He was also glad Gordon had a nice woman to care for him in ways Gordon's mom never did. At least, that's what Kenji assumed. He'd never met Gordon's family, even after ten years of friendship. It wasn't clear why, other than Gordon mentioning at one point they were "dicks," but he didn't know exactly what that meant. Certainly, it couldn't be that they were mean to *Gordon*, who was, in Kenji's opinion, the best person on the planet.

Akiko pulled Gordon into the back, probably to stuff him full of the food she'd brought for lunch, and Kenji went back to work pruning. By the time he'd worked his way around the entire plant, which was about as massive as you could ever expect from a fern, he was a little sweaty from standing in the sun and his arms were surprisingly sore.

This time, when the door chimed, Rob walked in.

"Hi," Kenji breathed. It was far too sultry for a plant pick up, but oh well.

"Hi, Kenji."

"I have your plants!"

"Great," Rob said. He smiled and stepped closer to Kenji.

The two chatted about the store, Kenji pointing out new plants since the last time Rob had been there and Rob showing him pictures of the plants he already had at his apartment. Kenji felt giddy, flirting with someone who seemed to appreciate him for who he was, not who he pretended to be.

He had no problem finding dates and hookups, but it was rare for him to meet people outside of Titan-related events or apps where he used some well-curated Titan photos. It meant most people interested in him knew who he was or liked what he was about. It wasn't a bad problem to have, but it did send an extra thrill through him when he met someone in the wild.

Eventually, Kenji directed Rob to the counter where he rang up his order.

"I hope this isn't too forward, but do you want to go get a

cup of coffee or something?" Rob asked as he put his card back in his wallet.

Kenji blinked. "Right now?"

"Yeah. Sorry, I don't mean to put you on the spot. I just… didn't want to leave without asking."

"I would love to, but I'm on my way to work here in a bit."

"Work?" Rob asked, looking around the store.

"Oh, um. Yeah. Actually, let's walk and talk. I really do have to get going, but I wouldn't mind an escort."

"Sure. Lead the way."

Kenji and Rob walked towards the arena at the leisurely pace Kenji had set. They even stopped for a cup of coffee on the way. The sun was high and bright, so Kenji ordered an iced coffee, and he had to hold back a smile when he noticed Rob had ordered the same thing. It wasn't a big deal, of course, just a fun coincidence he was choosing to appreciate.

He didn't understand why his stomach was fluttering. It was just that he hadn't felt this way in years, hadn't wanted to explore where something went with someone. But for some reason, Rob was different. He was so unaffected by who Kenji was at work, it made their connection seem more sincere.

"I have to admit something," Rob said. Kenji was ready for the moment to be ruined, for Rob to say he was married or hated plants, but instead, he leaned in slightly and whispered, "I've never actually watched a full wrestling match."

He said it like it was a shameful confession, but Kenji couldn't help himself and broke into a huge grin.

∽

AKIKO ALWAYS GAVE Gordon too much food. He didn't hate it, obviously. She was a wonderful cook who just hadn't quite grasped how to cook for a normal number of people. But it was flavorful, delicious food, and she was always open to showing him how to prepare it, so he didn't complain.

Occasionally, though, she would push him to eat when he really didn't want to. He hated the thought of hurting her feelings, so he ate his fill until eventually he had to stop, wishing he could come up with a better excuse than "I'm not hungry." At least Kenji had the excuse that he ate a strict diet most of the time, but she knew Gordon didn't operate that way, and she took full advantage of that.

He'd come to Kiko's intending to ask Kenji to help him with building a larger enclosure for his iguana, Peony, but Kenji had been busy trimming a plant. So Gordon, unable to say no to Akiko, had found himself whisked into the kitchen instead. It was okay, though—he'd heard the door chime a couple of times, so he was sure Kenji was busy with customers.

Besides, Gordon wanted to spend as much time as possible with Akiko because of her health, because while she hadn't shared any specifics, he suspected their time was limited. So, sitting with her, letting her fuss over him, and being force fed a delicious meal, was no hardship for Gordon. He patted his belly, thanking her for the meal, and pushed his worries from his mind.

"Are you here to sweep my Kenji-kun off his feet?"

Gordon laughed and she smiled at him. As if Gordon had that ability. As if he hadn't been hoping for years that he'd gather the strength to make that happen.

"I wish." He smiled at her sadly. "I wanted to take him to the lumber store with me, actually. Peony needs more room."

"Inside?"

"Yes. It's too cold here for him to live outside."

"I don't know why you bought that thing."

Gordon scoffed. "He's not a thing. He's a very nice lizard."

"Still," she said, offering to scoop more food onto his plate. He sighed and put his hand up to stop her.

"Kenji can't be around animals with fur," he said, quietly.

Akiko nodded in understanding, patting him on the shoulder before taking the empty dishes to the sink. When she returned, she slipped her hand around Gordon's arm and led him to the main part of the store. Her grip was light, and Gordon slowed his pace to allow her to keep up with him. He pretended not to notice how thin she'd gotten or how deliberately she moved.

They walked through the curtained doorway and Gordon expected to see Kenji there, hoping, maybe foolishly, he'd have time to go to the store with him before work. But the shop was quiet aside from the front door opening. The door chime jingled, drawing his attention to the doorway, and he saw something that felt like a knife to the gut.

A man, handsome and nicely dressed in a suit, with his jacket draped over his arm, was holding the door open with one hand and guiding Kenji out with the other. Neither Kenji nor the mystery man noticed Gordon or Akiko, and they took off down the street together.

Gordon's stomach sank and he must have made some sort of noise, because Akiko stepped closer to him and rubbed gentle, reassuring circles on his back.

"It's okay," she said.

Gordon nodded.

"We don't know who that is. It could be someone from Titan."

"Yeah. Could be," Gordon said, returning to the storeroom so he could start the dishes they'd put in the sink. He turned around, forgetting he'd left Akiko alone, but she'd already made her way back.

"Gordon-san," she said, sitting down at the table.

"Yeah?"

"Come sit with me."

"Okay."

It's not that Gordon didn't appreciate what Akiko was about to do. It's just that it was the same conversation every time. She'd tell him to be patient, but then tell him not to wait around for Kenji if someone else came along. She'd tell him Kenji really did love him, he just didn't realize it yet. All things that, years ago, fed his hope. Things that would keep him going when he felt like he couldn't handle another night of going to Kenji with bars, watching him disappear with men and returning later, just in time for them to head home and watch TV.

But now, all these years later, it just felt like a joke. An endless loop of promises he knew he shouldn't believe, but that he couldn't force himself to ignore.

"Do you want me to make you some tea?" he asked. "I got a new one. This one has toasted rice in it. I don't know if that's good or not."

"Sure."

He started the kettle and sat down next to Akiko, ready for whatever she was going to say.

"Kenji-kun is…"

Sweet. Warm. Driven and tenacious.

"He is oblivious."

Gordon burst out laughing.

"I don't think he is," Gordon said. "He's having a good time. That's okay."

"He is. But he loves you. He doesn't realize yet, how deep that love goes. But it's there, idle and waiting."

"I don't think it matters anymore."

She nodded. "I can't blame you for feeling that way. But I hope I am around to see the day he wakes up."

CHAPTER 4

KENJI CHECKED HIS PHONE FOR THE THIRD TIME SINCE HE'D arrived at the arena twenty minutes ago, his thumb swiping down on his email app to refresh his inbox, like maybe this time it would provide more information. Mike had set up a meeting with him and Anthony before their match started, which was unusual on its own, but the cryptic dribbles of information made it even more anxiety provoking.

He was pretty sure he wouldn't get released from his contract at the same time as Anthony, so he held onto that.

There was no additional information about the meeting, but he did receive a text from Rob asking if he wanted to get drinks later.

They'd been out twice since Rob had picked up his plants, and Kenji was really excited about it. He hadn't told Gordon yet, partly because Gordon was never particularly thrilled when he brought up guys he was seeing, but also... well, actually, that was kind of the only reason.

It was like Gordon knew none of his relationships would work out, and sure, that was always true, but it was embarrassing to bring up at this point. But things with Rob felt different! Kenji was excited and wanted to share that with his best friend, so he planned on telling him about it when they had dinner after his match.

Kenji looked up from his phone and saw Anthony sneak out of the room.

"Ant! Wait up!"

Kenji jogged to catch up with Anthony, who was already turning the corner from the locker room into the long hallway leading to the front lobby. It felt like it took a year to catch up to Anthony. His long legs and incessant need to do everything quickly and efficiently launched him miles away from Kenji within seconds. Kenji once counted how many tiles Anthony's strides cleared, and it was an unbelievable *six* to Kenji's much more reasonable four.

"You must have great cardiovascular health," he wheezed as he walked towards Anthony.

"I mean, I would hope you do, too," Anthony said, one eyebrow raised. He waited with his hands on his hips before glancing at his watch.

"You wear a watch?" Kenji asked.

"Yes."

"Nerd."

"Okay. Sorry I want to know what time it is sometimes, I guess? It also counts my steps. And I can read texts on it. Really, Kenji, have you never heard of a smart watch?"

Kenji didn't answer as he caught up to Anthony. The hallway leading to the offices was stretched out before them, its walls lined with photos of past Titan champions, frozen in victory. There was showcase lighting reflecting off old title belts and medals that Kenji hoped to earn one day, and he knew Anthony wanted it just as badly as he did—to be memorialized behind glass, untouchable and accomplished. Just being in the hallway lifted his spirits.

But, of course, any time he felt himself get excited about wrestling, the weight of the shop there to pull him back from the edge, stopping him from diving in headfirst. Akiko was waiting for him and counting on him, and that should be his priority. But God, he hoped he could find a way to do both.

But first, he had to attend the meeting. Kenji's preferred meeting would be short—Mike sharing the news that they were both chosen for CWA's annual training camp, an elite opportunity provided to only the most promising developmental talent. If selected, they'd train with CWA trainers and eventually participate in a few televised matches to showcase their skills, allowing CWA to get a read on the public's feelings towards them.

If that happened, it would be confirmation he was close to getting a CWA contract.

Unfortunately, Kenji had minor concerns that the meeting would result in the two of them being released from their Titan contracts and sent on their way to find new careers. Sure, it was unlikely, but the industry was finicky.

"Do you think it's bad?" Kenji asked Anthony, both of them staring ahead at Mike's closed office door.

Anthony didn't turn his head. "No."

"Well, whatever the news is, we're in it together. Right? I hope."

"Of course." Anthony smiled at him and raised his fist in a gesture of reassurance. Kenji bumped his knuckles against Anthony's before leaning forward and opening Mike's door.

"Knock, knock," Kenji said.

"Hey, guys! Come in. Come sit," Mike said, gesturing to the chairs in front of his desk.

"Hey, Mike," Anthony said, shaking his hand.

"I'll make this quick because I know you have a match in —" Mike glanced at his watch, "—less than an hour."

Anthony turned to Kenji, gesturing to Mike's watch with his head. Kenji glared at him.

"We do. I plan on winning tonight," Kenji said. He was the planned winner, so Anthony punched him in the arm.

Mike laughed. "Alright. Well, I have some fun news. Which is nice, because I just had to fire someone."

Kenji swallowed hard. He wondered who it was.

"Sorry, that probably wasn't appropriate. You don't know them. They work in the admin building and they kept stealing boxes of coffee. Long story. Anyway," he said, before putting on a huge smile, "the fun news is that both of you were chosen for CWA's training camp this summer. Not that I ever doubted it."

Kenji and Anthony grinned at each other and shook hands, which felt dorky, but Kenji was always nervous around Mike. He had no reason to be, Mike was great. He just really wanted Mike to keep him around, and it made him act more like Anthony, which was to say, a total square.

"That's great news, Mike, thank you so much. I can't wait to tell the kids," Anthony said, cool and calm. Very Mike-like.

"Do you think Fox will think it's cool?" Kenji asked.

"Shut up. He will, because I'm his dad, and he thinks I'm cool."

"Do babies that little have thoughts?" Kenji didn't know much about babies, but Fox seemed awfully small to give a shit about his dad's career.

Anthony and Mike laughed, but it was a genuine question. He couldn't tell if Anthony was serious. He would ask Gordon later.

"You guys head out in a couple of months, which means we'll be doing some rearranging of the schedules. Kenji, you'll be out of town more than usual leading up to it. I hope that's okay."

"Of course it is, yeah. Thank you."

"Anthony, you'll be joining him for all but one of those road trips."

"Perfect. Thank you, Mike."

"Alright, now get out of here. You start in forty minutes."

Kenji managed to contain his excitement until he heard Mike's door latch behind them, and then he let himself jump onto Anthony's back and ruffled his hair.

"I can't believe it!"

"This is wild," Anthony said. He looked happy in a way Kenji hadn't seen him in a long time. It made him smile.

Kenji was happy, too. Thrilled, really. He'd worked so hard leading up to the camp tryouts, which had only been possible because Gordon was willing to help Akiko out more, even covering some shifts at the plant store. He hoped Gordon didn't mind stepping in even more.

~

GORDON WAS ALWAYS surprised when he entered the Titan arena. It was just so much bigger than he ever remembered. The ceilings were endlessly high, there were seats for thousands of people, and in the last few years he'd had to walk longer distances from increasingly obscure, secret parking spots. There were always film crews set up by the ring and people running around with earpieces and microphones.

It was still surreal sometimes, attending matches and hearing people cheer for Kenji. He never had any doubt Kenji would become popular. In fact, Gordon knew he would eventually turn his contract with Titan into a full-time contract with CWA. Kenji claimed he wanted to quit and work at his aunt's plant store, but Gordon saw through his lies. Kenji was meant to do *this*, and everybody knew it.

The thought of Kenji someday moving to Boston, where CWA was headquartered, made Gordon a little nauseous. He hadn't lived more than five miles from Kenji since they met ten years ago, when Kenji was working part time as a barista and Gordon was studying for his master's degree. The moment he walked into the campus coffee shop and saw Kenji behind the counter, smiling and laughing with a customer before locking eyes with Gordon, his fate had been sealed.

Sadly, for Gordon, his fate was that he'd forever be in love with the person who eventually became his best friend.

As a general rule, Gordon was risk-averse, so jeopardizing what they had as friends by telling Kenji the truth about his feelings was about as unappealing as a wet sock on a cold day. They were just too close as friends, too perfectly balanced the way things were.

Well, that, and Kenji was about as far out of Gordon's league as anyone could possibly get.

But, as he often told himself, that didn't matter. Their friendship was more important than anything.

He settled into the seat Kenji had reserved for him next to the aisle. Seeing his name scribbled on the paper someone had taped to the seatback eased a little knot of discomfort in his chest. He preferred the aisle for comfort and hated being squished between people he didn't know. Gordon had mentioned his preference once, and Kenji made sure he'd never sat in a middle seat again.

Wrestling had never been part of Gordon's childhood, and while he found it totally absurd, it was also a lot of fun to watch. Greased up men throwing each other around the ring, acrobatic feats of athleticism, people freaking out over Kenji's existence in general. For Gordon, there was very little to dislike.

He leaned forward in his seat to watch the start of Kenji and Anthony's match and smiled to himself. He loved watching Kenji in any capacity, of course. But in the ring, he was transcendent, perfectly suited to the sport and the spotlight, and seeing him shine just made Gordon happy.

Even more thrilling than the action, though, was knowing Kenji wasn't just a character to him—Kenji was *his*, and the audience cheering for him would never know what they were missing. It was like a little bump of endorphins every time he thought about it.

Because while the audience loved Ken Vee, the cocky, womanizing crowd-pleaser with incredible technical skill, Gordon loved *Kenji*, the sweet, plant-loving, occasionally naïve man who once attended a work event as his date when Gordon had accidentally lied about already having one. He'd just wanted to escape an awkward dinner with his coworker and her "very single" daughter, but things had spiraled. Kenji had asked why he didn't just tell his coworker he wasn't interested, and Gordon's response was, "I panicked."

Kenji's entrance music started playing and Gordon watched him strut down the aisle. He still remembered when Kenji had asked if I'm Too Sexy by Right Said Fred was too on the nose, and… it really was. But he'd looked so pleased with himself, excited to lean into his gimmick: the sexy playboy whose charm could fool even the toughest officials into throwing a match in his favor. Gordon didn't really know what the rules were around entrance music, or if there were any, so he just told him to go for it.

Kenji had perfected his entrance by this point, ripping off

his sparkly, white vinyl vest every time the lyrics about being too sexy for his shirt came on. Gordon hid his face behind his hand whenever that part happened.

Kenji continued down the aisle, slapping a few hands on his way, winking at the people screaming his name, and tossing his jacket on the ground before sliding into the ring to his waiting opponent. Tonight, that opponent was Anthony. He thought Kenji and Anthony were on a tag team, but again, Gordon didn't fully understand any of this.

Anthony paced the other side of the ring, jaw clenched and angry. He glared at Kenji, then screamed obscenities at him and gestured offensively before the official came in and introduced the match.

There were various words Gordon understood in context, like one fall, pinfall, and submission, but every match seemed the same to him. Which wasn't a problem, to be clear. They were all fun.

The bell rang and Gordon just leaned back to watch. It was loud, sweaty, and a very nice way to spend his time. Kenji, flipping off the ropes onto Anthony. Kenji, tossing Anthony to the ground. Kenji, shirtless and damp. He smiled to himself, loving the juxtaposition of the man he was watching violently launch Anthony over the top rope of the ring, and the one who brought him home to meet his aunt because of a shared love of cooking.

"She is going to love you," he'd said. "I can't eat anything she makes when I'm training and she's desperate to feed someone."

He'd fallen in love with Akiko that night, partly because of the food, partly because of her connection to Kenji, but mostly because of her willingness to immediately welcome him into their family. He loved them.

As was often the case when he daydreamed about Kenji

and his aunt, Gordon couldn't shake the desire he had to be a more permanent part of their family. It always led him to think about how different his relationship was with his own mother, which was difficult.

It's not that she wasn't a nice woman. She cared, in her own way, she was just… Well, no, she wasn't *nice*, but he loved her anyway. But every time they spoke, which was more often than he cared to, she ignored anything he shared about himself, instead asking about future promotions or future Mrs. Whitakers, conveniently forgetting Gordon was happy in his current role or that he didn't date women. She occasionally offered a half-hearted apology, but not often.

He'd given up dreams of bringing Kenji home years ago, of course. The feelings he had for Kenji remained a secret from most of his family, especially his mother, because he just didn't want to open that can of worms. The only time he'd mentioned Kenji to his parents, they'd made him feel pathetic for spending time with someone so different from him—athletic, attractive, and social—as if Kenji's friendship was just a favor to him.

If she ever discovered his real feelings, or worse, if she found out he spent his free time sitting alone at Titan's arena, watching Kenji wrestle, she'd probably cry. But they wouldn't be tears of pity for her poor, stupid son, wasting his life pining after someone he could never have. They'd be tears of embarrassment.

After thoroughly depressing himself with the reminder that he and Kenji would never be more than friends and sinking further remembering his mother misunderstood or maybe straight up disliked him, he realized with some embarrassment that Kenji's match had ended. Two new people, neither of whom interested Gordon, were in the ring, bouncing off the ropes and colliding into each other. He made his way into the hall to wait for Kenji as he did every time he came to watch.

He glanced up from his phone a while later and saw Kenji walking towards him, smiling and waving. Kenji was charismatic and sexy, all hard lines and smooth muscles often wrapped in tight, white pants. But this more approachable version, in soft, comfortable clothing, freshy showered with his hair up in a lazy topknot, still warm from the water hitting his skin, his body begging to be held in Gordon's arms, if only for a moment… that was even better.

"You made it!" he said, bright and beaming.

"Of course I did," Gordon said. "You know I wouldn't miss it."

"Well, I'm still glad you made it. Did you still want to get dinner? I'm hungry."

"I always want to get dinner with you."

"Flatterer," Kenji said. He elbowed Gordon in his soft belly, which Gordon instinctively covered with his hand.

"You pick. I'm up for whatever," Gordon said, following Kenji down the hall.

The fresh air outside was a welcome reprieve from the overheated arena. Gordon's internal thermostat, which had started going haywire any time he talked to Kenji, was becoming a real problem. His brain actively ignored every reason Gordon had provided as to why being in love with Kenji no longer served their purposes. He wanted to be free from the agony he felt every time they spent time together, but he also refused to see him less, so his body rebelled by making him overheated and sweaty. If the goal was to make Gordon even *less* attractive, it was working.

The restaurant sign came into view after a short walk and Gordon breathed a sigh of relief. If nothing else, food and drink would be a decent distraction, even if it was at a crowded, hot bar with questionable sushi they both had a soft spot for. When they reached the door, Gordon held it open, and Kenji slipped in. Gordon squeezed his hand into a fist to stop himself from gently pressing it into the small of Kenji's back.

They settled at their table and discussed the match, Gordon doing his best to follow Kenji's animated retelling of the events of one hour prior. The server stopped by to take their order, and when she left, Kenji jumped right back in, barely taking a breath.

"All in all, I give your performance an A plus. Anthony looked exhausted, though. I almost thought he was going to stay on the ground for a minute, try to sneak in a nap."

"Yeah. Well, you know. Babies."

Gordon crinkled his nose and Kenji laughed.

"So," Kenji said. "Remember I was telling you about how I finally hit five stars on my island?"

"Animal Crossing?"

"Yeah!"

"I think so. Yes. I still don't really know what that means, but I remember you saying it." Gordon remembered everything Kenji said.

"It just means my island is really nice, Gordon, come on. Use that big brain of yours for something other than actuarial science."

Gordon laughed but felt weirdly self-conscious at the compliment. Kenji didn't really insult people, so it was *probably* a compliment. "I haven't been an actuary for a while, Kenj."

"Okay, I kind of knew that, but there's a finite amount of space in my head and it's currently full. What do you do now, then?"

"It's… something very boring. Tell me about your island."

"Wait! I forgot, I have more exciting news," Kenji said.

"Oh?"

The server dropped off their food and Gordon smiled at her in thanks before looking back at Kenji, who was grinning with an unnecessarily large smile.

"What's your news? You look very happy. Did you get some rare plant in?"

"No, I'm—oh, stop!" Kenji grabbed Gordon's wrist, the sushi inches from his mouth. "They gave you wasabi."

"Oh." Gordon frowned.

"Here." Kenji piled various rolls onto the side of Gordon's plate. "We can trade."

"You don't have to do that, I can eat around it."

"You can't eat around wasabi stuck to fish and rice."

"You need the food more than I do, you can just have mine."

"I'm sorry, last I heard, wasabi 'permeates everything close to it, and that includes my soul,'" Kenji said. He put a piece of Gordon's nigiri in his mouth.

Gordon laughed. "Okay, thank you."

"Close one."

Kenji hummed and turned his focus back to his dinner, arranging it away from the bit of wasabi on the side of his plate so Gordon could eat it safely. Gordon felt a flicker of warmth in his chest but forced himself to squash it down—Kenji's help didn't mean anything beyond friendship. He knew Gordon hated wasabi and acted accordingly.

"Anyway, what were you going to say before?"

"I'm going to Boston."

Gordon blinked at him, unsure what that meant. He knew CWA was headquartered there, and that if he ever got a CWA contract he'd have to move there, which he didn't like to think about. Maybe he'd misheard.

"Boston?"

"Anthony and I got chosen for the training camps!" Kenji was practically bouncing in his seat.

"Oh! Oh, shit. That's awesome, man. Congratulations."

That was good. Right? Kenji had worked hard to get ready for the tryouts. But it was one step closer to the contract he wanted. One step closer to leaving Portland.

It also meant more on Gordon's plate. The camp lasted an entire month, and there was no way Akiko could handle the store on her own for that long. But, if it meant Kenji was happy, he would suck it up and work more shifts there.

"Thanks. I'm really pumped. Anthony and I saw pictures of our apartment and everything."

"Nice," Gordon said, taking a bite of ginger. "I can't wait to see pictures when you get there."

Kenji was still smiling even after they'd finished discussing his plans, like logistics around the store and what help Akiko would probably need. Gordon even allowed himself to be the butt of several plant death jokes because Kenji was having such a good time coming up with them.

"Anyway, we have time. It's not like I'm leaving tomorrow. I leave in a couple of months."

"Right." Gordon nodded. That was good. He wasn't exactly ready to care for Akiko and an entire store while he worked full time. But any relief Gordon felt at the weeks laid out before him was destroyed seconds later when Kenji dropped a bomb on him.

"In other news... I met someone." He shoved the final piece of fish into his mouth and looked at Gordon with wide, sparkly eyes.

Gordon's mouth couldn't decide if it wanted to fill with saliva or go completely bone dry. It did neither, and then he choked on his tongue. He *met someone*?

"You met someone? Like... who? And when? You met a guy?"

Kenji didn't really *date* date. Gordon wasn't stupid, and he had fully functioning eyes. He knew Kenji had an active sex life, even if he chose not to think about it. But Kenji hadn't had a boyfriend in years. He'd had a few here or there, sure. Short-lived things that ended when he got bored. But Kenji wanted to focus on wrestling, and he'd told Gordon he wasn't ready to settle down.

"Yeah! He came into the store and we talked plants. Is that a sign, or what?"

"A sign?"

"Yeah! Like, it's meant to be, or something. I love plants, maybe I could love him."

"Love him? When did you meet this guy?"

"Relax. I'm kidding. I don't know him very well, but we've been out a couple of times."

"You don't know him very well?"

"Why are you repeating everything I'm saying? Stop that."

"I'm just surprised. You've never mentioned him. And you mention everything, like when Anthony cut his chin shaving and got blood on your shampoo bottle, or when Curt wore two different shoes to the gym. Things that, in my opinion, matter a whole hell of a lot less than you going out with some guy you don't know."

"Whoa. Relax, Gord," Kenji said, reaching to pat Gordon's clenched fist that was resting on the table.

"Don't call me that, please."

"Hey, okay, can we stop? What's happening here? Why are you mad?"

"I'm sorry. I'm not. I had a bad day at work. I didn't mean to get irritated."

"But you are irritated?"

"No. I'm fine. I'm glad you met someone."

The food sat uneaten between them and Gordon was kicking himself for making things awkward. He picked up his chopstick and poked at a fish egg.

"Okay," Kenji said. "Feels like maybe you're not, though."

"I am. I promise."

Kenji sat back in the booth and crossed his arms. "I know you're happy living the single life and everything. Gordon and Peony, bachelors forever! But lately, I don't know, I've been feeling like I wouldn't mind more than that. Someday. I'm getting old," he said, offering Gordon a small smile.

"Right. Thirty-two is getting up there."

Gordon did not love the fact that Kenji thought he was happy being single, nor did he love the idea that Kenji thought he and his pet iguana were destined to be single together, forever. He had a vision of himself growing old with an equally elderly Peony, feeding each other mashed up fruit and leaves.

"And it's surprisingly hard to meet people who want more than a hookup. Don't get me wrong, that part is pretty cool. But when I met this guy at the plant shop and he didn't even know who I was, I was like, whoa! I want to be more than Ken Vee, and that's hard when that's who people think I am first, you know?"

"I do."

Gordon knew it all too well, in fact, based on the social media comments and the chatter he heard every week at the arena. Kenji wasn't stupid, he knew he was attractive. But he was sometimes oblivious to the true effect he had on people. He had no idea how many people fawned after him, how badly they wanted him, and how every comment Gordon overheard chipped away at his heart, bit by bit.

It had always seemed inevitable that someday Kenji would

catch on and use his growing fame to get what he wanted. Gordon hadn't considered that it would be someone who saw Kenji for who he was outside of the ring that would pose a greater risk. He'd hoped for more time to be the most important man in Kenji's life, but the sinking feeling in his stomach told him the opposite. And it was probably time for him to think about what that meant for his own future.

CHAPTER 5

"Gordon," Victor said, waving his hand in front of Gordon's face. "What is going on over there? Did you hear anything I just said?"

"Shit, sorry. I'm distracted. What did you say? Something about risk?"

"I asked if you read the risk assessment briefing I sent out yesterday. The one we booked this meeting to discuss."

"I… did not. I'm sorry." Gordon's cheeks flushed and he looked down at the elaborate fern art on his latte. His brother, Victor, recently earned a promotion that meant Gordon reported directly to him, and he cringed internally knowing he'd already fucked something up. "I was at my friend's match and forgot this meeting was booked so early."

"Okay. I guess I can't be that mad if you're making me miss work to drink good coffee, but I really need to see some progress here."

"I know. You will," Gordon said. Then he looked up. "The office coffee isn't *that* bad."

"It is," Victor said. He took a sip of his coffee and groaned, accentuating his point. "Still better than mom's, though. How does she mess it up so badly every time?"

Gordon smiled briefly, but the mention of his mom brought a familiar tension to his shoulders.

"Oh, come on," Victor said.

"What?"

"I saw that. You tensed up at the mere mention of mom."

"Well," Gordon said, a bitter chuckle escaping. He picked at his napkin. "I mean, yeah."

"She's not so bad. She sucks at saying the right thing sometimes, but she means well."

"Yeah. I'm just on edge. Ignore me."

Victor frowned at him but didn't force any further conversation around their mom, which was appreciated. Gordon looked outside at the rain pouring down and grumbled quietly, not looking forward to the short walk back to the office.

"Ready to head back?" Victor asked. "If we're not going to discuss the briefing, I could use this time to catch up on some other stuff."

"Sure. I'll meet you there. I have to make a call."

"You're coming to dinner next week, right? Mom said you haven't let her know yet."

"Yeah, I'll be there. Six on Thursday, right?"

"Like always."

Victor gave Gordon a stupid salute and took off, leaving Gordon at the table to peel his tightened fingers off his phone. He needed to call Akiko to set up time to discuss her finances. She trusted him, though he wasn't sure why. He didn't have any actual training in anything financial, he just happened to earn a lot, which made her think he knew what he was doing. But he didn't mind. He'd help her with anything.

"Hi," he said when she answered.

"You called me back. Domo!"

"Of course. I wanted to set up time to talk about your finances."

"Yes. Kenji is going out of town Thursday. Do you want to come to the store for lunch then? I made your favorite."

Gordon waited for her to elaborate, but she didn't. "Everything you cook is my favorite," he said.

"Exactly." He could hear her smiling. "Be here at eleven, okay?"

"I'll be there."

Whether it was simply because his job was boring or because he had a lot on his mind, each minute of his morning flowed into the next with mind numbing monotony. He attended countless unnecessary virtual meetings where his presence was a formality at best. He sent a handful of emails and caught up on his annual employee trainings. He signed a single check for his boss. Not counting his brother, he saw two people over the course of the morning, and neither of them said hi.

Most of the company's employees worked from home, but for whatever reason, Gordon went in almost every day. As a member of leadership, he felt like he should be in the office. He read a business journal once, and it said something about leading by example and visible leadership, and he just kept doing it. Because that's what Gordon did. He stuck with the expected, the familiar, the low risk.

Maybe tomorrow he'd rebel and work from home. Maybe he'd even sleep in until eight o'clock so he could just roll out of bed. Maybe he'd call in sick, order an unhealthy lunch, and veg out.

He wouldn't do any of that, of course, because he was predictable and pathetic and boring, but thinking about it gave him a little thrill.

. . .

"So, how's the store doing overall? Do you have your P&L and bank statements?"

"I printed everything out here," Akiko said. "I think we're doing fine."

Gordon spent a few minutes going through the statements and it was true that she wasn't losing money, which gave Gordon some comfort. But between the store and her meager social security checks, she was mostly breaking even with just a bit leftover for savings. He schooled his face, forcing himself to look focused and not at all worried.

"Well," he started. "You're doing okay. Breaking even is better than losing money, but it's not exactly the cushion I'd like you to have. Will you please consider letting me pay the loan? You can pay me back if you want. I won't charge you interest."

Akiko wouldn't look at him, instead her gaze was set on the printed reports as her small fingers shuffled the papers.

"I'm sorry. I know you've said no several times. I'm not trying to offend you by offering, I'm just worried. I want you to be able to retire. Kenji wants you to be able to retire," Gordon said.

"I know."

"The offer is on the table, okay? But I'll stop asking you."

"Domo." Her eyes were twinkly, he hoped not with tears.

Gordon sighed and leaned back in his chair. "Are you okay?"

"Let me feed you," she said. "I made you stew. Nikujaga. It has potatoes."

"That sounds great," he said. He helped her up and walked her to the small kitchen she had set up in the back of the store, doing his best to ignore the way she avoided the question.

She'd never been married, and when she first opened the store, it was one of a kind and she worked long hours. The storeroom was set up so she could cook and eat there, and even sleep there occasionally on the old futon she now used as a couch.

The entire room was littered with tchotchke she'd collected over the years, art made for her by a young Kenji, and photographs of plants she'd grown and was particularly proud of. Gordon's favorite item in the back room was a framed photo of him posing with Kenji on Gordon's graduation day. Akiko displaying it in the store made his chest feel warm. It was a silly photo, and Gordon looked particularly hideous, but Kenji didn't, so he loved it.

She bustled over the counter, pouring the warming stew into two misshapen bowls Kenji had created in a high school ceramics class. He smiled down at it and she gave him a knowing look.

"So, this Rob…" she started.

"Ugh," Gordon said. He shoved a potato in his mouth to avoid saying more. "Oh, this is good."

She smiled at him, her eyes turning into pleased little crescents.

"I'm okay," he said.

Her doubt was obvious. "Are you?"

"Yes."

"Mmm. I don't think so. You've only eaten one potato."

"Why are you so worried about this now? I've been in love with him for my entire adult life. This isn't new territory for me." He ate a second potato and grinned at her. Proof he was fine.

"Why don't you tell him? You've kept this secret for years, and for what?"

He barked out a laugh. "What kind of question is that?"

"What?"

"He has a boyfriend."

"Tsk. For one month," she said, her voice softer and weaker. "You only had nine years to tell him before that."

She laughed quietly, then pressed her napkin to her lips before a rough cough escaped. An attempt at saying more was interrupted by further coughing that racked her tiny frame. Gordon rushed to the counter to pour hot water from the kettle and set a cup of tea in front of her.

"What is going on with you? Please, tell me. I'm really worried about you."

She sipped the tea slowly and carefully before she cleared her throat. "What is there to tell? I'm dying. I don't think that's a secret."

The words settled like stones in his stomach. He knew she was sick, of course. He even knew it was incurable, but she still saw her doctors frequently, not that she let him or Kenji in the appointments. He stupidly assumed that meant she was undergoing treatment. That she had years left with them.

"You aren't—you're *dying?*" he asked.

"Well, sure. We're all dying."

"You know that's not what I meant."

"My doctor thinks I have a few months left. Maybe six. There aren't many good treatment options left and I'm tired, Gordon."

"I know, but…"

Her small, wrinkled hand reached out and covered Gordon's larger one. "It's going to be okay. I've made peace with it."

"You have to tell Kenji," Gordon said.

"No! No, absolutely not. He'll quit Titan and stay with me full time. That is not an option. He's finally happy and excited.

You know he said Mike is going to send him to CWA for a training camp?"

"I know," Gordon said. He gave her a soft smile, so proud of Kenji, but it melted away seconds, Akiko's prognosis suffocating any lightness he felt when he thought of Kenji. "You can't keep this from him. He deserves to know."

"I'll tell him soon. Please promise me you won't tell him. I want to have time to talk to him about it, and he's heading out of town soon."

"I won't, but—"

The chime of the front door interrupted their meal, and Gordon turned to see who walked in. He was on the wrong side of the table to see the door, but he heard a familiar laugh that caused a flood of conflicting emotions to pass through his body. He stood to greet Kenji and let him know they were in the back room, but Kenji beat him to the punch and passed through the curtained doorway, his smile big and bright. Rob was on his side, his arm casually framing Kenji's strong shoulders.

Gordon's heart skipped a beat, but this time it wasn't fluttering at Kenji's presence. It was something sharper and more painful, a combination of holding this new secret and being face to face with Rob.

"Hey! Didn't mean to interrupt," Kenji said. "Are you guys done with the finance chat?"

"Yes," Akiko said. "Have a seat, Kenji, Rob. Have some stew."

Akiko and Gordon looked at each other, neither of them showing any emotion, but Gordon could tell Akiko pitied him. Gordon gathered up the bowls he and Akiko had used and helped her to the counter. He managed a tight smile at her that she returned.

"I thought you were going out of town, Kenji," Akiko said.

"We were, but Rob had a last minute vet appointment for his rat, so we're heading out later."

"He's a gerbil, Kenji," Rob said, patting Kenji's hand. "They're not the same thing. I've told you this." He laughed condescendingly and winked at Gordon, but Kenji didn't seem to notice. Gordon gritted his teeth.

Akiko placed two bowls of stew in front of them and Kenji lit up, turning to Rob. "This is my favorite."

"It smells great. I don't eat potatoes, but I'll eat the meat."

Gordon looked back to Akiko and their eyes locked again, and she gave him another knowing smile.

"Anyway, we went and saw that screening of that movie about the circus, you know?" Kenji said, squeezing Rob's hand.

"The Circus?" Gordon asked.

"Yeah! That's the one."

"What did you think of the ending?"

"I didn't get it. You don't even find out what happens, it just… ends. I thought the film broke."

Gordon heard Rob sigh, like they'd already discussed this. "Like I said, sweetheart, that's the point." Rob's voice was thick and impatient. "You're supposed to fill in the blanks."

"I don't know about all that. But I liked it anyway. It reminded me a lot of the chaos of the indie circuits."

"Maybe it wasn't the movie for you," Rob said, shoving a piece of beef into his mouth.

"Maybe Kenji can watch whatever movies he wants," Gordon said.

Rob narrowed his eyes at Gordon before smiling, which Gordon assumed was for Kenji's benefit. "He certainly can." Standing from his seat, he turned to Kenji. "I'll be right back, I need to drain the snake before we go."

Nobody spoke during the time it took Rob to leave the

room. Kenji was slurping stew happily, Akiko and Gordon were rinsing dishes, their sides touching.

"He is awful," Akiko said under her breath. Gordon tried to stifle a laugh.

"*Stop*," he said.

"We're all thinking it," she said, as she scrubbed remnants of stew from the pot.

Gordon turned to look at Kenji, who was scrolling through his phone, blissfully unaware their conversation.

"So, Kenj, where are you guys off to this week?"

"All the Titan guys are heading to McMinnville. We decided to make a big thing of it, the guys and me."

"Is everyone bringing their partners?" Gordon asked.

"No," Kenji said. "But Rob said he wanted to go. I guess he has some old college friends down there he hasn't seen in a while."

"It's an hour drive. He could visit them any time."

"I know, but he wanted to show me off," Kenji said, winking. "Can't blame him."

Gordon rolled his eyes but couldn't help but smile, because he understood. He would show Kenji off every second if he was Rob.

"Hey." Gordon sat down across from Kenji at the table.

"Uh, hey." Kenji sipped more broth and gave Gordon a questioning look.

"Finances are okay. But I wanted to show you this cash flow projection report I mocked up on my phone. This one shows what your cash flow would look like if you paid off the loan today. This one shows what it looks like if you wait five or six years to pay it off in full. Look how much more money you'd have in five years if it was paid off today."

Gordon studied Kenji's face for a moment, hoping for a smile or a flash of understanding. Instead, Kenji's expression darkened, and he set his bowl down with a surprising amount of force. It splashed broth onto Gordon's hand, and he tried to wipe it off, already regretting what he'd said.

"I told you, Gordon, you are not paying off the loan. Stop asking. I'm literally begging you at this point."

"It just makes so much more sense for me to do it. I have the money! It's just sitting there."

"It makes sense to *you*, because you don't have any emotional tie to paying it off. This loan will get paid off when I save enough or when I earn my CWA contract. If we have to pay a bit of interest in the meantime, it's worth it to me."

"But…" Gordon didn't actually have a rebuttal to that, he just didn't understand why Kenji was so unwilling to bend on this.

"Paying this off with my money will prove to me that I made it. Okay? Like a big fuck you to my parents and everyone who ever doubted me. You don't have to get my reasoning, but you do have to respect it. Akiko and I love you, but this is not your store, and it's not your loan. We've discussed it, and she's fine with waiting until I can pay it off."

"Okay," Gordon said. "I'm sorry."

"Stop asking about it. Please."

"I will."

"Ugh, now my soup is all cold and spilled."

"I'm sorry." Gordon got a napkin and wiped up the rest of the spilled stew, then took the bowl to get him some more.

In the time that he stood up and walked to the stove, Rob had returned. Kenji gave a hurried goodbye and gathered his things, the two of them slipping through the curtained doorway and out the front door before Gordon even had a chance to react.

He glanced to Akiko who was watching him, her face soft but knowing.

"Oops," he said, his voice quiet.

She smiled at him. "It's okay. He's following his pride. It's not personal."

"It felt pretty personal."

"Well…" She shrugged and leaned back in her chair, her silence saying exactly what Gordon already knew.

CHAPTER 6

GORDON'S CHILDHOOD HOME WAS RIDICULOUS. IT LOOKED LIKE one of those houses owned by a pleasant, welcoming neighborhood family in a 90s movie. The kind where it was implied they had a normal income, even though there was absolutely no way it was affordable on anything less than mid six figures. But the mom managed to stay home and serve orange juice to her family every morning, and she fed all the neighborhood kids sandwiches after school, and they called her "Mrs. B." Gordon always liked the idea of that kind of family.

Unfortunately, Gordon's family home hadn't felt like that at all. He certainly didn't begrudge his mother for having a fulfilling career, or his father for working hard and retiring early. But parts of it would have been a nicer alternative to his reality.

He grew up in a house where kids were only allowed in certain rooms, and when they hosted dinner parties, he wasn't supposed to talk, let alone participate. He couldn't remember having a friend over his entire childhood, and his mom made it clear things were better that way. His house growing up was a place his mom felt comfortable offering their endless cruel comments and nitpicking, most of which was reserved for Gordon. His dad wasn't as brutal as his mom, but his apologies and comforts only went so far.

That's why his desire to bring Kenji home for family dinners had lasted about fourteen seconds before he never considered it again. Sure, the idea of showing up with a guy like Kenji on his arm was tempting. Kenji was a living contradiction to every judgment and doubt Gordon's mom had sent his way over the last thirty plus years. But he couldn't do that to Kenji, no matter how much he wanted to, or how willing he knew Kenji would be to play that role for him on a random Thursday evening.

Instead, he suffered through monthly family dinners his mom scheduled through her assistant. His siblings were always there, which was better than facing his parents alone, but both of them were closer to his mom than he ever was, even when he had put in a greater effort.

His brother, Victor, was his parents' golden child. In hindsight, it was a terrible idea to get Victor hired at the same company he worked for. His string-pulling had set Victor up in a position to move up the ladder quickly, surpassing Gordon's senior director role and landing in a C-suite position within six months of employment. Gordon didn't even *want* a role like that—too much pressure, too volatile. But his parents looked at any career stagnation or brief pause in upward movement as a failure to meet his potential. Victor's success just added additional items to his parents' ever-growing list of Gordon's perceived inadequacies.

His sister, Amber, was similarly successful professionally, but still unmarried, much to the chagrin of their parents. She wasn't interested in marriage, as far as Gordon knew, but it didn't stop them from setting her up repeatedly via networking events.

He was close to Amber in ways he wasn't with the rest of his family. She'd been the first person he'd come out to, and she'd been so excited that he finally expressed interest in *anyone* that she'd demanded they rate everyone in his graduating class together. She was the only one who knew anything other than the bare minimum about Kenji, and he'd even showed her photos of him on the Titan website. He swore up and down he was just Gordon's friend, but he was pretty sure Amber could see through his lies.

Anyway, he wasn't angry with his siblings for their successes or their parents' excitement around them. They were victims of the same upbringing he was, and it wasn't their fault. But it still made family gatherings unpleasant.

He made a mental note to sit next to Amber at dinner, hoping he could participate in conversations that way, since his mom made sure to guide the conversation at every dinner. The topics never varied. Pressuring them for grandchildren was second only to chatting about business and career goals. The dinners often led him to wonder why she even wanted grandchildren, since raising her own children hadn't seemed like an enjoyable part of her life.

He stepped through the front door into the immaculately clean foyer and placed his shoes on the rack inside the closet, out of sight. The house smelled lovely, which wasn't surprising. For all her faults, his mom was a phenomenal cook, perhaps the only thing the two of them had in common. His stomach rumbled in anticipation as he turned the corner to the kitchen and saw his mom leaning over a pot of something. He didn't even care what, it just smelled delicious.

"Hi, mom," he said gently, trying not to surprise her.

"Oh, Gordon! You're on time," she said, smiling, poking at whatever she was cooking. "Please grab the thyme from the fridge. It needs more."

He smiled at her, *this close* to reminding her that he'd never been late to a family gathering, and actually it was Victor who was chronically late. It wasn't worth it, though, so he quietly grabbed the thyme and set a few sprigs next to the stove.

"Where are Victor and Amber?" he asked.

"Oh, you know them. Busy at work, I'm sure they're running a bit behind."

"Sure. Can I help with anything?"

"You can fix the salad."

Gordon pulled out all the vegetables he thought made sense to put in a salad: spring mix, carrots, bell pepper, cucumber, snap peas, and celery. Spread out on the counter, the items filled him with apprehension. Not because he didn't think they'd taste good, but because he was worried his mom would zero in on some stupid vegetable he shouldn't have taken out and make him feel like an idiot for assuming it was okay to use. Probably the celery. Celery could go in salads, right? He felt like it could.

After washing the vegetables he'd grabbed, he chopped them into salad-appropriate sizes, setting aside scraps Peony would enjoy. When his mother left to get the door, he felt his shoulders loosen and he breathed out a sigh of relief and let his mind wander back to Kenji. But unfortunately, that meant he was thinking of Rob, too. He sighed again, louder this time.

"Whoa, big sigh from a big guy," Victor said. "What was that about?"

"Nothing." Gordon chopped harder, imagining Rob's head was the carrot's top—decapitated and tossed into the bin. A little dark, maybe. He paused to smile, then cut off the carrot greens and shoved them in a baggie to take home.

"Okay. Well, let me know if you need help."

"I would never ask you for help in the kitchen. You can't even make toast."

"I guess my plan worked, then!" Victor poured a glass of wine and shoved it in Gordon's direction, raising his eyebrows. "Cheers."

"You know I don't drink."

"Why don't you give this to Brie?"

"Who's Brie?" Gordon asked.

"I don't know, she came with Amber."

"Is she here?" Gordon asked, perking up. He kind of wanted to talk to Amber tonight. About... things. Like what she might do if someone she had feelings for was dating a douche, and what she might do if that douche didn't even deserve the *worst* guy on the planet, let alone the best.

"Yeah, she just walked in with Brie, who is... a friend, I guess? A woman her age."

"Oh," Gordon said, deflating a bit. So much for his evening's plan.

With the salad finished, Gordon cleaned up the counter and washed his hands before heading to the living room to greet the rest of the family and, apparently, Amber's friend. She was a cheerful-looking, short, dark-haired woman wearing a colorful cardigan and a black, too-short-for-his-mom skirt, which he liked a lot.

"Oh, Gordon!" his mom said, smiling widely and approaching him with her hands out before grabbing his face gently. It was a gesture she had never done before, and one that left him more confused than anything. "This is Brie, Amber's coworker. She's new to town and had nowhere to go tonight, so I invited her. Why don't you two have a seat and chat?"

Brie's eyes opened wide and she scanned Gordon up and down before her face crumpled slightly, which was mortifying on its own, but nothing compared to the fact that his mom had apparently planned this without telling anyone.

Gordon offered a small smile, then gestured to the couch, encouraging Brie to sit down. Her expression had shifted into something a little more good-natured, maybe embarrassed that her disappointment had been so visible just moments earlier. She placed her hands on her knees, which were hidden under some sparkly stockings Gordon thought were fun and pretty. They reminded him of Kenji's white costume tights, which had threads of glitter and gold sewn throughout.

"I'm gay," Gordon blurted. He was eager to nip the awkward tension in the bud and it just… came out. "I'm sure you're a very nice person, and I love your sweater, and I'm sorry you were led here thinking you were meeting someone more… your type. Or potentially interested. But I get that I'm not, and I'm also… not."

Brie was quiet for a moment before she laughed. It was an oppressive, husky, booming laugh. It was so loud it must have filled every corner of the house, and if she'd been closer to the windows, he was sure it would have rattled them. He *loved* it. It made him wish he could force attraction to her, if for no other reason than having that laugh in the family forever would infuriate his mom.

"That is so funny," she said, wiping her eye. "And to be clear, it wasn't that. You're great, very cute. I didn't realize I was coming here to be set up, that's all, and when your mom introduced you, you looked like you were going to throw up. I thought about breaking through your front windows to escape."

"Oh, my God," Gordon groaned, putting his face in his hands.

She cackled again, and Gordon did too, the sound of their laughter mixing in relief from their shared embarrassment.

"Can I get you a glass of wine?"

"Oh, no thank you. I'll take a sparkling water, if you have it," she said, tucking her short hair behind her ear.

"Come with me to the kitchen, we have a few options."

He led her to the kitchen and opened the fridge, pulling out a few cans of sparkling water.

"Lemon, lime, or… ugh, lavender-pineapple. That sounds awful!" He held a can of each up for Brie to choose. She laughed her big laugh, and he couldn't help but laugh, too.

"I think it sounds awesome. Lavender-pineapple, please."

"It's your funeral."

"Thank you. Cheers?"

He tapped her disgusting seltzer with his much more palatable lime one. "Cheers. Thanks for coming and putting up with all of this."

Amber joined them in the kitchen shortly after and they chatted light-heartedly about the menu, Gordon taking the opportunity to brag about his salad. He confirmed with both of them that celery *was* allowed in salads, no matter what his mom had said years ago. When they were called to the table, Gordon realized he'd ignored his mom's request for him to set out the silverware, and it gave him a tiny buzz.

He squeezed between Brie and Amber on the short end of the table, armored from his mother, and spent the next hour rubbing elbows and sharing stupid stories that grew more and more absurd. They laughed nonstop, with Gordon doing his best to make them laugh harder with each anecdote, usually Kenji-related. He had years of them up his sleeve and had managed to curate a list that sounded innocent enough to his family.

Dinner passed quickly and easily, and he couldn't remember a night where dinner with his parents had felt so effortless. He chose not to focus on how depressing that was, and instead, leaned into her friendly warmth and tried not to feel guilty about enjoying his evening so wholeheartedly when he knew nothing his mom wanted would come of it.

"I'M TRYING to make this my summer of EDM," Amber said, fiddling with the Bluetooth speaker on the counter. "Do you mind if I put on a playlist while we do the dishes? I'll have to rescue Brie shortly. I think Victor may have found her."

Gordon knew his family would hate to hear even faint EDM coming from the kitchen, so he readily agreed. "Poor thing. But yeah, put on whatever. I'll wash, you dry?"

"Perfect."

The low bass from Amber's music and the flowing water was like white noise, wiping Gordon's mind clean of the feelings that usually came from family dinners. Amber's presence helped, of course. She talked a lot. Not about anything particularly important, but he didn't mind. Several times during their conversations his mind drifted to Kenji and what he was up to tonight. He was in McMinnville, but he hadn't reached out at all. He hoped that wasn't their reality now—him seeing Rob, with no time for Gordon.

Amber glanced up at him and he noticed her story had stopped mid-sentence. He pretended not to notice and handed her a serving platter. She nudged him with her hip.

"You've been rinsing that platter for like twenty seconds with a silly grin on your face," she said. "The soap is gone, Gordon. And now my story about the ant hill outside my apartment will never be finished."

"Sorry," he said, eyes focused on the soapy water.

"You're thinking about him again! Do you ever stop?"

"It's not usually this bad," he confessed in a whisper. He kept his voice low. "He's seeing this new guy, Rob. That's why

I was hoping to see you tonight, but with mom inviting Brie…"

"Oh," she said. "Say no more. I've been there, and yeah, I'm sorry about that. I told mom it was weird."

"Hey, Gordon," Brie said, walking into the kitchen with Gordon's phone in her hand. "Your phone has been ringing off the hook for like five minutes. Call after call. I tried yelling for you, but *somebody* put their Summer of EDM playlist on. Do you ever listen to anything else?" Another cackling laugh erupted from Brie, which had comforted him all evening, but not now.

"Hey! I do, but—"

"Wait, where's my phone? Who's calling?" Gordon asked, his voice tinged with urgency. He didn't get phone calls very often. Who called people anymore, anyway? Why didn't they just text? Unless something was wrong.

Akiko.

His stomach dropped, and the pan he was scrubbing slipped from his soapy fingers, clattering in the sink, splashing grimy water over his shirt. He heard Amber and Brie murmur something as he grabbed his phone and ran through the living room to the front porch. His heart was beating hard enough for him to notice, but he still hesitated, almost afraid to see who called.

As he was scrolling through his missed calls and texts, all from Kenji, the phone buzzed in his hand again. It was Kenji, again. Gordon's stomach dropped, he just knew something was wrong.

"Kenji?" he said.

"Gordito!"

"Kenji, what's going on? Why did you call me so many times?"

"Umm," he said, then said something to someone away from the phone.

"Christ, I thought Akiko died!"

Gordon heard the phone shuffling, presumably Kenji's hand moving it closer to his ear or face.

Oh, he was drunk.

"What? Why?" Kenji asked. Then he laughed and mumbled something about his muscles. Gordon grumbled.

"Kenji—"

"My Gordito. I need you, please."

Gordon's breath stalled momentarily. He certainly wasn't stupid enough to think Kenji meant what Gordon was hearing, but it still made him stumble.

"Ken—"

"Do you know where Rob went?" Kenji yelled.

"What? Where are you? I thought you were with the guys in McMinnville."

"I am in McMinnville, but Rob didn't want to go out with the guys. We went out with his college friends."

"Okay, well did he go get a drink or something? Are you at a bar?"

"I'm at… umm…" Kenji's voice sounded further away, and Gordon heard the phone fall.

Gordon pinched the bridge of his nose, listening to garbled voices and background noise coming through the phone.

"Kenji."

More garbled voices, more background noise, more of Kenji's laughter and guys commenting on his arms. He wouldn't be surprised if Kenji wasn't wearing a shirt.

"Kenji," he said, louder.

"Gordon," Kenji said, mocking Gordon's voice.

"Oh, my God. This isn't funny. Where are you?"

"I'm at… Well, I don't know. Can you come get me? I can't find Rob."

"Come get you? In McMinnville. Where you are with Rob, but not with Rob. And clearly wasted."

"I'm not wasted!"

Gordon stood up and paced around the porch, drilling his thumb into his eye socket so he didn't scream.

"Dude."

"Rob left, I think? We met a guy, and I thought it was going to be a whole thing with us this evening, but they left and now I don't know where he is. And I could walk back to the hotel, but I can't remember the name." Kenji sighed.

"Okay, can you call Curt or Anthony? Did Mike go down there?"

"I did but they didn't answer. Mike didn't come down. I think Anthony went home after the matches."

"And Rob is missing."

"Yes. That's what I'm telling you. I need you, please. Can you give me a ride home?"

Gordon glanced back at his parents' house, then at his phone to check the time. He'd spent three hours there, which seemed sufficient. He'd had a good evening, meeting Brie and avoiding his mom. It was only an hour to McMinnville, and if he left now, he could bring Kenji back to Portland before too late.

"Yeah, okay," Gordon said, sighing. "Give me an hour and a half or so. I'm at dinner."

"Oh, shit! Sorry. Like, *dinner* dinner?"

"I'm not sure what that means, but just dinner with my parents. My mom set me up with Amber's friend."

"What?! Peggy Whitaker, the matchmaker!" Kenji laughed. "I love this. Who is he?"

"Ah, *she* is a nice woman named Brie. But, actually, she's really—you know what? I'll explain when I see you. Or maybe tomorrow, when you're… um, normal."

"I am normal!"

"Don't leave the bar," Gordon said. He pushed open the door and walked back through the living room to grab his stuff from the kitchen. "Actually, send me your location because I feel like you're going to leave the bar. But don't. I'm serious. I will be mad if I get down there and you're gone."

"I love you so much, my sweet Gordito," Kenji said with a slur, his heavy breath blowing against the phone.

"Alright."

"Hey, everyone! Tell Gordon you love him!"

Gordon heard a half-drunk chorus of voices yelling about how much they loved him and smiled before he grabbed his keys.

KENJI HAD CONVENIENTLY FORGOTTEN to tell Gordon that it was the weekend of the annual UFO festival in McMinnville, which wasn't a problem, but it meant parking was a beast. He didn't know the town well enough to stray from the main roads, and there were people wandering the streets. Kenji's pin had stayed put, at least.

He walked through the crowds with some people dressed like aliens and others who were almost certainly on something, feeling a little jealous of their detachment from reality. Several people touched him as he passed by and he cringed, wishing, once again, Kenji had never met Rob.

By the time he finally reached the bar, he could feel the bass of the music drifting into the street. He double checked the name, confirming he was at the right place. Based on the music, he had assumed it was some sort of club, though McMinnville wasn't exactly known for its bustling nightlife and club scene.

He stepped inside and scanned the bar, looking for Kenji. He hoped it'd be a quick in-and-out; he did have to work tomorrow. He didn't see him, mostly because the bar was packed with alien fanatics. It was impossible to see even ten feet ahead of him with all the bodies, and it was so loud he could barely hear anything, but he did hear Kenji—holding court, like usual. His laugh was booming across the bar and Gordon followed the sound of it.

He shoved someone to the side when they got a little handsy, and there was Kenji. In one piece, safe, fully clothed. Gordon breathed out a sigh of relief before heading towards the group of people enchanted by his friend. There must have been a dozen people touching him and laughing at his jokes, and Gordon couldn't help but smile. Kenji was charismatic and effortlessly inviting, and loving him meant it was fun to see him in his element, even if it made Gordon itch to imagine being on the receiving end of that much attention.

"Gordon!" he yelled and pointed at Gordon. Every head turned to look at him. "Guys, Gordon is here, look!"

"Gordon!" the crowd shouted, like he'd just arrived at a party in his honor. They cheered and hollered, but Gordon groaned, as any hope he had of leaving on time was quickly squashed.

Kenji hopped off his stool and shoved his way through the crowd, stumbling towards Gordon with his arms outstretched. He wrapped them around Gordon and squeezed tightly, crushing Gordon's lungs, before pulling back to balance him upright.

"Whoa, sorry!" Kenji said. "You're here!"

Gordon patted Kenji's back like he was meeting a new dog.

He was uncomfortable, touched on all sides by people passing by him, welcoming him to the party. If Kenji hadn't been there, he would have run away ages ago.

The crowd lost interest in Kenji immediately after he found Gordon, which was a relief. Kenji looked disappointed for a split second before his face lit up. Gordon's heartrate picked up, hoping it was excitement around his presence making him look like that. But of course, it wasn't.

"Rob!" Kenji said.

Rob appeared out of the crowd, a faint smirk on his face and a man following close behind.

"Ohhh," Kenji said. He stage whispered to Gordon, "That's the guy we were going to go home with."

Gordon's stomach rolled at the thought. "Got it."

He marveled at Kenji's casual dismissal of Rob's disappearance. He'd left to do unspoken things with the man who now stood at their side, and Kenji didn't seem to care. Gordon knew Kenji had helped set the boundaries of their relationship, but when he imagined being Rob, having Kenji the way he did, choosing someone else even temporarily seemed impossible to imagine.

"What are you doing here?" Rob asked, his arm sliding over Kenji's shoulders.

"You left me without saying anything. I asked Gordon to come get me."

"Baby," Rob said, drawing out the vowels. He nuzzled into Kenji's neck. "I told you I'd be right back."

"But you didn't come back. And I don't know where the hotel is."

"He called me about ten times. You couldn't even let him know you were leaving for a bit?" Gordon asked, nodding his head in the direction of the other man.

Rob shrugged, his arm still draped over Kenji, casual but possessive, a smug laugh escaping his lips.

"I wouldn't expect you to understand," he said, rubbing his hand down his firm stomach while staring at Gordon's softer one.

"Well," Kenji said, oblivious to Rob's gesture. He squeezed Rob's hand that dangled over his bicep. "I understand, and still don't want to be left hanging."

"I'm sorry, baby. Next time, okay?"

Gordon cleared his throat.

"Problem, Gord?" Rob asked.

Gordon sighed. "God, you are incredibly unpleasant. There's no problem, but Kenji asked me to come get him. I have work tomorrow, so I need to head out."

"Sorry you came all the way down here," Rob said.

"He doesn't have to leave yet! I mean, unless he wants to."

Gordon was taken aback, although he wasn't sure why. He'd come down to pick up Kenji because Rob disappeared. Rob had reappeared, so Gordon was no longer needed. It should have been a relief because now he could go home and get to bed on time. But thinking that made him feel like a colossal loser.

He wished he wanted to stay, but he really didn't.

It wasn't the first time Kenji had chosen someone else over him, and it probably wouldn't be the last. But for some reason, this time cut a little deeper. Maybe because Rob had embarrassed him, or maybe because Gordon had left his comfort zone for nothing. He didn't want to dwell on the reason. He just wanted to go home.

"Yeah, I have stuff to do tomorrow, so it's probably better if I head out. Text me when you're back, okay?"

The walk back to the car felt like a slow unraveling, his feelings and composure coming apart bit by bit. He could only imagine what everyone was saying about him back at the bar, how obvious his feelings for Kenji must be. Rob certainly picked up on it, he all but called him out on it. Knowing he was probably telling Kenji how pitiful he was made him want to shrink down and disappear.

CHAPTER 7

Kenji was on his third day of a four-day break from Titan, which was so unusual he couldn't remember the last time it had happened. He was still feeling guilty about Gordon driving all the way to McMinnville to pick him up only to turn around immediately when Rob showed up again.

But Gordon told him he didn't mind—that it wasn't too bad a drive, and making sure Kenji was in good hands was good enough for him. Kenji hadn't bought that, and had apologized more than once, eventually causing Gordon to snap at him, begging him to leave it alone. He had, for Gordon's sake, but still couldn't stop thinking about it.

And that's how he ended up behind the shop, walking the grassy strip along the alleyway, searching for dandelions that had gone to seed. He had an idea he hoped would show Gordon just how much he appreciated him, even if he wasn't allowed to bring it up again.

He'd already prepped a few buckets of soil inside the shop, which had been nice. He'd forgotten how much he enjoyed working in the dirt. When he was younger, the plant shop had been a peaceful, happy place, but as his wrestling career developed and he learned what running a business actually entailed, the reality became overwhelming. Lately, his time at Kiko's had been all about worrying. Money, customers, keeping things going, learning everything he needed to know. The stress had drained the joy from it, but he kept telling himself it was worth it. That if he put in enough effort, he could make it work. He owed it to Akiko to do that.

He felt similarly about his relationship with Rob. Things had started out fun, but the more time they spent together, the more Kenji realized Rob wasn't the kind of person he'd ever pictured himself with long term. He didn't find Kenji's occasional gaffes charming, and his indifference toward wrestling was actually more of a medium-level dislike.

But Rob was different than his past boyfriends in a lot of ways, and Kenji wondered if that meant he should try harder. That maybe the reason all his relationships fizzled was because he kept picking people who thought he was funny, or people he had things in common with. That maybe if he just committed to this one, really gave it time, he'd prove to himself that love wasn't about instant connection—it was about effort. Even if, deep down, he wasn't totally convinced.

Akiko's head popped up behind the sales counter when Kenji reentered the shop, puffy dandelions in hand, and she shrieked.

"Ah! What are you doing with those?" she asked.

"I need your help with something, in the back."

"Put those in a bag! I don't want those seeds planting themselves anywhere. Why would you bring a weed inside?"

Kenji grimaced. "Oh, um. Sorry. Can you hand me a bag then?" He started walking towards her and she made another noise, making him stop in his tracks with his hands up.

She shuffled towards him, grumbling and shaking her head before opening a bag and throwing the dandelions inside.

"What are you doing with those?" she asked again.

"Gordon told me Peony isn't eating. And that he loves dandelion greens, but the store hasn't had them lately, so I thought we could grow some."

Akiko's face softened. "I see."

Kenji put the dandelions in the bag and closed it, rolling the sides down. "Can you help me with this?"

Moments later, they were both squatting next to the buckets of soil. Kenji watched his aunt dig in the dirt, something he'd grown up watching her do. It was like the earth was a natural extension of her body, and she seemed so at peace. His heart squeezed with affection. She and Gordon were both so generous and thoughtful, which is how he'd ended up here in the first place.

He wondered how long it had been since he did something really special for either of them, but he came up blank. Then he thought of how he couldn't think of a single time Rob had done something thoughtful for Kenji that didn't also directly benefit him, and he frowned, wondering if maybe they did suit each other after all.

Akiko looked up at him when he'd stopped digging. "Oh, what is that face about?"

"Just thinking."

"Hmm. How are things going with Rob?" she asked, as if she'd figured it out. She looked back down to the dirt where she'd formed small holes to drop the seeds into.

"Oh, they're okay, I guess. I don't know."

"Not good? No wedding bells in your future?"

"Jeez!" He laughed. He pulled out a small selection of dandelion seeds and dropped them in, a few in each hole. "It's still early. But no, I don't love him. Yet."

"I think you would know by now if it was heading that way, no?"

Kenji felt defensive and he wasn't sure why. "I don't know."

"Hmm." She spread a thin layer of dirt over the seeds Kenji had planted, then looked up, locking eyes with him. "Love can be tricky, you know? Sometimes it hides in plain sight until you're too blind to see it."

He didn't know how to respond to that, but a small smile tugged at his lips. Earlier that morning when Gordon was heading to work, he'd asked Kenji to hand him his belt. Kenji glanced at it twice without realizing, and Gordon rolled his eyes before he told him to get his eyes checked.

Gordon would definitely know if he was in love. Kenji wasn't sure he would, even if it was staring him in the face.

He glanced up at Akiko and nodded, then watched her pat the soil down.

"Can you hand me that watering can, please?"

He handed it to her and watched her water the seeds before she stood up to wheel the portable grow lights to the buckets.

"There we go. We should see some sprouts in a week or two."

"Okay. That sounds fun. I'll hide them from Gordon."

She smiled at him before heading off to the front of the store where she started tidying the checkout counter. Kenji cleaned up the mess they'd made, sweeping up the leftover dirt and tossing the rest of the dandelion seeds underneath it, hoping to smother them. He moved the dandelions and the lights behind some storage bins, knowing Gordon would have no reason to enter that area.

The sun was beginning to set, and Kenji glanced at a clock, grateful to see it was past closing time. He hurried to the door to lock the deadbolt and turn off the open sign and found

Gordon standing outside with a bag of takeout. He held it up and waved.

"Hey! I wasn't expecting you," Kenji said.

"You always say that, but I'm here like five days a week." Gordon gave him a look, then glanced around before lighting up when he saw Akiko sweeping. "Akiko-san, I brought you dinner from that restaurant we saw on TV!"

She paused mid-sweep and made a noise of excitement.

"You guys made dinner plans?" Kenji asked, trying not to feel hurt.

"I brought enough for you. It's for all of us."

Of course he did.

"Oh. Thanks."

The three of them settled in together in the back room, Gordon and Akiko pointing at various dishes and discussing ingredients Kenji didn't know anything about. He glanced up at Gordon's face, and it was excited and animated, chatting with Akiko.

"You guys are really into this restaurant, huh?" Kenji asked, teasing, but still feeling a little left out.

"Food is an experience, Kenji," Gordon said, way too seriously and in an unfamiliar accent.

Akiko laughed. "He said that on the show!"

Gordon grinned at her and she elbowed him before serving him food from the different takeout boxes.

"You guys are huge dorks." Kenji took a bite of a brown and yellow thing and made a throaty noise. "Okay, I get it, though."

He leaned back in his chair and just enjoyed listening to the two of them talk, realizing that for the first time in a long time, he felt content. He wasn't trying to figure out what came next in his career or what the future held with Rob. He was just happy to be there with the two people he loved most.

CHAPTER 8

WILL "GANYMEDES," ONE OF TITAN'S LONG TENURED WRESTLERS, had set his cup on the edge of the coffee table, precariously balanced in a way that made Gordon incredibly anxious. He'd set it there haphazardly when Amber squished herself in between the edge of the couch and Will's thigh before wrapping her arms around his bicep.

"Gordon," she said, "I cannot believe you've never brought me to one of these parties."

"I don't think they happen that often, believe it or not. It's a wholesome crew."

"Wholesome! I am not!" Will turned to Amber and whispered something in her ear that made her giggle, and Gordon could only assume it was filthy. He was almost glad Amit had taken over the playlist, blasting his experimental, electronic something or other that made it impossible to have a normal conversation.

Gordon looked around the room—it was wall to wall with wrestlers and their friends, plus a few young people he assumed were fans, based on their wide-eyed expressions and unbreakable bonds with the walls.

Kenji was missing. Well, Kenji was *probably* off with Rob in some bedroom. But with an effort he'd perfected over the last couple of months, Gordon ignored the imposing thoughts of what they were doing, and with whom, and focused on the people he was sitting with.

But then he watched Will's hand creep up the inside of Amber's thigh and took it as a sign it was time for him to move along. He pushed himself up, groaning quietly before stretching his back. He felt a hundred years old and totally out of place at this party full of young, athletic people, but Kenji was leaving for Boston soon, and he hadn't given up hope they'd find each other again in the midst of the chaos.

Maybe one of the wallflowers would want to chat in the meantime. He scanned their faces and then felt about *two* hundred years old, and a little concerned they were too young to be there. But even if they had been older, none of them interested him. And truthfully, he doubted they would find him interesting, either.

His feet carried him through the living room and into the kitchen where he grabbed a sparkling water from the cooler, passing the lavender-pineapple for a much less horrifying grapefruit.

"Gordon!" Kenji said. "I'm glad you didn't leave!"

"I'm not going anywhere," he said. "Just getting something to drink."

"Hand me one of those, Gord," Rob said, his hand outstretched. Gordon dug through the cooler and found a can of lavender-pineapple and placed it in his hand without a word.

"I just had to talk to Rob about the store, and Amit's music is making my ears bleed. We were on the deck out back. It's nice out there," Kenji said.

Gordon heard Rob's can pop open, followed by a disgusted

grunt. He smiled to himself before turning to Kenji, handing him a can of grapefruit.

"What's going on with the store?"

"Well, I don't think my aunt can deal with it all by herself. I asked Rob if he could stop by a few times a week to check on things, tidy up, water a fern or two. That sort of thing."

"Okay. I can help too, you know."

"No need." Rob dabbed at his tongue with a napkin. "Ugh."

"Do you even know anything about plants?" Gordon knew the answer, but unfortunately couldn't stop himself.

"A lot more than you, I assure you."

"Rob loves plants! It's how we met, remember?" Kenji said, leaning into Rob's shoulder.

Of course, Gordon remembered. He remembered everything about Kenji and the events of his life, no matter how painful they were for him to recall.

For example, he remembered every single night out they'd had where Kenji left with someone else, and every one of Kenji's attempts at playing wingman, which almost always ended with him landing the affections of the few men Gordon had expressed interest in.

He remembered every time Kenji met someone he liked enough to bring home to Akiko, and every time Kenji was there when Gordon did the same, though his excitement for Gordon never felt particularly enthusiastic. That hurt, but it was fine. For Gordon, those men were just tepid placeholders for what he really wanted, and each of those relationships would inevitably end because it was unfair to offer only half his heart to anyone else.

So yes, he remembered when Kenji met Rob, though he wished more than anything he didn't.

"I just know Rob is busy with attorney things. I can hire a

temp worker or two. Curt works with some kids at his side gig who would love the money, I'm sure."

"Oh, huh. Actually, that—"

"That's not necessary, Gord," Rob said, cutting Kenji off.

Gordon narrowed his eyes, just the slightest amount. He hated the name Gord and hated it even more when it came out of Rob's mouth.

"And besides," Rob continued. "You know how Kenji is. He turned down your offer to pay the loan because he doesn't want your money. It surprises me you keep pushing it."

"Okay, Rob, that's not cool," Kenji said, a hand pressed against Rob's chest. "Gordon, I didn't mean any—"

"What is your problem, man?" Gordon asked, stepping closer to Rob, Kenji in between them. "I'm trying to make sure things don't fall apart while he's gone. Something I don't think you can be trusted to take care of."

"Gordon, I appreciate—"

Rob put his hand on Kenji's chest and stopped him gently. "He's made it clear he doesn't want that from you, and you keep trying to weasel your way in. He doesn't want to owe you."

"He wouldn't *owe* me. Akiko is my family, too."

"Guys, stop," Kenji said.

"He'd rather figure out his own way. Right, baby?"

"To be honest, none of this is your business," Gordon said.

"Well, it might be. I'm not going anywhere."

"This is so stupid. Whatever. You're both acting like idiots. Rob, come into the living room." Kenji walked out of the kitchen, leaving Rob and Gordon alone.

Gordon watched him leave, wanting to follow him to apologize, regretting what he'd said. But Rob's comments put him on the defensive. He just hated him so much.

He turned back to Rob. "You know you're just a temporary distraction."

"You'd like that." Rob smirked at him.

"Well, obviously." Gordon laughed.

Rob sighed and stepped back to lean against the counter. "You know everybody sees it, right? Except him, somehow. But come on, man. Look at him and look at you." Rob looked down at Gordon's shirt, the same shirt he'd dropped a strawberry on when he arrived, leaving a stain over his left nipple. Rob cocked his head and tapped the tip of Gordon's nose. "Messy, messy."

Gordon clenched his jaw, then his fists. He'd sparred with Kenji enough times to know the basic beats of a fight, though he didn't think he'd manage to take Rob down with any success. But the impulse was there, boiling over. And for the first time in his life, he didn't care to stop himself.

He pulled his fist back and swung before landing a surprisingly solid punch against Rob's cheek. The force of it caused Rob to lurch backward and his eyes flew open, but it was a short-lived moment of pride for Gordon, because Rob closed the space between them again in seconds.

Gordon felt the full weight of Rob's body pummel him to the ground. The wind was knocked out of his lungs, and he instinctively brought his arms up to cover his face. Shouting erupted around them, but he couldn't make out what was being said. Out of nowhere, the pressure on his body lifted as Rob was dragged away.

It was a party full of wrestlers, of course, all of whom lifted people of Rob's size multiple times a day. Still, Gordon was impressed at the speed with which Rob disappeared from his line of sight, and when he sat up and rubbed his eyes, he realized Rob was gone entirely.

Will and Niall appeared from the ether and kneeled beside

him, grabbing him under the arms and lifting him to a standing position before shuffling him into the corner to get ice for his aching hand.

"Dude," Will said. "What were you thinking?"

Gordon hissed when the bag of ice touched his knuckles, which were already discolored and bruised.

"I don't know," he whined, regretting his actions already. "I wasn't, really. He's just so punchable. What does Kenji see in him?"

"He's hot," Niall said, the look on his face telling Gordon it was obvious. "And desirable. Confident. Rich, I think? Nice ass, even better than mine. I think half the people here want to take him into the back and see what else there is under there. I wouldn't mind being a fly on the wall."

Will shot him a look and jammed his elbow into Niall's ribs, a pained scoff slipping from his lips.

"What? Some people get off on that!"

"Okay, TMI, dude," Will said, rolling his eyes before adjusting the ice pack on Gordon's hand, causing him to wince. Will gave Niall a look and said, "Also, maybe Gordon isn't interested in the details of your sex life, hm?"

Niall shrugged, a small grin spreading across his face.

"Alright, well, thanks for the awesome pep talk, Niall," Gordon said.

"You know I'm kidding, buddy. Rob sucks. He's hot, sure, but what a piece of shit. I tried to get him to guess the winner of the 2001 Hour of Wreckoning match earlier, you know? I put it on just to have some fun. He said he couldn't choose because he didn't know any of their stats. Then he said if we were betting money, which we were not, by the way, he was at a disadvantage. That match is over twenty years old! Who the fuck cares?"

Gordon smiled at Niall's outrage.

"Believe me, man, *none* of us like him. I'm not even convinced Kenji likes him, if you want to know the truth. Especially not now," Niall said, pointing at Gordon's hand.

Gordon's stomachache lessened slightly. "Okay."

"Hey, Will, you know what Gordon said when I made him pick a Wreckoning winner at his first Titan party?"

"No, what?"

"'Which one could beat Kenji?' Very cute, right? But that was like four years ago and Kenji was so tiny, so the answer was all of them."

Will laughed. "Aw. That is cute."

Gordon wanted to curl in on himself and die.

"He ended up picking the first guy out."

"Okay," Gordon said. "Again, thanks for the pep talk, Niall."

Niall patted Gordon on the head and took off towards Amit, whose music had somehow become even worse.

"So, um, are you okay?" Will asked, looking over Gordon's shoulder towards the living room, undoubtedly looking for Amber.

"I'm fine. Go on," Gordon said. He hadn't even finished his sentence before Will had disappeared.

With his pain sufficiently numbed by the ice resting on his hand, the reality of what had just happened began settling on Gordon's shoulders. There was no way Kenji would want to spend the rest of the evening with Gordon now, not after what he did.

His thoughts spiraled and the evening's events replayed over and over. Rob's smug grin and antagonistic comments, Kenji's attempts at placating the two of them, the punch he landed on Rob. That part wasn't so bad, actually, but the rest of it made him feel like shit.

He moved to the backyard where it was quiet and cool,

before settling into a padded lawn chair. He let his head fall back against the cushion and closed his eyes, wondering how long he could stay out there before Will asked him to leave. He thought about Amber and hoped she was having a better night than him. The text she'd sent him ten minutes earlier, the one asking if he could take her car home because she was staying the night, had all but confirmed it. Gross.

His thoughts were interrupted by the sound of the sliding glass door opening and closing in quick succession. Someone settled into the chair next to him, the wood creaking under what sounded like a solid frame. Kenji.

Gordon looked over and saw him, his face bright in the moonlight. There was no anger in his face, but no warmth, either. Just a neutrality he wasn't entirely comfortable with. Neither of them spoke, but Gordon wanted to break the tension. What *was* the right thing to say after you punched your best friend's boyfriend, he wondered.

"So," Kenji said, tapping his fingers on the armrest of his chair, "I've never heard of you punching anyone before."

"Yeah. Does it do anything for you?"

Kenji laughed, the sound immediately releasing Gordon from his spiral of worry.

"What the fuck, man," he said, still laughing. "Don't let him get under your skin, okay? I know he's an asshole."

"Then why..." Gordon stopped short and mulled over what he really wanted to ask. He wasn't sure he wanted to know the truth behind why Kenji was seeing Rob, especially if it was for all the reasons Niall said. "Nevermind."

Kenji's laugh faded, but he was still smiling. "I don't know. I mean, he's not my future husband, Gordon. You know that, right?"

"I'd hope not. What if my best man speech was just me talking about how the other groom has a weak jaw?"

"There are no expectations with Rob. We're having fun, just... semi-committed, regularly occurring fun. I'm not looking for anything more than that. Not with him, anyway. And I don't think he feels that way about me, either, which is why that entire argument was so stupid. Both sides of it."

Gordon tried to prevent his heart from soaring at the prospect of a looming end to Kenji and Rob's relationship, but he failed.

"Who knows, maybe I'll meet someone better in Boston."

That helped, and he felt his heart crash down to Earth.

"So, are you heading out?" Gordon asked. He hadn't seen Rob hovering around the doors, but that didn't mean anything.

"Not unless you want to."

"You're not staying with Rob tonight?"

"God, no. Not after embarrassing me like that. You're everybody's favorite. Mike would probably fire me if he found out I left with Rob."

"I think Jim is everybody's favorite."

"He doesn't count. No ex-Titans. And seriously, after tonight? You definitely are."

"Okay," Gordon said, smiling up at the stars.

"I'm going to miss you when I'm in Boston. It'll be weird to be away from you for so long."

"Yeah."

Gordon took Kenji's words and tucked them away deep inside where he was sure they'd pick at the edges of his heart over the next month. Kenji wasn't serious about Rob, he knew that now, but somehow it didn't comfort him the way he would have expected. The joke Kenji made about meeting someone in Boston had been light-hearted, but it confirmed what Gordon had known for years. But for some reason he'd refused to fully accept it, instead feeding his hope with every touch, hug, or inno-cent comment.

Gordon didn't want to be in love with Kenji anymore. There was no catalyst, no especially difficult moment. It had just grown too heavy for him to carry, too secretive and painful. But his body had been holding it for years, and he didn't know how to exist without the weight of it.

It sometimes felt like the only future free from these feel-ings was one free of Kenji all together. But that was impossible, at least for now. Akiko needed him, and he needed her.

At least Kenji's absence over his month in Boston would give Gordon the space he needed—a clean break to figure out who he was without spinning endlessly around Kenji, bound by his gravitational pull.

CHAPTER 9

Things had blown over with Rob for the most part, though the argument with Gordon lingered in the back of Kenji's mind. He wished he hadn't left the kitchen, and he wished he knew exactly what the impetus had been for Gordon punching Rob, but neither of them had given him the details.

He'd invited Gordon out to play pool at a bar near the arena because things hadn't blown over quite as quickly with him. They had spoken every day and seen each other the normal amount, but Gordon felt distant, and Kenji was hoping going out would give them both a chance to regain some normalcy before he left for Boston.

His trip was approaching quickly, and he was feeling uneasy about it all—leaving Akiko, where things stood with Rob, asking so much of Gordon and believing him when he said it was all under control. But he trusted Gordon, so he was forcing himself to let go for the evening.

Gordon left Kenji by the bar to grab a pool table, then racked the balls quietly and arranged them carefully. Kenji watched from his spot at the bar as a man stopped by and chatted with Gordon for a moment. He felt his stomach tighten when Gordon laughed at something the man said, a laugh that was usually hard earned by strangers, but it loosened when Gordon pointed over to Kenji and waved. The man walked away after leaning in, saying something else that made Gordon smile and nod slowly.

Drinks in hand, Kenji approached Gordon.

"Who was that?" he asked.

"Who? The guy I was just talking to?"

Kenji nodded and sipped his beer.

"Christian," Gordon said.

"Okay. Who is Christian?"

"Uh, that guy? I don't know, he just stopped by and said hi, and asked if I was playing with anyone," Gordon said, giving Kenji a bemused look. "Is that okay?"

Kenji schooled his face, realizing he was being weird. "Yes, of course. Your break."

He grabbed a cue and watched Gordon set up his shot. He did his best not to look over to Christian. With a quick flick of his wrist, Gordon completed the break, and the balls scattered across the table, two solids finding their way to a pocket. He grinned at Kenji, who glared back at him.

"Gross. I'm stripes, I guess."

They took their respective turns and the game went quickly. Kenji was relieved the conversation was flowing freely, like maybe their friendship would regain its balance. It probably helped that Gordon was winning, which he did every time, but it still made him annoyingly happy.

Kenji felt his phone vibrate and checked to see who had texted.

"You can get that," Gordon said when he caught Kenji shoving his phone back in his pocket.

"It's okay. It's just Rob."

Gordon settled into a stool at the tall table next to them.

Kenji joined him, the familiar scent of Gordon's jacket—floral, but clean, and maybe whatever lizards smell like—grounding him. Kenji swiped through his phone to show Gordon photos of the apartment he'd be staying in with Anthony, an open loft with huge windows and a price tag he was glad he never had to pay attention to. Gordon told him about Victor's latest requests at the office, this time, a bagel slicer that Victor thought Gordon should purchase instead of having the office manager pick one up on her next snack run.

Kenji's phone vibrated again, on the table this time, and he winced.

"Seriously, dude, just answer him," Gordon said, shaking his head. "I'll survive. I'm over it."

"Okay, sorry."

Gordon's gaze fell to the bar, where the man from earlier was leaning on the counter, chatting with the bartender. "I'm going to go get another soda water. I'll be right back. Do you want another beer?"

"Just a Coke for me, please."

Kenji watched him go, and the same tightening he felt earlier returned when Christian smiled as Gordon approached before introducing him to the bartender, who appeared to be a friend.

Kenji pulled his phone out and replied to Rob, who had asked if they were still getting together. After tapping out a reply, he let his mind wander to more pleasant things, like what it would be like in Boston and what connections he'd make. He'd finished imagining his debut match, which he most definitely planned to win, when he noticed Gordon standing even closer to Christian than he was before.

Gordon leaned against the counter and laughed at something the bartender said. Kenji's hand tightened on his empty beer glass but loosened when Gordon approached him with fresh drinks.

"So, what are you and Rob up to tonight?" Gordon asked.

"What?"

"You and Rob? I just assumed you guys were making plans," he said, pointing to Kenji's phone.

"Oh, yeah. We're getting dinner later."

"Okay…"

"Sorry," Kenji said. "I'm tired and spacy. Do you want to play another round?"

"Sure," Gordon said, nodding. He grabbed his drink and walked back to the pool table, leaving Kenji in his seat.

Kenji rolled his shoulders to shake off the weird energy he was feeling, something he was blaming on being tired and nervous about the rest of the summer—he thought Boston, mostly, but also leaving Akiko. And Gordon.

"Alright, I'm about to kick your ass," Kenji said.

"I think we both know that's not true."

Their game progressed predictably, Kenji losing horribly. Gordon went quiet eventually, looking towards the door over Kenji's shoulder. Kenji turned around and saw Rob, who had not actually been invited.

"Hey," Rob said, approaching the table. He nodded to Gordon, who nodded back.

"Rob," Gordon said.

"What are you doing here?" Kenji asked.

"I thought we were getting dinner."

"It's not even five!"

"Thanks for the warm welcome, sweetheart."

Gordon smiled into his glass and took a sip of his drink.

"Sorry." Kenji set his cue against the table. "I just meant I wasn't expecting you so early."

"How badly is he losing?" Rob asked, looking to Gordon.

"Pretty bad," Gordon said, landing a ball in a pocket. "But that's normal."

"Anyway," Kenji said, "we'll be done soon and then we can go. If you don't mind, Gordon."

"I'll be fine. I have to get Peony some food anyway."

Kenji leaned against the table and watched as Gordon sank the final shot, disappointed the game ended so early. He really needed to get better at pool.

"Good game, Kenj. Kind of," Gordon said, smiling. He grabbed their glasses, balancing them in his hand so he could take one trip to the bar. "See you later, guys."

Rob slid his arm around Kenji. "Ready to go?"

"Sure," he said, watching Gordon walk to the bar.

It didn't feel like he'd managed to fix things with Gordon completely, and Rob showing up early ruined any chance he'd had to do it. For a second, he imagined an afternoon where Rob hadn't showed up, and he and Gordon had been able to play a few more rounds or go home to watch a movie. It sounded so much better than going to have dinner and conversation he wasn't in the mood for.

Before they walked out the door, Kenji took one last look at the bar and saw Gordon paying his tab and felt his shoulders loosen.

Outside, the air was stale and muggy. It smelled like exhaust and stale beer and it was too bright. Kenji shoved his hands in his pockets.

"Italian okay?"

"Sure, that sounds good," Kenji said.

"Who was that with Gordon when we left?"

Kenji huffed. "I don't know. Someone he met in there."

"Hmm."

"Hmm what?" Kenji asked with more bite than he meant

to. He kicked a rock down the sidewalk and watched it bounce instead of looking at Rob.

"You spent a lot of time watching him when you guys were playing pool."

"No I didn't," Kenji said.

"He was hot. I don't blame you."

"He was fine, but that's not why I was looking at him."

Rob smiled. "I knew it."

Kenji glared at him. "I wasn't *looking* at him. I was trying to figure out if Gordon... nevermind. I don't know."

"What?" Rob asked. He stopped in the middle of the sidewalk for a second and grinned. "Ohh. You were jealous."

"I was not jealous. I just didn't know who he was, and he ended up talking to Gordon at the bar for a while. I was curious."

"Right."

A customer on his way out of the restaurant held the door for Rob and Kenji. They offered him quick smiles in thanks before they walked in. The air conditioning was nice, but Kenji was mostly grateful for the forced silence, since Rob couldn't continue their conversation at the host stand.

He wasn't *jealous* of Christian. He just didn't like that Gordon's attention was on someone else when they were there specifically to patch things up. That was all.

The waiter took them through the restaurant and sat them at a table in a corner, isolated and away from the window. Rob sat down across from Kenji and smiled again. "Okay. Just don't break his heart."

"What are you talking about?"

"Should we get an appetizer?"

. . .

WHEN KENJI GOT HOME from his date—the long, boring date, during which he could not focus on Rob and just wanted to get home—he walked into the house and saw Gordon on the couch with his computer propped on his lap. The room was dark, but Kenji could see remnants of whatever delicious thing Gordon had made for dinner in the nearly empty bowl next to his calves. He glanced up and smiled at Kenji, his face washed out by the light of his computer screen.

"You're home early," he said, closing his laptop.

"Yeah, I guess so. Didn't feel like going out, I guess." He plopped on the couch next to Gordon and took the computer, tossing it to the ottoman. "Stop working. It's so late."

"I'm trying," Gordon said. He stretched his arms up over his head. "Victor has a bee in his bonnet about something stupid."

"A bee in his bonnet?" Kenji laughed.

Gordon grinned at him. "Want to watch a movie?"

"Okay," Kenji said. He tugged at the piping of a couch cushion. "So, um. What did you do after I left?"

"Went to the pet store."

"Oh, you didn't stay at the bar?"

"No?" Gordon looked at Kenji for a second, then sighed at his phone, which was vibrating with a call from Victor.

"Oh. Okay." Kenji sat back on the couch, his grip on the cushion loosening.

"Anyway, is a comedy okay? I don't want to have to use my brain."

"Sure." He put his feet up on the ottoman next to Gordon's, knocking the bowl to the ground. "Oops."

Gordon's phone vibrated again, a text message this time.

"I should probably deal with this," Gordon said, grabbing the bowl from the floor.

Kenji glanced over and saw the texts coming in from Victor. He even texted rudely.

> Victor: Did you send the updated report?
>
> Victor: This isn't what I asked for.
>
> Victor: I need you to fix this.
>
> Victor: Are you ignoring me?

Gordon typed out a response and sat forward on the couch. He barely had time to set the phone down before it started ringing.

"Want me to throw that in the garbage?" Kenji asked.

"Yes, please," Gordon said. "Ugh, I'll be right back."

He walked into the kitchen and answered with a clipped, "Yeah?"

Kenji tried to focus on finding a movie out of respect for Gordon, but Victor was making it hard. He couldn't hear the details of what Victor was saying, but he could hear him yelling.

"It's late," Gordon said. "I'm watching a movie."

Kenji heard more murmured yelling and Gordon making noises of acceptance. He wasn't pushing back at all.

"Alright, the language really isn't necessary. I did hear you," Gordon said.

Kenji glared towards the kitchen.

"I'll get it sent over as soon as I can." Gordon hung up but didn't come back to the living room right away. Kenji found him standing by the counter, gripping the edge.

"You okay?"

"Hm? Oh, yeah. Just work stuff."

Kenji bumped into Gordon's shoulder. "The movie is waiting for us."

When they got back to the living room, Gordon took his laptop out and started working on something. The report Victor said he'd messed up, he assumed, which looked fine to Kenji.

"It's so late. Do you really have to do that now?"

"Yeah, unless I want to hear from Victor again," Gordon said, chuckling sadly.

Kenji didn't say anything, but he spent the rest of the movie stewing over the way Victor spoke to Gordon—so loud, and what Kenji could only assume was entitled. He thought about how Gordon was so willing to take care of the stupid report on his day off, how Victor hadn't even hesitated to demand Gordon's time, like he just expected it. The more he thought about it, the more he realized Gordon had been downplaying how much Victor sucked. Kenji didn't even know him, but now he hated him.

Kenji glanced over to Gordon and saw the concentration on his face, wishing he could do something to protect him from Victor—like, maybe punch Victor in the face. He settled for scooting closer to his friend, pressing their thighs together, and hoping his presence would be as grounding for Gordon as Gordon's always was for him.

CHAPTER 10

KENJI STOOD IN FRONT OF ROB'S FULL-LENGTH BEDROOM MIRROR buttoning his ugly, maroon shirt that was snug in a way he wasn't used to. He glanced down at his phone to check how many hours he had left before he was allowed to go home and change. They hadn't even left the house, so realizing he had another six hours before he'd be in his bed almost made him cry.

He'd promised Rob he'd attend some event as his date because he was trying to network his way into a new role at a competing firm. Or something. Kenji didn't really know, even though Rob had spent twenty agonizing minutes explaining the purpose of the evening, the names of people they were likely to meet, and basic ground rules for behavior, which had made Kenji want to scream.

If he was honest with himself, he would admit that things were not working between the two of them. But it was hard to end things for a variety of reasons. Kenji felt stupid for thinking Rob was different somehow. But he'd been so caught up in the excitement of their meeting, he didn't want the embarrassment that came along with quitting so soon. Plus, they really did have a good time together, even if that was sort of the extent of it.

"You look good," Rob said, fixing Kenji's tie and patting him on the chest. "Crooked. I got it."

It made Kenji feel guilty, even though he suspected Rob felt similarly.

"Thanks."

"What's wrong? You look… off," Rob said, brushing a piece of lint off Kenji's shoulder.

"Nothing's wrong, I'm just a little nervous. My shirt is tight and everyone you mentioned seems awful."

Rob shrugged. "Yeah, they are. But it's just something I have to do to get what I want. You understand that, right? It's like how you have to go to shitty towns all over the Pacific Northwest to get to the big leagues."

"That's not really fair. The fans are fun. Also, there are no leagues in professional wrestling," Kenji said.

Of course, Rob didn't know that. He didn't know anything about Kenji's life.

"I know that. It's a figure of speech."

"Oh."

"You said you'd go. Can you just do this for me? People will love you!"

"Yeah, I know. I'll go."

Rob gave him a quick kiss and left the room before yelling back that Kenji should do something with his hair. Kenji was left staring at himself in the mirror feeling like his hair looked just fine. It was clean, but maybe Rob wanted it tied back? He put it in a low ponytail and headed out towards the living room where he found Rob holding two pairs of shoes. His toes pinched after he put them on and he wished more than ever he was at home with Gordon and Akiko, not in Rob's sterile downtown apartment.

The event was being hosted at a hotel downtown in a ball-room that looked like something out of a movie. He'd never attended an event quite like it. Most events he attended that could be considered "events" were at Titan, so he knew most of the people already, and those he didn't, knew him.

But Kenji was a social guy. He enjoyed meeting new people and finding common ground. The variety in types of people he met every week was one of his favorite things about wrestling. He figured, worst case scenario, he would find a few people who are interested in chatting about stuff he understood, and he'd just stick with them all night if Rob had stuff to do.

Rob took Kenji's hand and placed it on his arm then gave him a quiet smile. He really did look handsome. Kenji smiled back and held on as Rob walked them around the space, intro-ducing him to a dozen people he'd heard of in passing but never actually met.

Kenji was met with raised eyebrows after introducing himself and sharing what he did for a living, many of the people he spoke with glancing back at Rob or sharing quiet laughs and looks with each other. Kenji didn't understand what had been funny, but that wasn't uncommon, so he rolled with it.

"Sweetheart," Rob said, pulling him off to the side.

"What's wrong?"

"Please don't tell people you're a professional wrestler. Or a wrestler. Or any combination of words that implies you commit acts of violence for a living."

"Why?"

"Just tell them you're a business owner. It's not even a lie, you do pretty much run Kiko's."

Kenji laughed, because that was far from accurate. Akiko owned it, and Gordon had been more involved than Kenji for more than a year now. In fact, over the last few months, as he had increased his ring time with Titan, the idea of overseeing Kiko's had gone from being something he was entertaining for the sake of family to feeling like a suffocating nightmare. He hadn't told his aunt yet, but it was on his list of things he needed to get to. Eventually.

"I do not run Kiko's."

"Just… please, for me?"

"Okay, fine. Am I allowed to like wrestling?" Kenji asked.

Rob rolled his eyes. "Just talk about other things tonight. Plants? You love plants."

"I do love plants, I guess," Kenji said. His shoulders slumped slightly.

"Perfect. Thank you, sweetheart. You being here, looking like that, is all you need to do."

Kenji grunted in agreement before he was pulled back into the crowd. He followed Rob around for twenty minutes, too afraid to talk in case Rob hated what he said, worried he'd be scolded again. Rob barely acknowledged Kenji, briefly checking over his shoulder, offering him small smiles and winks as he continued his conversations with colleagues.

The worst part was that Kenji just didn't care that much. He wanted to go home to Gordon and Akiko, to spend time with them before he left for Boston. But he'd told Rob he'd stay, so he did.

"Hey, I have to go do some networking. Go get yourself a drink, and I'll be back in twenty minutes. Okay?"

"Okay. I might step outside and get some air," Kenji said, adjusting his suit jacket.

Kenji wasted no time before he left out the ballroom doors, shoving open the heavy doors to the outside. The event was downtown, so there weren't any private areas to escape to, but there were stairs leading up to the hotel. He sat on the edge of one and pulled out his phone. He had a few texts from

Gordon, including a photo of Peony sitting at the table with Akiko, who was glaring down at him.

Akiko looked frail and sick in the photo and Kenji's stomach tightened. He hated how much he'd been gone, relying on Gordon to keep things together. He felt like he had let her down. But he also knew she would brush him off if he tried to apologize. Her support was endless and pure. Kenji felt his nose tingling as if he was about to cry, so he rubbed his face and dialed Gordon's number.

"Hey, man. How's the party? You're on speaker," Gordon said when he answered.

"Hi Kenji!" Akiko chirped from the background.

"Hi guys. Oh, it's about what you'd expect."

"How did you get Akiko-san to sit with Peony?" Kenji asked. He laughed again, looking at the photo of the two of them. "It looks like they're having a conversation."

"Well, you've missed a lot lately. Peony laid an egg."

"One egg?"

"For now. I called the vet. Apparently, it's normal, I just have to give him more calcium and UV light or something. I'm taking him in, and they'll tell me what to do."

"Will he have more?"

"I think so? It explains why he's been such a bitch lately, though."

"Wait, does this mean Peony is a girl?" Kenji asked, really hoping that wasn't a ridiculous question, but he was at least ninety nine percent sure it wasn't. But he also knew seahorse dads carried their young.

"I guess so."

"I can't believe I'm an uncle! When do they hatch?"

Gordon chuckled a little bit. "I mean... they're not fertilized, Ken," he said gently.

Kenji heard Akiko laugh in the background and smiled

briefly. "Tell her to leave me alone. I'm already being tortured at this party."

"What's going on?"

"Oh, nothing. This just isn't my scene. Apparently, I'm not allowed to talk about wrestling."

The phone made a shuffling noise and Gordon's voice was clearer when he spoke again. "I'm sorry, you're not *allowed* to talk about wrestling? Says who, Rob?"

"Well, you know. He has people to impress, or something," Kenji said, wishing he hadn't mentioned it. It was bad enough to hear it from Rob, he didn't need Gordon thinking he was pathetic on top of it.

Gordon groaned and yelled something to Akiko he couldn't quite understand, like he'd put his hand over the phone. He was quiet for a minute before he said, "She says she doesn't like Rob at all."

Kenji laughed and rubbed his eyes. "Oh, my God. I know, I know."

His smile fell when he heard someone walking down the stairs then standing in front of him. It seemed like a bad sign that he'd rather be on the phone with Gordon than be at a party with his... Rob.

"Why are you outside? These steps are filthy."

"Hey, Gordon, I gotta go. Tell Akiko I love her, okay? And Peony. And Peony's child."

"Yeah. Talk to you later," Gordon said.

Kenji's shoulders slumped and he looked up to Rob.

"Can you come back inside, please?"

"I kind of want to go home, if that's alright. It seems like you're doing great on your own," Kenji said.

"What? Why?"

"It's just not really my scene! I don't know. I'm not even allowed to talk about my job or stuff I like. Why am I even here?"

Rob rolled his eyes. "I want you here. I want people to know you."

Kenji sighed. "I don't know, Rob. This has been really fun, this thing between us, but I'm going to Boston soon. Maybe it's just bad timing, too much going on in our personal lives, you know? It's hard to put as much into this as we need to, being so busy."

Rob's face pinched and he sat next to Kenji on the dirty step. "Don't say that. What if we just put a pause on things when you go to Boston. We're both dealing with work stress, but I like you, Kenji. Don't throw it away just because of... this," he said, gesturing to the hotel.

"Oh. Well, um, okay." Kenji didn't want to make a scene, but he was sort of hoping Rob would breathe out a breath of relief, and maybe they could laugh about how ill-suited they were. Instead, Rob leaned into him.

"I still want to help with the store," Rob said. "And I'd like to get you to the airport like we talked about."

"I thought you had a conference," Kenji said. "I already asked Gordon to take me when you said you couldn't."

"It got cancelled. Can you un-ask Gordon and let me take you, please? I'd hate it if this thing was the last time we hung out before you left."

Kenji bit his lip, thinking about how to make it work, and realized he could go out to dinner with Gordon the night before he left instead of getting breakfast the day of his flight.

"Okay. Yeah, that sounds good," he said, with a confidence meant to ease Rob's mind. But deep down, he was nervous about running this by Gordon. He knew Gordon wouldn't mind—he never did—but part of him dreaded telling him. "I'm still heading out, though."

Rob smiled at him before leaning over to kiss his cheek. "That's okay. I'll see you in a couple of days."

Kenji headed to Gordon's house and ran up the stairs with a smile on his face, happy to be home, looking forward to joining them for whatever TV marathon he and Akiko were in the middle of.

When he pushed the door open, he opened his mouth to say hi but stopped himself when he saw Gordon and Akiko asleep on the couch. Peony was asleep on his favorite branch. The TV was playing some cooking competition show they both enjoyed. It was a sweet scene, but he was sad he'd missed their evening together. He picked up a blanket Gordon had folded on the back of his couch and draped it over Akiko before patting her thinning hair and taking himself to bed.

CHAPTER 11

"SO, SHE'S MOVING IN WITH YOU FOR THE MONTH?" AMBER asked. She was crunching on some sort of dried coconut topping sprinkled over a quickly melting açai bowl from the place around the corner from Gordon's house. They'd managed to find a spot in the shade for the impromptu dog park picnic she'd suggested, but it was still scorching. "That's probably good. She's pretty sick, huh?"

"Yeah, you could say that," he said, chuckling slightly. "And of course I'm okay with her being there. I want her there. Kenji wants her there."

"Hmm."

"What?" Gordon asked, watching Amber's dog chase the ball he threw. "Uh oh. I hope she comes back."

Amber squinted her eyes, trying to find the ball. "How did you throw that so far? Gordon, are you hiding some muscles under there?" She squeezed his arm.

"How quickly you forgot my years of rec league softball. I even made it to the state championship a couple times, remember? It was very healing for little Gordon."

"Aww. Yeah. You were so cute when you played t-ball,

though."

"I wasn't. Anyway, I don't know how much I told you, but I had to quit because Kenji's schedule was leaving Akiko alone more than we were comfortable with."

"Is he really gone that much?"

"He is now, yeah. Partly because his boss sends him to extra matches with other promotions to up his online engagement. CWA wants him to be more well-known, or something, before they're willing to give him a contract. I don't know how it all works, exactly. Just that he's been gone a lot the last couple of years."

"What happens if he gets a contract?"

"He'll move to Boston."

"Will she go with him?" she asked.

He didn't think she meant it rudely. But Gordon knew, based on previous conversations, Amber was worried Kenji took advantage of him. Which he didn't, by the way. Gordon never minded helping.

"Well, no. She has her doctors and stuff here. She's not in any shape to move."

"Oh, yeah. Of course."

"She also has the store and everything."

"So, she'll stay here and run the store, and Kenji will fly back when he can?"

"I guess so, although the first couple of years I don't think he'll be here much." He ate the last of his açai bowl and grimaced. The ice in his had melted from the heat, leaving behind a warm fruit soup. "I'd probably have to run the store if he left. She can't handle it on her own anymore and she's not… you know. She's not going to get any better."

Amber nodded and squinted into the sun again, whistling to call her dog back.

"So, you'll work full time, take care of Akiko, deal with

mom, *and* take care of four hundred plants, something I know you both suck at and derive no pleasure from. And Kenji gets to go live his dreams in Boston?"

"It's not like that," he said.

She shrugged. "I don't know Kenji at all, so it might not be. But I do know you're in love with him and you'll do just about anything for him. I just hope he returns the favor sometimes."

"Of course he does," Gordon said.

"I believe you."

"And I like doing things for people."

"Okay."

Gordon crossed his arms and leaned on the trunk of the maple tree he was standing under. He had no interest in defending his behavior to someone who barely knew the dynamic of his friendship with Kenji. But he worried that made her comments even more poignant.

"It's too hot. I'm going to walk back and get this lady out of the heat. See you at seven, right?" she asked, clipping the dog's leash to its harness and taking off, leaving Gordon under the tree to digest.

GORDON'S HOUSE WAS MODEST, the kind of place that wasn't particularly impressive, but felt like a real home. It was the opposite of the house he'd grown up in, which is exactly what he'd wanted. Three bedrooms, two bathrooms, and a small yard that needed some TLC. Preferably hired TLC, since Gordon killed plants by breathing on them wrong. The path out front was overgrown and ugly, but it led to a covered porch he liked to sit on when the summer evenings cooled off.

Inside, a few walls were lined with bookshelves that held a mix of old textbooks he never tossed and other books he never read. He had a few framed photos of his family, Kenji, Peony, and Akiko dotting the surfaces, but in general, the house gave a minimalist vibe without the nice aesthetic.

He still liked it, even if it was more house than he needed on his own. But better than being too small, since he thought he might have a roommate someday. Or a partner. Or maybe a really big dog, once Peony died and mammal-allergic Kenji moved to Boston full time. But he didn't really want to think about that right now, still reeling from the brief conversation he'd had with Amber.

Did Kenji take advantage of him? He'd never really thought about it, because he was happy to take care of him. Kenji was busy, and his goals kept him occupied. Who was it hurting if Gordon ran errands and covered for him when needed? Akiko kept him fed, Kenji was always grateful, and Gordon liked feeling useful.

Satisfied with his conclusion and relieved to know he was not being taken advantage of by his best friend, he trudged up the steps at his house, nearly crying tears of joy at the promise of air conditioning ahead. The door was unlocked, which meant Kenji was probably inside eating something or napping, though his car wasn't there. If he'd had anything worth stealing, Gordon would have felt nervous opening the door.

As he pushed the door open, it snagged on something—a shoe, maybe. Gordon squeezed his way through and saw Kenji's gym bag and other shoe near the table, allowing him to breathe a sigh of relief.

He kicked the door closed and made his way to the kitchen, hoping he'd find Kenji, but the room was empty. But there were scattered seltzer cans around, two of them half full, a sure sign Kenji had been there at one point.

"Kenji?"

He poured out the rest of the seltzers, knowing Kenji wouldn't finish them if they were even slightly flat, and walked down the hallway to his bedroom where he found the door slightly ajar. He nudged it open with his toe and glanced in, stopping short when he saw what was there.

Kenji was sprawled out on his stomach, shirtless and half tucked under the sheet of Gordon's bed. It wasn't even close to the first time he'd walked in on him sleeping there, but it made him pause every time. Gordon watched him breathe for a few moments, reveling in the almost painful intimacy, before forcing himself to walk away—quietly, of course, because if he was sleeping in the middle of the day, he probably needed it.

He decided to follow a recipe Akiko had given him that he'd learned was a favorite childhood comfort meal. Her health had been dwindling faster than he'd expected, and soup was a good way to get her to eat. Since he had no control over any other aspect of her life, he was feeding her as much as he could, afraid that if he didn't, she'd go to sleep and never wake up.

He gathered up the ingredients he needed—broth, vegetables, chicken, mushrooms, precooked rice—and used gentle hands to spread them out on the counter, trying to keep the noise level down so Kenji could sleep.

The spread reminded him of the first time Kenji brought Gordon home to Akiko after just a few months of friendship. She'd cooked him a feast with so many different options he'd been visibly awestruck. She had been so tickled by Gordon's reaction that she gave him cooking lessons for months, just the two of them standing side-by-side in her small kitchen while Kenji was off working one of his various part time jobs or enjoying the dating pool.

Eventually, their time together shifted from teaching to just enjoying each other's company and producing a good meal, which Kenji was always happy about when he got home.

Gordon's focus shifted when he heard footsteps heading towards him. His stomach fluttered when he saw him.

"Hey," Kenji said, stepping into the kitchen, looking sleep rumpled and cute. His eyes were squinty from sleep. "Did you get new sheets?"

"Yeah, you said the other ones made you itchy. I put those in the guest room." He smiled sadly at Kenji, struggling to hide the heaviness he was feeling knowing Kenji was leaving soon.

"Oh, okay. Well, they're nice."

"Glad you like them," Gordon said. He rolled his neck trying to work out a kink. He'd been going nonstop for weeks, and it was catching up with him.

"What are you making?" Kenji asked before stepping towards Gordon, reaching out to massage his neck. "Let me get that."

Gordon steadied his breath and squinted at his phone screen so he could focus. "Um, zosui?"

"Oh, nice. She'll love that," Kenji said, rubbing harder.

Gordon set his phone down and leaned into Kenji's touch. "What are you doing?"

"Your traps are very tense. They're like little bricks in there."

"I've been on my feet a lot. None of my muscles are used to it, I guess," Gordon said. He let out an embarrassing whimper.

Kenji laughed and pressed even harder, digging his thumbs into the muscles of Gordon's back, one on either side of his spine. "I wish I could take you to Mitch at work. He sometimes does massage even though I don't think it's technically part of his job. I think he just likes to touch me."

"What? Who is this guy?"

"I'm kidding! He's a physical therapist. Very professional. I asked him how to massage a neck because I noticed you've been rubbing yours in the evenings lately."

Gordon shuddered and stepped away from Kenji before he embarrassed himself. He cleared his throat and said, "Thank you. Feels a lot better."

"Hey, can you get me to Rob's later? I gave my car to Will to keep while I'm in Boston. I need to get there at nine or so. He said he could drop me at the airport tomorrow after all."

Gordon immediately deflated, going from the high of being touched by Kenji to this horrible reminder of Rob's existence. "What? He can? I thought you wanted to get breakfast with me before you left."

"I know, but that was when I thought Rob couldn't make it."

Gordon huffed out a laugh before turning back to his cutting board. He sliced a few mushrooms. "Okay."

"Are you mad?" Kenji asked, moving in to stand next to him.

For reasons beyond Gordon's understanding, Kenji looked genuinely surprised.

"We can get dinner tonight instead, right?" he asked.

"No, we can't. I'm going to a show with Amber at seven. I agreed to go with her after you asked me to drive you to the airport, because I knew I'd have that time with you."

"Well, can you meet up with her after, or something?"

"Can I ditch her last minute, make her go to a concert alone, and then ask her to hang out with me once we're done with dinner? No," Gordon said. He wanted to laugh, but Kenji looked serious. And confused.

"But…"

Gordon paused, waiting for something reasonable to leave Kenji's mouth.

"Sorry. I can't cancel on her." Gordon shrugged. But part of him wanted to. He couldn't believe this was the last interaction he and Kenji would have before they were apart for an entire month.

"Fine."

"Fine?"

"Well, I'm kind of annoyed we don't get to spend any time together before I go," Kenji said.

Gordon set his knife down and turned to him. "How is that my fault? You're changing the plan here, not me."

"I just feel like this is an extenuating circumstance. Amber would understand if you couldn't make it."

"Rob would understand if I took you to the airport."

"Maybe… But either way, he lives closer to the airport. It just makes sense for him to take me."

"Yeah, I don't know what you'd do if you had to spend an extra ten minutes in the car," Gordon said, chopping again. Green onions this time, so he could be aggressive about it. "Wait, what do you mean, maybe?"

"What?"

"You said 'maybe' when I said Rob would understand. Would he not understand?"

"I mean, he'd understand, but he probably wouldn't like it. He's a little jealous of you, I think."

Gordon huffed a sad laugh. "Right. I can totally see why."

"I'm serious! He says you're like my other boyfriend. The one I ignore him for." Kenji waggled his eyebrows.

"Don't you guys have like, an open thing going on? Why would he care?" Gordon asked, not that he wanted the details, and not that he cared what Rob thought. Mostly.

"Sure, in some ways. But he knows you're good to me. I'm pretty sure he thinks I'm going to leave him for you. He thought I was jealous of that guy you talked to at the bar the other day. And to be honest, I don't even think he even likes me that much, it's more like a pride thing. Like, if he can't have me, no one can."

"Oh." Gordon's stomach tensed up, a mixture of hurt and ridiculous hope.

"Not that that you would have me."

"Right."

Kenji looked relieved, like maybe the tension had passed for him. It hadn't for Gordon. If anything, he felt worse now.

"Well, can I borrow your car, then? I have to get my bags from home before I go over there. I can drop you at the venue! That could work," Kenji said, proud of himself for figuring it out, regardless of how bad of a solution it was.

"And how do I get my car back from Rob's?"

"Uber?"

Gordon took a deep breath in and looked back to his ingredients. He started throwing them into the heated broth so he didn't have to look at Kenji, whose presence and questions were distracting him in the worst way. He was probably messing up the recipe, and if he did that, Akiko wouldn't eat it. If she didn't eat, she'd get weaker. If she got weaker, she'd die sooner. He couldn't fuck this up.

"Careful!" Kenji said. "You splashed broth on me."

"Maybe Rob has a shirt you can borrow," Gordon said. He threw the lid on the pot and turned it down to simmer before heading into the bedroom to pick an outfit for the evening.

His sheets were still twisted from Kenji's nap, piled up in the middle of his bed. It was a miserable reminder of everything he was trying to avoid thinking about. Kenji, not in his bed, not even in Portland. The money he'd wasted on new sheets so Kenji could stay there more comfortably. The spare bed dressed in the old, scratchy sheets, waiting for Akiko to move in, and the hope that her skin was less sensitive than

Kenji's. The fear that he couldn't do any of this. What his future would look like if he lost both of them.

He felt Kenji's presence before he turned around. He smelled the familiar shampoo and laundry detergent and Icy Hot that made up Kenji's signature scent, and it made his chest ache.

"What is your problem?" Kenji snapped. "I'm not allowed to spend the night somewhere else, or what?"

"Of course you are."

"Then what was that about?"

"I just…" Gordon looked at his feet, unsure why he felt the need to do this *now*, but he did.

"What?"

"Do you ever think about how much you ask of me? And how little you give back in return?"

"What is that supposed to mean?"

"I cleared my schedule for you. You told me Rob couldn't get you to the airport, so I made sure I was available. I made plans with Amber knowing we'd spend time together tomorrow morning. And now that Rob can take you, you change our plans without even letting me know. Because you expect me to be fine with it. Right? As long as Kenji gets what he needs, fuck everybody else."

"What the hell are you talking about?"

"And then, for some reason, you tell me Rob doesn't like me? Then asked me for my car to get to his house because he's driving you to the airport in the morning. Instead of me."

"It's not—"

"*And then,*" Gordon continued, angry and hurt beyond anything he'd ever felt from Kenji's behavior, "I get to spend twenty bucks on an Uber to get my car from your boyfriend's house at eight in the morning so I can get to Kiko's to open for the day, because nobody else is there to do it."

"It was just an idea. I'll take the fucking Uber, Jesus."

"It's not about the car, Kenji!"

Kenji rolled his eyes.

"You didn't even consider that maybe I'd *want* to go to the show with Amber. You just assumed she would understand if I ditched her for you. Which she wouldn't, by the way."

"Okay, so go to the show with Amber! I don't care."

"Of course you don't."

"Oh, my God. You are being such a bitch."

"Why? Because I'm telling you no?"

"Because you're making this a huge deal when it really doesn't need to be! But whatever, I'm going home to get my stuff and taking an Uber to Rob's, I guess. Thanks for your help."

"See, that's what I'm talking about."

"What is?"

"Amber told me you take advantage of my willingness to do things for you because I'm—" Gordon cut himself off, unsure where he was heading with that sentence, but sure he didn't want to say anything he couldn't undo. "Just because."

"What, you were gossiping about me with Amber?"

Gordon threw his hands in the air. "That's what you're taking from this after everything I just said to you? That I gossiped about you? No, Kenji, I didn't gossip about you. I told her about how I was feeling about something, and she talked to me about it." Gordon pushed his way through the door frame, escaping back to the kitchen to stir his soup.

"Why are you acting like this? Is this about Rob?" Kenji asked, clearly angry but, again, looking genuinely confused. It was a face Gordon was beginning to hate, because it seemed to appear only when Gordon wasn't bending to Kenji's will. "This weird jealousy thing doesn't look good on you. I shouldn't have to work this hard to keep you happy."

Gordon felt like he was on fire. To keep himself from saying something he'd regret, he focused on pouring the rice into the soup and setting back it to simmer.

"I know I'm not your boyfriend, okay? Believe me. But maybe the one you do have can help you out, huh?"

"I didn't realize I was inconveniencing you so much," Kenji said.

Kenji was doing so much more than inconveniencing Gordon. He was wielding a tiny pickaxe, chipping away at his heart with his indifference and unknowingly cruel comments about the limits to their relationship.

"Text me when you land tomorrow, okay? I have to shower before I head out."

"Gordon, come on."

But Gordon was emotionally drained and physically incapable of subjecting himself to more of this conversation that would inevitably end with him apologizing for things that weren't his fault. Kenji didn't demand apologies, or even expect them, but Gordon had learned long ago that the easiest way to move things along was to take the blame and then forget it ever happened. He recognized the irony of ending up in this situation for the exact reason he'd tried to avoid it, but he pushed the thought aside and shut himself in the bathroom. Kenji was gone by the time he came out, but he'd pulled out a jar of sesame seeds from the spice cabinet—Akiko's favorite topping—and set it by the stove.

∼

KENJI STOOD at Rob's door, suitcase in hand, the strap of his carry on bag digging into his shoulder. He'd slipped in behind another resident to bypass the locked front doors to the apartment complex, which had been difficult and annoying, but not as annoying as it was to stand in front of the door to a seem-ingly empty apartment. After an initial unanswered knock, he'd checked his phone to see if Rob had reached out, but he had no notifications at all. He knocked again.

After a few more minutes of waiting, he tried calling Rob. Twice. There was no answer and the texts he'd sent were unread. He stood there, unsure what to do, frustrated but not entirely surprised, because... it was Rob. Being ditched by Rob didn't bother him, if he was honest. If anything, this would be a good excuse to end things once and for all. But it forced him to see his behavior from Gordon's perspective, and that was something he realized he'd never really done before.

He left the building, luggage in tow, and called a car to take him back to Akiko's house. Calling Gordon wasn't an option, not after the argument they'd had. The argument outlining the very behavior Rob had just pulled on him. It stung more than he wanted to admit.

Akiko's house was already dark, and she was asleep by the time he got there. He had an early flight and now he had to get up even earlier to find a way to the airport. Part of him was tempted to wake her before he went to bed, just to say good-bye, but Gordon would be by the following day to move her in while he was gone. He wanted her to get as much rest as she could.

He settled on leaving her a note on the counter before heading to his room, telling her he loved her and that he would see her when he got home.

CHAPTER 12

GORDON SAT AT THE POINT-OF-SALE DESK AT KIKO'S WITH HIS work laptop open in front of him and a handful of boring reports open. Victor's tiny face was tucked into the corner of the screen.

"It's not the same thing, Gord," Victor said.

"How is it not the same thing? You're literally at mom and dad's beach house right now. I can see the ocean."

Victor turned to look out the large window behind him and had the decency to look sheepish. "Okay, so it is the same thing. But people have noticed you haven't been at the office much. It's not so much that you're working remotely, it's that you don't usually do that. People rely on you there."

"Okay. Well, that's not really my problem. I manage a team of engineers who haven't been into the office in two years. They don't need me there, and I am needed here."

"Wait, where are you? That plant store?"

Gordon lifted a small creeping fig he'd successfully repotted and couldn't wait to tell Akiko about. He flashed Victor a genuine smile. "Yes."

"I'm confused."

"It's temporary. I'll be back to the office soon."

Victor sighed.

"What?" Gordon asked.

"I mean, I'm your boss. You're putting me in a difficult position, here."

"Why? I'm getting all my work done. I haven't missed any meetings. I have some help here for days I really need to go into the office. What's the issue?"

"I thought you were just working remotely. What if everyone else found out you have a second job and I let you work remotely from it? *My* job would be at risk."

The door chimed and Gordon clenched his jaw. It was the worst possible time for someone to walk in. Fortunately, they stepped towards a bookshelf and started flipping through books, chatting quietly.

"Okay, I get that," he murmured.

"Great. So, we'll see you at the office tomorrow, then?"

"No. If I can't do this then… I think I need to take some time off."

"Gordon." Victor leaned back and Gordon could see his shoulders and upper body. His arms were crossed.

"I'll email you the dates. Okay?"

"Oh, sure. I can at least make up an excuse better than 'has to work at a plant store.' How do you feel about breaking a thumb?"

"I don't care what reason you give if I can take the time off. I'll be back in a couple weeks."

Victor raised one eyebrow. "Wait, you're serious? I was kidding."

"The store is important to me."

"More important than your job?"

The customers in the store had moved on from the book-shelves and Gordon did his best to flatten his expression,

DROPKICKS AND DANDELIONS 111

worried he'd snap at Victor and scare them out of the store. The store wasn't more important, no, but that was only because if he lost his real job, he wouldn't have any income or health insurance. He had some savings, but Gordon wasn't the type of person who could quit a job without something lined up.

At the thought of quitting, he swallowed, realizing his job mattered for another reason, too. Without it, perhaps worryingly, his only purpose would be helping Kenji and Akiko. Even he knew that wasn't a good idea.

"Can you just be my brother for a second, not my boss?"

"Uh, sure," Victor said.

"I've told you about my friend Kenji, right? His aunt owns the plant store, but she's terminally ill and he's out of town for a month."

"Okay?"

God, he hated Victor sometimes. "Well, they need help." *Obviously.*

"And why is that your problem?"

"It's not my—God," Gordon pinched the bridge of his nose. "Because I care about them? I have the ability to help out, and I love them. I want to help."

Gordon watched Victor huff out a small laugh and shake his head before he picked up his phone and started scrolling.

"I'm sorry, am I boring you?"

"You can't just take two weeks off with no notice. Especially not for this."

"I didn't want to take any time off!" Gordon realized he'd raised his voice when the customers all turned to look at him. He mouthed *sorry* and turned back to Victor, speaking quietly again. "What if I just shift my hours? I have some kids who help out here in the afternoons and evenings. I can work later and take calls remotely if they come up."

He heard Victor sigh again and shuffle some papers on his desk. "You're already on West Coast time. That sounds challenging."

"Please?"

"Fine. But seriously, if anybody asks me about this, I can't guarantee I'll cover for you. And if this becomes an issue, or you fuck this merger, I can't defend you here. I'll email HR and copy you for a temporary schedule approval. But only for two weeks, Gord."

"Thank you." Gordon felt his body loosen. "I'll be back in the office soon."

After ending the call with Victor, Gordon turned his attention to the customers in the store and tidied up a bit.

Working at the store was overwhelming. Every evening when he went home to Akiko his tank was completely empty, and for two weeks he'd done pretty much nothing but work and care for Akiko before flopping on the couch to watch TV or attempt to read the same ten pages of a book.

Some earlier customers had needed help processing an online order, and he'd stared at the screen for two full minutes trying to remember the steps to complete it and couldn't figure it out. He finally asked them to fill everything out on a phone order form so he could take care of it later, and if their card was declined, well, he'd just pay for it out of his own pocket.

He'd never spent this much time alone at Kiko's. He'd helped out plenty, but someone was always there to help *him*. He rotated and watered plants to the best of his ability, but was generally convinced he was doing it wrong. Case in point, the plants he'd paid the most attention to were the ones faring the worst. Brown, crispy bits; wrinkled, kinda-green bits; a fuzzy coat covering a couple dozen leaves; a mushroom. All within two weeks.

He could call Kenji for help, but then he'd know Rob

wasn't helping at all, and Gordon was nervous about getting between them. He could ask Akiko, but that seemed like the last thing she needed on her plate, if she was even capable.

It was all fine. Temporary. Kenji would figure it all out eventually.

The thought should have reassured him, but instead, it made him sad. Because Kenji was already figuring things out. In Boston. And Gordon didn't know what that meant for any of them.

CHAPTER 13

ONE THING KENJI HAD UNDERESTIMATED WHEN HE DECIDED ON this career was the number of matches he'd be in that were just... unhinged. They defied any logic and only existed because of writers in the throes of a fever dream or influenced by some sort of mind-altering substance.

Most matches were small and lasted a few minutes, playing some minute part in an overarching storyline. They ended with little fanfare, never to be thought of again. Other matches started in one end of the arena, the locker room or hallway, and ended in the ring, telling a larger story and fully narrated by announcers. Those matches hyped up rivalries and progressed wrestlers' angles.

But this one, three weeks after his arrival in Boston, was the unhinged kind.

During the match, a six-man tag team battle, Anthony and Kenji had been tossed into a dumpster midway through. There was no explanation for why a dumpster was in the CWA arena, but that didn't stop the writers from moving forward with it.

Anthony and Kenji were slated to lose the match, but not

until they'd spent ten minutes inside the dumpster while the other four wrestlers, all from CWA, duked it out in the ring.

"This isn't so bad. Kind of cozy," Kenji said from inside the dumpster, sitting on a black garbage bag full of God knows what. He couldn't see Anthony's face, but he heard him smiling somehow. "My pants are going to be ruined, though."

"I've had worse matches, I guess."

"Have you?"

"My first indie promo still uses fire."

"Jesus."

"Fun, though," Anthony said.

"This would be nicer if they hadn't had them put actual trash in here. Mike would never. I hope we don't still smell bad when we go to the barbeque."

Anthony groaned. "I'm tired, man. I was going to stay in."

"We have to go! Our first big CWA match! The barbeque is like, *the* summer event. I bet we can pull so many guys. Or whoever."

"I'm married," Anthony said. He sighed and dropped his head against the side of the dumpster.

"Happily, clearly." He nudged Anthony's thigh with his foot.

"Aren't you seeing Rob, anyway?"

"I was, kind of. Half seeing. We broke up, but it had kind of petered out, to be honest. I'm zero percent heartbroken."

"What happened?"

"It just fizzled out. We both knew I was leaving for a month, plus he was a dick to Gordon at Will's party. I ended it after we got here."

"Ah. And how did Gordon feel about Rob?"

Kenji laughed, loud enough that it echoed off the walls of the dumpster.

"That good, huh?"

"He hated him. He never told me that directly. But he did punch him. I was able to piece that together myself," Kenji said, tapping his temple at the dark blob he assumed was Anthony.

"Wait, Gordon punched Rob?"

"You need to hire babysitters more, man. Will's party was wild. Mostly because yes, Gordon punched Rob!"

"Wow. Who would have thought?"

"Anyway," Kenji continued, "he's never really liked any of the guys I've dated, no matter if it's serious or not. I mean, he's polite, but he's protective, you know?"

Anthony didn't respond.

"Maybe he doesn't like them because his own relationships always fizzle out?"

"Kenji," Anthony said.

"Hmm?"

"You are actually dumber than I thought."

"It's just a theory!"

"You know why his relationships always fizzle out, right?"

"No, actually, I don't. I've just always assumed he hasn't found the right person because he's too good for all the dudes he dates." Kenji shrugged.

That part was true. Kenji had met Gordon's boyfriends in the past, and they'd always been fine. Bland, boring, cute, he guessed, but not *enough*. Gordon deserved the best guy.

"He is, huh?"

"Yeah. Like that guy I told you about. The one who chatted him up at the bar before we came out here."

"I thought you said he didn't even get that guy's number."

"He didn't, that's my point. He probably saw what I saw, which is that he was nowhere near Gordon's league."

"That's nice, I guess. But that's—"

The sound of a truck engine rumbled inside the arena.

"Um," Kenji said, turning his head, attempting to identify the source.

"But that's not why his relationships fizzle out," Anthony said, louder, over the noise of the truck.

"Okay, Einstein, why do they, then?" Kenji yelled back.

"Oh, my God. He's in love with you, dumbass!"

The top of the dumpster opened and light spilled in, Anthony's face finally visible. He was looking at Kenji like he couldn't believe his stupidity, and maybe a little scared about what was about to happen to them.

The truck tilted the dumpster onto its side, spilling Kenji and Anthony onto the ground in an inelegant heap. An icy spray of water, courtesy of the two remaining CWA wrestlers, rinsed them of garbage juice before they were thrown into the ring and pinned almost immediately.

Kenji was grateful, despite the quick end to the match. Anthony's words lingering in his head made it impossible to focus, and all he wanted to do was go back to the apartment and ask him what the hell he was talking about.

OF COURSE, when they got to the apartment, Anthony disappeared into the closed off bedroom, probably to call his family, leaving Kenji alone in the loft.

He'd called Gordon as he got ready for bed, and so far, their conversation was about as detached as he'd feared it would be. He was worried he'd ruined everything by being an asshole before he left for Boston. Or maybe by being an asshole in general. For years.

"The dandelions are really coming in," Gordon said through the phone. "Are you sure she should be growing them at the store? What happens when the puffball seeds infiltrate all the other plants there?"

"Well, she won't let them get to that stage," Kenji said, smiling at the full sentences Gordon was finally giving him.

He hadn't talked to Gordon on the phone much since he'd arrived in Boston, mostly bypassing him and calling his aunt directly. He'd hit the ground running at CWA, spending time with the other wrestlers and working with the trainers, and things with Gordon were awkward, so he just didn't try.

But every evening when he got back to the apartment, he listened to Anthony talk to his kids on the phone and felt an unfamiliar emptiness in his chest. He was beginning to hate the distance between himself and Gordon. Physical, of course, but also emotional.

Gordon's apparent indifference felt like a slow, painful breakup. He tried to think of a time he'd felt worse after breaking up with an actual romantic partner and drew a blank. Usually, he was almost relieved to be alone. It meant more time to do whatever he wanted, and very often, that meant hanging out with Gordon. But now he had no one to turn to.

"I can't believe you guys managed to hide them for so long," Gordon said.

"We were determined."

Kenji was on top of the enormous bed he'd be sleeping in for duration of his time in Boston, rubbing his hands on the clean sheets. "You should see the size of my bed. You could fit like four of me in here."

"Hmm."

"So, how's she doing today?" Kenji asked, worried the change in subject had been too abrupt. He hoped talking about Akiko would get him to engage more.

"She's okay. Sleeping a lot. I met with the financial advisor and ran some errands, went to the pharmacy."

"Busy day. Did you have work?"

"I took the day off," Gordon said.

"Oh, okay," Kenji said. Gordon didn't say anything else. "I had a match tonight. I sat in a dumpster."

"Nice. Televised?"

"Yeah, I think so. Definitely online somewhere."

"I'll see if I can find it. Akiko and I will watch."

"Okay. Um, hey Gordon?"

"Yeah?"

"Are we okay? Like, as friends?"

"Of course."

That was about as convincing as it was when Anthony told him he was okay with Kenji putting his toothbrush in the same drawer as his.

"I broke up with Rob," Kenji said. He hadn't mentioned it yet, mostly because it felt weird to text Gordon about that alone, but also because he… didn't care. It wasn't top of mind for him. He wished he'd broken up with him before he left, but Rob had been missing in action until after Kenji landed in Boston. When they finally spoke, it seemed like the feeling was mutual, despite what they'd discussed before Kenji left.

Gordon didn't say anything in response, which was unexpected. He thought Gordon would at least say "nice."

"Gordon?"

"I heard you. I can't say I'm upset about it, because that dude sucked. But I'm sorry. It's never fun to break up with someone."

"No, it's not fun. I'm a little worried about the store, I guess, but he promised he'd continue keeping an eye on it."

Gordon was quiet again. "Alright. Sounds good. Well, Akiko is asleep right now, so I can't get her the phone. I have a call to make, so I'm going to let you go."

"Oh. Yeah, okay."

Kenji curled onto his side in his giant, empty bed and frowned while he waited for Anthony.

CHAPTER 14

BOSTON WAS SO HUMID. EVERY TIME KENJI LEFT AN INDOOR SPACE, it was like walking into a wall of water. The idea of living there full time was losing appeal with every step, and he still had six blocks to go before he'd reach the train he and Anthony were taking to the CWA barbeque. Kenji's pink linen shirt was sticking to his chest, and he was tired and sore from the matches earlier in the day. It made the walk more miserable than usual, and he was dragging.

"Remember to hydrate," Anthony said.

"Doesn't walking in air like this hydrate you by osmosis or something? God, this is awful."

"I'm serious. Especially if you're going to drink at the barbeque."

"Okay, jeez. I'm hydrating." He took a drink of water from the bottle Anthony handed him. "How late do you want to stay?"

"We can play it by ear. I'm not going to drink, so feel free to do whatever. I'll get you home safely."

"Thanks, daddy."

"Stop."

"Sorry."

The backyard was already buzzing by the time they arrived, with dozens of wrestlers and their friends scattered around, drinking fancy things and eating tiny appetizers off silver trays. Kenji looked down at himself and worried for a moment he was underdressed, but then he saw one of CWA's talent wearing no shirt at all—just tight, lime green swim trunks. Kenji looked better than that, even if it was just a linen shirt and chinos.

"Do I look okay?" he whispered to Anthony.

"Yes. But I don't think anyone is going to care what we're wearing. Or that we're here at all, for that matter."

They stood on the edge of the party taking it all in, trying to find a starting point, when Anthony elbowed Kenji, nodding at a man who was walking in from the other side of the yard.

Dom, the man he was pointing out, was one of CWA's top stars. He was tall and scary and ridiculously ripped. Almost *too* muscular, if that was a thing, though Kenji wasn't convinced it was. But Dom's intimidating appearance belied his true nature, which so far had been helpful and surprisingly kindhearted. He'd made Kenji's time in Boston much less terrifying than it could have been by taking him under his wing during their first week together.

Beyond that, Dom was a bit enigmatic. He rarely spoke about anything other than wrestling or weightlifting, and most of his interactions involved showing off his body or playfully harassing other people.

So, Kenji didn't know much about him aside from the fact that he was nice his first week and that he was *extremely* good looking. He figured that was why Anthony pointed him out, because he may have talked about Dom more than was appropriate. But he kept it to their apartment, and Anthony swore he didn't mind.

"Man alive," Kenji said, blowing out a breath. "I just don't get how he looks like that."

Anthony laughed and grabbed two plates of something from the server walking by them. "Canapé?"

"What is a canapé?"

"This one looks like smoked salmon and crème fraiche. That's a little cracker."

"What's the green thing on top?" Kenji asked, popping it in his mouth.

"Chive."

"Oh, there's horseradish in there, too. I'm glad Gordon didn't eat that," Kenji said, frowning as he said it. Gordon continued to be distant, not replying to his texts right away and not talking to him on the phone other than when Kenji called to talk to Akiko. And those conversations were difficult in their own right, with all three of them refusing to acknowledge the progression of her health issues, dancing around them with lighthearted chit chat instead. He wondered if Gordon knew more than he was letting on, or if Akiko had confided in him. Part of him hoped so, because he wanted Gordon to have time to prepare for what they all knew was coming.

He missed them both, of course. But this disconnect from Gordon was a feeling he wasn't used to, and he didn't understand where it was coming from.

"Hey," Kenji said, grabbing a glass of fizzy wine from a different server passing by. He took an iced tea for Anthony and handed it to him. "What did you mean in the dumpster yesterday?"

"You'll have to be more specific."

"You said Gordon is in love with me."

"Oh! Yeah. What I meant was that Gordon is in love with you."

Kenji glared at Anthony and sipped his wine. "Fuck off."

"I can't tell if you're being serious," Anthony said. "Did you really not know?"

"I can't tell if *you're* being serious. Gordon has never said anything like that to me."

"Well, you know Gordon."

"Yeah, I do. A lot better than you."

"Well, no offense, but a stranger could figure it out after spending about thirteen seconds with you two. How this is news to you is beyond me."

Kenji waved at someone across the lawn, trying to focus on something other than the prickly feeling of his skin, but Anthony continued talking.

"But what I meant is that he's not exactly busting at the seams to put himself out there. Remember when we went to that club and that guy asked him to dance, and he faked a knee injury so he could sit in the booth?"

"Yeah," Kenji said, laughing. He smiled at the memory. "Aw. He's just not that into clubs. Plus, that guy was not good enough for Gordon. He could probably sense it."

"You didn't even talk to that guy!"

"Well, I saw him!"

"In the dark. From the back."

"Well, I'm sorry, but he didn't look good enough."

A frisbee landed at their feet and Anthony threw it back to Dom.

"Wow, you're really good at throwing frisbees."

Anthony sighed audibly, louder than a normal sigh. It was definitely directed at Kenji. "Ken?"

"Yeah?"

"Have you ever considered that maybe you're a little in love with Gordon, too?"

"No." It felt weird somehow, like he was being caught in a lie.

"Why haven't you guys ever hooked up, anyway? I've never understood it."

"I don't know. He asked me out when we first met, but we wanted different things. I didn't want to get tied down, you know? I was only twenty-two. He wasn't much older than me, but he wasn't interested in sowing his oats, and that's all I wanted to do. And then I just kept doing it for most of the next ten years."

"Huh," Anthony said. He scrunched his brow. "How many oats would you say you've sowed?"

"I don't know. Fifty?"

"*Fifty?!*"

"That might be an exaggeration. It could be more than that, too. It's not like a keep a diary." Kenji caught himself looking at Dom again and wondered if he'd be interested in being added to the list. But then he saw a woman jump on Dom's back before they were both dumped into the pool, so he turned his attention back to Anthony. "Anyway, like I said. We had different goals."

"Well, I'm surprised. That's all."

"Fifty guys over ten years isn't that many, Ant. Five a year. Less than one every other month."

Anthony rubbed his eyes. "I meant about Gordon…"

"Oh. Well, I didn't want to hurt him. I still don't," Kenji said.

"I get that. He's a good dude."

"Yeah, I know that," Kenji said, his voice clipped.

"Have you ever thought about revisiting it?"

"I… no, not really. Things are good between us as friends."

"For you, maybe," Anthony said, a quiet chuckle under his breath.

"I'm sorry, do you and Gordon sit around and talk about this, or are you just pulling this out of your ass? Do you have some sort of secret loyalty to Gordon I'm unaware of? I don't think it's any of your business."

"You're right. I'm sorry."

Kenji watched the party, pretending to look interested in anything at all that wasn't Anthony, whose gaze was fixed on Kenji. He tried to watch the pool volleyball game, the cute server making their rounds, and the makeshift wrestling ring a few kids had put together with jump ropes, but nothing stuck. He couldn't stop thinking about Anthony's words. *For you, maybe.*

What did that even mean? Kenji was sure Gordon wasn't in love with him—that was ridiculous. He supposed it was possible he'd retained some simmering attraction. Kenji *was* hot, after all. But Gordon was cute, too, and it was nothing more than that. Gordon had plenty of chances of to admit he had deeper feelings for Kenji over the years and he'd never mentioned it. Not even once.

His mind drifted, uninvited, to thoughts of Christian, the guy Gordon talked to for five minutes and hadn't even exchanged numbers with. The sour feeling in his stomach around Christian's existence at the bar had been confusing at first, sure. But regardless of what Rob said, Kenji knew it had just been displeasure at someone else taking Gordon's attention. Kenji was needy, he knew that, and he liked being the center of attention. Especially Gordon's.

But what if that wasn't the reason? The thought made him feel sweaty, beyond what the heat and humidity was doing to him.

This was all too much thinking for Kenji. He pushed it from

his mind and turned towards the ruckus he was grateful to hear approaching from his left. Dom, drying off his arms and legs, was walking towards them with his tag-team partner, Monty, an ex-Titan who wrestled under the name Romeo. He and Kenji had worked together before Monty moved to Boston. Kenji could hear them yelling back and forth, something about balance and lifting.

"Hey, man!" Kenji said, giving Monty a brief hug. "It's good to see you. You look good!"

"You, too. It's fun to see you here! Welcome to Boston. Kinda. I mean, welcome, but also this is the worst time of year to visit. I think."

"Yeah, I'm figuring that out. But it's okay, we go back soon," he said, smiling at Anthony.

"Thank God," Anthony said. "I'm not used to—"

"Okay, we came over here for a reason," Dom said, interrupting the conversation. "I am going to take you, Kenji, and Romeo here is going to take Anthony. We are going to bench press you guys, and whoever does more reps gets one hundred dollars."

"Uh, I'm sorry?" Anthony asked.

"I love it. I'm so in," Kenji said.

"I don't think that's possible. I weigh like two hundred and thirty pounds." Anthony was glancing around at the other three men trying to get them to reconsider, but Monty was already cracking his knuckles and stretching his back, staring back at him with a big smile.

Dom scoffed and shook his head. "Anthony, Romeo can bench press three seventy five. So can I."

"Okay, well, it's different when you're lifting a human! It's like carrying a bag of water. It's way harder than lifting an iron bar in a controlled setting."

Dom practiced picking Kenji up a couple of times. "It's not so hard."

"That's not the same thing. And you're not even going to be on a bench! It's not even a floor press. It's a lumpy, uneven, bag of water ground press."

"Well, I think if we focus and try really hard, we can do it," Monty said.

"The key is for you to stay very straight, like a barbell," Dom said. He turned to Kenji and pointed a finger at him. "If I drop you because you're flopping around, it won't be my fault, and I will make you pay for half of Romeo's winnings."

Kenji nodded eagerly. "Yes. That seems fair."

"I—what? No, it doesn't!" Anthony said. "I'm not paying anything if you drop me, Monty."

"Okay. I'm not going to drop you, though. I think we're going to win."

Kenji stared at Anthony, pleading with him telepathically to agree so Dom didn't think they were boring. He heard Anthony sigh in defeat, so he rubbed his hands together and smiled before turning to Dom.

"I'm ready! Oh, wait!" Kenji said. He looked to the woman standing near Dom. "Can you take a photo of this? I want to be able to show my friend."

She smiled and nodded before Dom and Monty laid down on their backs in the grass. They were laying with their heads near each other, legs splayed in the other direction. It was like twelve linear feet of muscles and brawn. Kenji didn't hate it.

"Okay, Kenji. Come here," Dom said. "Give me your thigh."

"Um. Anthony, come here and just lean on my hand. You don't have to, like, give me your thigh, or anything."

Kenji lifted his leg and placed it into Dom's waiting hand. He breathed deeply, willing his body not to react, but Dom's hand was so high, *dangerously* high, with his index finger inching way too close to Kenji's junk.

"Oh, God," Kenji whispered, squeezing his eyes shut. If his body did betray him, it was not his fault.

Dom shifted his hand slightly, solidifying his hold on Kenji's leg. His other hand grabbed Kenji's shirt, pulling his torso towards his palm until Kenji stiffened his body and legs. Straight like a barbell, like Dom said. He finally allowed his eyes to open and looked for Anthony, who was being held above Monty's head. They smiled at each other and Kenji took a deep breath so he wouldn't laugh and make Dom angry.

"Hey," Kenji said.

"Hi."

"Guys, do not talk right now. Kenji laughs too much. He will squirm and mess up my grip."

Dom was straining under Kenji's weight, but he was surprisingly steady. Dom lowered his arms, and Kenji felt his hip bumping Dom's chest, then he felt Dom push him back up to the starting position.

Monty tried to do the same but managed it with much less finesse. Kenji could see him struggling, and Anthony was looking at the ground with inevitability. Dom was getting ready to lower his arms again when Anthony screamed and toppled out of Monty's grip, landing face down with his abdomen on top of Monty's chest. He groaned and rolled onto the grass.

"Ow, God, my face! I fucking told you guys!"

"Ugh," Monty said, and curled into a ball.

"Told me what? I won!" Dom said, hopping to his feet. He flexed his biceps at them and smiled. "Thank you, Kenji. You have made my night. Rome, you will pay me tomorrow."

"You're welcome," Kenji said.

The woman who offered to take photos handed his phone

back to him and disappeared with Dom, who appeared to be searching for food.

"Sorry, Monty."

"It's fine! Sorry I dropped you on your face," Monty said, rising to his feet slowly. "Hey, how's your aunt doing, Kenji? I heard from Mike she's not well. I'm really sorry."

Kenji's chest warmed with Monty's concern for Akiko. She had visited Titan dozens of times over the years, some of them during Monty's short-lived career there. She'd always enjoyed chatting with him.

"Oh, yeah. Thank you. No, she's not well. She's okay right now, but you know how it is."

"Yeah."

They chatted a bit longer, each filling the other in on gossip from their respective Portland friends and discussing how CWA had been for Monty so far. His phone rang and he put his finger up to signal he'd be right back, but when he walked off, Kenji predicted they wouldn't see him again that night.

"I thought you said Dom was really sweet," Anthony said, rubbing his shoulder where he'd twisted his arm in the fall.

"He is! Just competitive, I guess."

The two of them headed towards the larger groups, ready to mingle after their eventful start to the party. Hours later, they found themselves back on the outskirts with a small group, laughing and chatting and drinking from half-empty cups. By the time they left, Kenji was pleasantly buzzed, but missing home. On the train, he took his phone out and sent Gordon a few photos from the evening, but Gordon didn't respond.

∼

IN THE WEEKS since Kenji left, Akiko's health had declined rapidly. The cancer, which had been slow-moving for years, seemed to have accelerated, or maybe that was just the way cancer went.

Gordon had moved Akiko into his house, tucked away in the back bedroom he'd been using as his home office and that currently held Peony's enclosure. She asked for Peony to stay so she could watch him, and Gordon did his best to make the room comfortable for her, placing fresh flowers on the bedside table, and buying a new, cozy bed set, shoving the scratchy sheets Kenji hated so much into the back of the linen closet.

But the reality of her mortality hung in the air. The oxygen she'd been prescribed took up already limited floor space and the home nurse's cart took up even more, all of it undoing the pleasant effects of anything he bought.

"I'm okay, Gordon," she'd told him. "I'm not scared."

But Gordon was. For a lot of reasons. He was going to miss her, of course. She'd filled a need he hadn't realized he'd had: the warm comfort of a mother figure. It was confusing, because he had his own mom, but Akiko loved Gordon for who he was and for what role he played in Kenji's life. Her love was never transactional. He never felt like he was disappointing her, unless he didn't stop by to eat her food often enough, and that had an easy solution. It was just pure, unadulterated love, and it had no strings attached.

His relationship with his own mother was at its best when he kept his distance, where they didn't try to provide any emotional support to one another. He knew she loved him, but her love was riddled with expectations to which he never measured up. It was exhausting to know he'd never be the son she truly wanted, so their relationship suffered.

All of that meant losing Akiko was more than just losing a friend. It was like losing the surrogate mother he'd never realized he needed but had been blessed with for more than ten years.

After their last appointment with Akiko's doctor shortly after Kenji left, he'd told them her prognosis had shifted, and it was likely she had just a month or two left. There were no guarantees, it was possible she'd live much longer. But Gordon heard what wasn't being said: it was also possible she wouldn't make it that long.

He didn't know what to do about telling Kenji. For now, he was trusting Akiko with guiding his decision.

Gordon watched her sleep all day and into the evening. Panic crept in when she didn't wake up for dinner or to watch Kenji's match. He checked on her periodically, each time the exact same thing. Her breathing was more rapid, the oxygen wasn't helping as much, she couldn't keep her eyes open.

Her nurse wasn't scheduled to stop by for a few days, so he called her doctor to ask what to do.

CHAPTER 15

Kenji rolled over to shove his face in his pillow, a little hungover, but mostly just exhausted from his evening out with Anthony. His head was achy, and while he would normally appreciate the peace, things were quieter than usual. None of Anthony's predictable morning noises filled the space.

Anthony was an obnoxiously routined man—the coffee machine always went on at seven, he would do one of his yoga videos while it brewed, he would drink his coffee while doing the New York Times puzzles, then head out for a run. He *always* made it back by eight-thirty for a shit and a shower. Kenji could set his watch by it. For it to be seven thirty with no sign of Anthony's puttering was unusual, to say the least.

"Ant?" Kenji called from his bed, drawing out the first letter in a whine.

Anthony didn't respond, and Kenji groaned into his pillow before sliding his feet to the floor and walking towards the kitchen where he kept his phone overnight.

Gordon once said something about improving sleep hygiene by keeping screens off—or in another room entirely—to limit middle-of-the-night distractions. As much as he hated to admit it, it really worked. But now it meant he had to get out of his cocoon and haul himself two rooms away.

He was initially relieved to see Anthony was there, alive and well. But when Anthony turned around, Kenji's relief quickly turned to dread. Anthony's face was pale, and his eyes were wide open, staring at Kenji with an uncharacteristic intensity. He was on the phone with someone, but not speaking.

"What's going on?" Kenji asked, reaching out to Anthony. He started worrying more when Anthony didn't respond and just looked at the counter. "Are the kids okay?"

"Yeah," Anthony said to the person on the phone. "I'll have him call you."

Anthony set the phone down and looked back to Kenji. His face had softened some, but he looked almost… scared?

"You need to call Gordon," he said.

"Okay. Um, why?" Kenji asked, scrambling for his phone. He turned the screen on and saw four text messages and about ten missed calls from Gordon starting at midnight the previous night. Nine o'clock Gordon's time.

Gordon: Call me

Gordon: Please call me when you see this.

Gordon: Stupid fucking sleep hygiene. Your phone is in the kitchen. Hopefully you didn't make Anthony do that. I'll call him too.

Gordon: I'm okay, just call me.

KENJI'S HANDS WERE TREMBLING. Obviously, something was wrong. Peony died, or the store burned down, or Gordon lost his job, or... other things Kenji refused to accept as possibilities.

"Kenji, hey," Gordon said, a bit breathless.

"Hey, what... what's going on? Are you okay?"

"I'm okay. Um," Gordon took a shaky breath. "You need to come home. Now, I think."

"What? Why?" Kenji felt Anthony step towards him and guide him to a chair, leaving his hand on Kenji's shoulder after he sat down. He felt a small squeeze.

"Akiko is in the hospital, I brought her here last night. She's okay right now. Sleepy. But, um, her doctor suggested I call you."

"Why?" Kenji asked. "Just tell me what's going on, Gordon, please."

Gordon paused. "She's dying."

Kenji's breath caught in his throat, Gordon's words hitting him like a physical blow. His chest felt tight, and if it wasn't for Anthony's hand still squeezing his shoulder, grounding him, he would have thought he was floating away.

"She's *dying?*" His voice cracked miserably, his question so quiet he wasn't sure Gordon even heard him.

"Yeah," Gordon said, his voice calmer than Kenji felt. "Not immediately, but it's time for you to come home."

"I—okay, I have to, um..." Kenji looked around, unsure what he was trying to find, but desperate for something to focus on.

"Mike already got your ticket changed. I called him last night."

"Okay."

"I think you leave this afternoon your time. I'll be at the airport to pick you up tonight."

"Okay."

"We'll be okay, Kenj."

"Okay," Kenji said. "Wait. You can't pick me up tonight, I'll take an Uber. You can't leave her alone."

"She'll be okay. We have some time. The doctors said we do. She's on oxygen and stuff."

"What stuff?"

"I don't really know. Pain meds, I think?"

"Oh."

Kenji had a thousand questions he wanted to ask about prognosis, timeline, and what the hell had happened in the last three weeks since he left his very ill but certainly not dying aunt in Portland, but the words wouldn't come.

"Go pack," Gordon said. "I'll be here."

"I'll call you when I land."

He hung up and set his phone on the table. Anthony sank down slowly into the chair next to Kenji, leaving his hand on his shoulder.

"Ken?" he said, gently.

"I, um. I have to go home. I think my aunt is dying?"

Anthony nodded. "Just take what you need for now. I'll pack everything else up and check it with my bags when I fly home."

"Yeah, okay."

"You don't have to figure anything out right now, just get a backpack and put some underwear and a toothbrush in there," Anthony said with a soft smile.

Kenji nodded, but everything felt too big and over-whelming for him to even stand up.

"Okay, I'll go get your stuff packed up. Go drink a glass of water, okay? Your flight leaves in a few hours, so you need to get going."

"I'm sorry," Kenji said. To Anthony, but also in a more

general sense. Sorry he left his sick aunt back home in Portland, sorry he hadn't been able to retire her and let her enjoy her life the last few years, sorry he was four thousand miles away thinking about this stuff and not at her bedside, telling her to her face.

"Don't apologize. Just go drink some water. You need to leave in twenty minutes."

CHAPTER 16

GORDON'S DAY DRAGGED ON IN LONG, MISERABLE MINUTES. AKIKO slept most of the day, which was bittersweet. She needed to rest, but Gordon wanted to talk to her and tell her everything he'd ever wanted to say to her. To thank her for being in his life, for giving him Kenji on whatever level she had. And he did say it all, but she was too tired to engage. Her eyes stayed closed, but she squeezed his fingers occasionally. Her soft, pale hand was so tiny in his, and he kept it there all day, gently placing it on the soft blanket he'd brought from home only to take lighting-quick trips to the bathroom or to get himself some water.

She woke up some time in the afternoon and turned her head to look at Gordon.

"Hello," she said, smiling at him. The tubes in her nose prevented her from smiling normally. It was a small, particularly cruel reminder that the once vibrant, active, funny woman he knew had slipped away, now replaced by this feeble body and tired mind.

Something beeped, a monitor alerting the nurses that her blood pressure was low. Helpful information for someone, he supposed, but not him. An apologetic nurse rushed in and turned off the alerts and Gordon gave her a small smile before focusing back on Akiko.

"Hi," he said, squeezing her hand. "Nice to see you."

She half-smiled at him again, her eyes blinking slowly.

"Kenji is on his way. He got a direct flight. He should be here in a couple of hours."

"Good," she said. Her voice was so weak Gordon had to strain to hear what she said.

"Um… I hope he makes it. But if he doesn't, I just want you to know how much he loves you. I know you know that," he said. She smiled at him, her eyes squinting slowly but happily. "You're the most important thing in his life. And I love him, and I'm… He'll be okay when you're gone. I'm going to do my best to take care of him, even though it—"

She put her hand up, interrupting him. "I know."

Gordon nodded, happy to hear her say it, even with so many words unspoken. He was happy he could tell Kenji later.

She spoke again and her voice faltered. Whether it was from emotions or illness, Gordon wasn't sure. "He loves you."

"Okay."

Gordon swallowed roughly, then laid his head on Akiko's bedside, her soft hip pressing into the waves of his hair. Tears fell slowly and steadily from his eyes onto the bedding. He looked at their hands intertwined and tried to memorize every bit of her fingers, from her immaculately kept fingernails to the wrinkles of each knuckle. He counted the tiny freckles she had on the back of her hand and committed each age spot to memory. Then he closed his eyes, and because he'd been awake since the previous night, he managed to fall into a light sleep with Akiko's hand in his hair.

~

KENJI DIDN'T BOTHER CALLING when he landed, too afraid Gordon would leave Akiko's bedside to pick him up. He'd only brought a carry-on bag, so he ran directly from the gate to the taxi area outside the main terminal. He slid into the back seat of the first car he saw and mumbled the hospital name. The driver didn't say much as he pulled away from the curb, probably sensing Kenji's need for silence based on his puffy eyes and tense body.

His heart pounded as the driver pulled up to the hospital, and after a promise of paying on the app, Kenji ran through the front doors, his legs carrying him faster than he could process. He ended up in front of the elevators and realized he didn't know what floor she was on, and it was so late the information desk wasn't open.

The hospital lobby was empty, the only other people there similarly frantic or upset. None of them could answer Kenji's questions about where they room the dying aunts who had taken in a teen boy after his parents divorced and offered no explanation as to why he had to move out. They certainly couldn't offer him any answers about why his parents got to continue living, happy and healthy last he heard, but his aunt who had done nothing but bless the world with her presence was dying at the age of sixty-eight.

Panicking, he sat down on a bench and put his head between his knees. He felt paralyzed, incapable of figuring out what to do. It seemed simple enough—call Gordon, figure out the room number, visit his aunt. But the reality of performing those tasks was so much harder.

He looked up when he heard footsteps and sucked in a breath.

"Gordon," he whispered.

He was there, walking towards Kenji with his sweet face,

so worried and kind. His arms were outstretched, inviting Kenji in.

"How did you know I was here?" Kenji asked. He pressed his face into Gordon's shirt and sniffled. "Sorry. Snotty."

Gordon chuckled and Kenji could feel the vibrations echo inside his head, warm and familiar.

"You shared your location with me. I'd been tracking you, but I fell asleep. When I woke up, you were on 84, and I figured that meant you were serious about me not picking you up. I respected your wishes."

Kenji choked out a laugh, watery and wet, into Gordon's shoulder. When he pulled away, a spot stayed behind on his shirt. "Sorry," he said.

"Anyway, I saw you stationary on the map and figured maybe I'd catch you in the lobby." Gordon said, tilting his head to look at him. "She's on floor six. Come on. She'll be happy to see you."

Gordon directed Kenji to Akiko's room and excused himself to buy two cups of coffee from the twenty-four hour cafeteria on a different floor. Kenji appreciated Gordon's obvious effort to leave them alone, though he was a little scared to see Akiko.

The glass door to her room slid open quietly and Kenji walked in to see her curled up on her side, oxygen tubes in her nose, monitors silent but lighting up the room. She didn't wake up right away, so he sat with her and held her hand and told her all about his time in Boston. She always loved hearing his stories, and she'd been so proud of him.

She woke up eventually, with heavy eyelids, but she managed to focus on him. She didn't say anything and seemed exhausted. Kenji was too scared to ask the nurses if that was because it was late or because she was dying.

"Hi," he said.

"Hi."

"I'm scared."

She gave him a small smile and started speaking, so quietly he couldn't understand her at first. "Take care of my plants."

He smiled a little. "Of course. Um, I don't know how much of my stories you heard. But I'm glad Gordon was with you while I was in Boston. I worried about you a lot, but I knew he was taking care of you. It meant I could focus on my matches. I'll have to think of a way to thank him."

She nodded slowly, her head never leaving the pillow.

"He loves you," Kenji said.

"I know," she said.

She said something else, but he didn't understand. He blamed it on her medication-fogged mind and focused again on the finality of these moments. His lip quivered, so he bit it, not wanting to upset her. She squeezed his hand gently and Kenji took it as permission to be sad. He blew out a big breath and held her tightly, afraid to let go.

A doctor knocked on the door before entering the quiet, low-lit room.

"Hello," she said. "Oh, hi. We haven't met. I'm Dr. Louden. I'm the hospitalist on duty tonight. I've been checking on Akiko, here. She's your mom?"

"I'm Kenji. She's my aunt," Kenji said, looking over at her. "But kind of mom-ish."

Akiko grinned behind her tubes.

"He's also her medical proxy," Gordon said, entering the room behind the doctor, holding two cups of coffee. "We finalized the paperwork a few weeks ago."

"Great," Dr. Louden said. "Thank you for letting me know. I'm here, Akiko, to discuss moving you to comfort care. It looks like Kenji made it, so I'll put the orders in for what we talked about earlier."

Akiko nodded, and Kenji looked at Gordon, panic stirring in his gut. "What? Already?"

Gordon looked back at him sadly, and Kenji realized he didn't really have anything else to say. He just wanted to pause time or stop this from happening at all.

"Sorry." His eyes filled with tears, and he sniffled.

"I'll give you some time," Dr. Louden said.

Kenji sat down in a chair next to her bedside and rested his head on the wall.

~

ONE THING GORDON learned about being present while someone remarkable dies is that time ceases to have any meaning at all. Sitting with Akiko while her life faded away had turned time into a cruel paradox where the seconds dragged on, but slipped away so quickly he was desperate to slow them down.

The evening's hours passed, the sterile room bearing witness to every human emotion. Objectively unfunny things became inexplicably, stomach-achingly hilarious, causing laughter to erupt out of them at unexplainable times. When Gordon suggested requesting additional morphine to ease Akiko's discomfort, Kenji threw his book at him in anger, then broke down crying as that anger gave way to bone-aching sadness Gordon wished so desperately he could fix. They ordered food thinking they were hungry, but felt nauseated by it when it finally arrived.

It was maddening to know a person who had shaped their worlds so significantly was there, physically present, but halfway gone, never to be with them again in any meaningful way. She was leaving and they were staying, forced to accept the new reality of their lives. If they were lucky, they'd be without her for fifty years, and this would be their final memory of her until they finally joined her in whatever afterlife may or may not exist.

But as devastating as it all was, Gordon was grateful to have experienced it. Especially with Kenji.

Akiko died in the early morning hours, just as the summer sun was peeking up over the hills in east Portland. It felt incongruous with their reality, like it should have been cloudy and dark, but instead they had to deal with birds singing and children laughing and the sun feeding all the world's flowers.

Gordon stood by the door letting Kenji have a few moments of privacy to say his final goodbyes. He watched him lean down and kiss her cheek, a gesture she was never comfortable with. It made him smile knowing Kenji did it for himself, just because it made him feel better.

Neither of them spoke as they made their way to the car, but as they exited the hospital doors, they were hit with a wave of heat. Gordon knew it was shaping up to be hot, and Kenji didn't have air conditioning. He usually stayed at Gordon's house during heat waves, but Gordon worried about inviting Kenji into his home where Akiko had been for the last few weeks of her life. He was going to suggest going to Akiko's house, but Kenji spoke first.

"Can we go to your house? I don't want to go home," Kenji asked.

"Yeah, of course."

After a silent car ride, Kenji mumbled something about smelling like airplane and disappeared into the bathroom. Gordon was so exhausted he thought he might collapse, but the sheets on Akiko's bed needed to be changed before Kenji was done in the shower, and he knew if he sat down, he'd never get up.

He stood in the spare room for a moment, glad it had

remained mostly empty during Akiko's time there. Autopilot took over and he managed to change the sheets, giving Kenji the softer ones he'd purchased. He barely remembered changing the pillowcases before going into his own room and falling into a deep sleep.

It wasn't uncommon for Gordon to have dreams about Kenji. Pointless dreams where they discussed Gordon's boring job, or nonsensical dreams where they ran through a forest made of pencils and candy canes. Occasionally he'd get lucky, and his brain would bless him with something a little more physically engaging, though the letdown after waking up wasn't always worth it. But his favorite dreams were the ones where they'd just exist in domesticity, lying in bed, cooking dinner, or reading next to each other.

The dream he was having now was one of those. The best kind, where he could practically feel Kenji's warmth and weight against his body, securely tucked into his chest. The haze of sleep faded slightly, and he squeezed his eyes shut, desperate to stay in that moment just a little longer.

But as he woke up more, the weight of Kenji's body stayed put. He heard a soft noise and woke fully, with real-life Kenji wrapped around him, sniffling.

He looked down and saw Kenji curled into his side. He looked so tiny somehow. Like a sad, lost little kid who didn't want to be alone. Kenji must have noticed Gordon wake up, heard his head moving on his pillow or noticed the change in his breathing, because he pressed his face into the undershirt Gordon had been wearing for two straight days, and sobbed.

Gordon didn't even think, he just wrapped his arm under Kenji's body, pulled him into his chest, and let him cry.

CHAPTER 17

When Kenji was finally brave enough to venture over to Kiko's, he stood in the doorway, frozen in place, afraid to face the store without her and afraid to see its state after he'd been out of town. But somehow, it looked better than it had in months.

Every leaf seemed greener, and the desk was organized and clean. Even the windows sparkled. It was like going back in time fifteen years, when Akiko was at her prime and Kenji just visited on the weekends.

He just couldn't understand it. Akiko had been so ill, even when he left. Gordon didn't know anything about plants. He and Rob were nothing to each other.

"Wow," Kenji said. "It's… did Rob do all this?"

Gordon's face tightened slightly, giving away the answer before he spoke. "Um, for the first couple of days."

Kenji walked through the store and noticed new labels written in familiar handwriting, shoved into previously unlabeled plant pots. Plants Kenji knew all about, but that someone less familiar with botany wouldn't. He glanced at Gordon, who was digging his finger through some dirt in the pot of a peace lily near the window.

On the counter sat a notebook, and Kenji wasted no time flipping through it, hoping it was something Akiko left for him.

But it wasn't from Akiko. It was something even more incredible—a notebook full of watering guidelines, light requirements, and feeding suggestions for dozens of plants in the store, the same familiar handwriting documenting each one. He looked up to Gordon again, who was looking back at him sheepishly, wiping the dirt off his finger on his pants.

"I just didn't want you to come back to a bunch of dead plants. I'm bad with them, but I'm not a murderer."

Kenji didn't laugh. He just stared at Gordon before flipping to the end of the notebook, smoothing his hands over the pages. He looked down and found a few sketches of plants he didn't even know Gordon could *name,* let alone draw. On each page was a plant Kenji had mentioned giving special attention to. The giant fern in the corner, for example, which wasn't even rare or difficult to care for, he just loved how big it was and hoped he could grow it even bigger. The sketch was terrible. Underneath it, he'd written, *very big, look into plant growth supplements?*

He'd only mentioned it to Gordon once.

Kenji looked around the store again. It made his chest ache seeing it this way, so clean and neat. The pain deepened when he thought of Gordon sitting there alone, researching and tracking, for no reason other than the fact that the store was important to two people he loved.

He made his way to the nursery where even the smallest, most fragile propagules were thriving, each with a personalized nameplate using names Kenji had suggested as a joke in passing.

"You did all of this?" Kenji asked, gesturing broadly. "The labels? And the…"

"Well, plus a couple of teenagers I hired through Curt. They helped a few hours a week. And I didn't label the plants at first, but then I overwatered a couple times, and put the Apidista in the sun—"

"Aspidistra," Kenji corrected with a whisper.

"Aspidistra."

Kenji crossed the room and stood in front of Gordon, who was biting his lip and squeezing his hands into fists next to his thighs.

"I'm sorry if I overstepped. I mean, I know it's just a store so that's probably stupid, but like I said, I just didn't want you to come back to a bunch of dead—"

Kenji didn't let him finish. He squinted at Gordon, trying to see him more clearly. "How could I have missed you?"

"What?"

"You were right in front of me, and I was blind to it. Just like she said."

Without letting Gordon respond, Kenji stepped forward, close enough to hear that his breathing had sped up. Kenji saw the fabric of Gordon's shirt moving with the pounding of his heart, so he placed his hand there, trying to calm him. But if anything, the physical touch made it worse, and Gordon squirmed.

"Um," Gordon said, his voice just a whisper between them.

Kenji's hand reached up and cupped Gordon's jaw, as natural as anything between them had ever been, then kissed him softly. He felt him suck in a breath, but a second later he felt Gordon's hands on his sides. They were cautious at first, just the tips of his fingers grazing his ribs. As he deepened the kiss, Gordon's grip tightened around the fabric of Kenji's shirt, pulling their bodies together. He moved his own hands around to Gordon's back and felt the soft muscles under his shirt tensing beneath his touch.

Gordon sighed into Kenji's mouth and the kiss increased in intensity. Every breath between them was more frantic than the last, and Kenji started walking the two of them backwards towards the storeroom. He bumped into a cardboard box on the ground, almost tripping them both, and the moment was broken long enough that Kenji let out a quiet laugh. He reached out to grab Gordon, to close the space between them again, but he stopped when he saw Gordon's face. It was flushed, with kiss-swollen lips, but he looked upset.

"What's wrong?" Kenji asked, suddenly realizing he had basically assaulted Gordon. He threw his hands up to his face. "Shit, I'm so sorry. I just…"

"No, um," Gordon said, still slightly breathless. He looked over Kenji's shoulder to the futon they'd been headed to seconds earlier. "Let's go sit, maybe."

The back room looked the same as it always did, but it smelled like remnants of the spices used for whatever stew Akiko had been teaching Gordon most recently. Kenji's stomach tightened realizing he'd never smell her cooking again.

"Nikujaga?" Kenji said under his breath.

"Yeah. She put a bunch in the freezer. Minus the potatoes. She said I have to boil those myself."

Kenji laughed briefly before sobering, hit by a piercing wave of grief, then overwhelming embarrassment at what he'd done. Gordon seemed to notice and pulled Kenji down to the futon. Their thighs pressed together, and Gordon held his hand.

"I am really glad you did that," Gordon said. "Like, more than I think you can understand. Which is why I can't believe I'm saying this, but… we shouldn't do that again."

"Why?"

Gordon looked at him, hesitating. Kenji tried to read his face to figure out why.

"I don't want you to act on feelings that might be… confusing because of everything going on. I would hate myself if I took advantage of you while you're grieving."

"You're not taking advantage of me."

"I just don't want you to regret anything."

"I'm not confused, and I won't regret it, Gordon."

"Listen. Um, I love you. Okay? But—"

"I love you too. Of course. I'd never hurt you," Kenji said. He shifted so they were facing each other, and Gordon swallowed. "What? You look like you're going to puke."

Gordon huffed out a small laugh. "No, um. I'm, like, *in love* with you. And if that kiss was because—" his voice cracked, and he cleared his throat before continuing, "—because you're upset and just searching for a distraction… I'm sorry, I just can't."

"I'm sorry, *what?*" Kenji asked, sure he'd misheard, but Gordon just stared at him, frozen. "You're in love with me?" He put his head in his hands and rubbed his temples.

"Oh, God. I'm sorry. I shouldn't have said that. There's a lot going on right now," Gordon said. "Not, uh, the best timing, maybe."

Kenji laughed weakly but didn't look at him again.

"It doesn't have to change anything. Your friendship is more important to me than anything, okay?"

Kenji tried to pay attention as Gordon continued talking about friendship and timelines and missed connections, but he'd stopped listening the second Gordon opened his mouth. His mind was too busy thinking back on conversations he'd had, strange comments from Akiko, and memories of the last ten years, scouring for any sign that what Gordon was saying was true, because there was just no way.

He thought of the earliest months of their friendship, back when Gordon had asked him out. Kenji had turned him down, not because he didn't like Gordon, but because they were looking for different things. Kenji was young and aimless and had just discovered wrestling and men. All he did was hook up and work out, which, admittedly, hadn't changed too much. But his desires had, somewhat.

But still, he'd never considered any of Gordon's behavior to be that of someone who had lingering feelings. Surely, if that had been the case, he would have mentioned it at some point.

Right?

But Kenji knew Gordon. He didn't do risky things. Asking Kenji out must have been terrifying for him, and Kenji's stomach ached imagining how sad Gordon must have been when he turned him down.

But he thought things were okay, because Gordon had continued coming to the coffee shop where they'd met, always an hour before closing, claiming he worked until then. When Kenji found out his real schedule and confronted him, Gordon simply shrugged and said he enjoyed walking him home every day, and Kenji was happy to have such a nice friend.

He thought back to the time Gordon was considering what pet to get after graduating with his master's degree, and how desperately he'd wanted a dog. Kenji was allergic to pretty much every mammal and he'd resigned himself to spending no time at Gordon's, a sacrifice he'd been willing to make if it meant Gordon was happy. When Gordon came home from the humane society with a three-legged, half-tailed iguana, Kenji chalked it up to him feeling bad for the little guy. Later, after borrowing Gordon's phone, he'd noticed *"best pet for people allergic to mammals"* and *"can people be allergic to iguanas?"* in his search history.

He remembered the apartment he'd lived in during his first ever road trip with Titan—the one with excessively leaky faucets, half attached cabinet hardware, and windows painted shut. Gordon had demanded to take care of Kenji's fish that week, and Kenji had agreed, even though it was weird and completely unnecessary. When he'd returned from the road trip, everything had been fixed. The faucets no longer leaked, the cabinet hardware was secure, and for the first time since moving in, he could open the windows wide enough to let in a cross breeze.

His stomach rolled again thinking of all the men he'd introduced to Gordon, each of them a fleeting and ultimately unimportant presence in his life. But Kenji had always thought it was fun for all of them to go out and spend time together. Kenji even had an expectation that every person he dated would accept Gordon as almost an extension of him, but he realized then he'd never considered if Gordon wanted that.

Poor Gordon had been there through it all, a constant presence in the background of Kenji's life, engaging and kind, rarely demanding more from Kenji or expressing discomfort from what must have been a painful part of his existence.

It made him feel sick. How had he been so stupid, and for so many years? And why didn't anyone *tell* him? He had wasted so much time.

Gordon loved him. It was so obvious now. More surprising, but just as obvious, was that Kenji realized he loved him too. The hatred he felt for anyone Gordon dated, the elation he felt when they were both single with ample free time, the way he was drawn to touch him and seek comfort from him, the way his body felt when anybody confronted him about his feelings for Gordon. Even his aunt's cryptic comments—she obviously saw it when Kenji couldn't.

Why did he have to realize it *now*, when Gordon was telling him they couldn't act on it?

In the end, all Kenji managed to say was, "Of course. Our friendship is important to me, too."

Gordon gave him a short nod.

CHAPTER 18

IN THE WEEK FOLLOWING AKIKO'S DEATH, THINGS WERE STRANGE. Gordon's existence in general felt off, and things between him and Kenji were strained. They'd both taken time off work, spending most of their time at Gordon's house, but they'd slept in separate bedrooms and did absolutely no kissing.

And that was okay. If their relationship would never progress to something serious, it was for the best that it never happened again. Gordon knew himself well enough to know his heart was too invested to explore something casual with Kenji. It was true when they first met, and it was even more true now.

Before Kenji left for Boston, Gordon had started imagining a life with less Kenji, to allow himself to move on from the painful feelings of unrequited love. But when Akiko died, he put it all on the back burner, determined to support Kenji through his grief, wholly and without a second thought. And now his feelings for Kenji felt deeper than ever before, which was pathetic and horrible, because he'd finally told Kenji how he felt, and the feelings were unreciprocated.

Neither of them had ever been great at deep conversations

about things like *love*, so it's not like Gordon expected them to have a long, drawn-out conversation discussing new boundaries to their relationship or if they should consider scaling back their friendship at some point. But their reality wasn't working either, just existing in a grief-fueled fugue state, things so tense that the slightest spark would ignite them without a moment's notice.

When they finally reopened Kiko's, Gordon ensured it maintained its sparkle with a manic need to distract himself from the shift in his relationship with Kenji. They'd opened the store hours earlier and it felt nice, like a slice of normalcy in an otherwise confusing time. Even conversation was flowing more easily, the change of scenery allowing them to forget the tension they'd been immersed in since their kiss.

Gordon glanced up from some paperwork he had to get done before a meeting the following day and watched Kenji tending to a fiddle leaf fig. He had recently learned those were temperamental decorative trees that didn't even produce figs when grown indoors, and as much as Kenji had tried to convince Gordon of their appeal, he just couldn't accept their popularity.

"I see you glaring at this poor tree," Kenji said, cradling a leaf with one hand, dusting with another, shielding the tree with his body. "Leave her alone."

"I just don't get it. No figs on a fig tree?"

Kenji gave a small scoff. "It *can* grow them indoors, it just sometimes chooses not to. We value choice in this plant store."

"I saw a video of one dropping its leaves because someone drove it to their new apartment during cold weather."

"You know, for someone who hates this plant, you sure know a lot about it. Just tell it you love it and move on with your life."

Gordon heard Kenji suck in a sharp breath. He knew it was

meant as a lighthearted joke and not a commentary on the tension between them, but the words themselves felt heavy and thick. A flicker of hurt passed over Gordon—a brief but visible wince—and Kenji's face fell.

"Oh, shit, Gordon, I didn't mean—"

"I know," Gordon said, looking back at his paperwork, pretending to write something. "It's fine."

"Gordon," Kenji said, and Gordon ignored him. "Look at me."

"What?" He said it with more bite than he meant to, but he was mortified at the reminder of Kenji's response to his confession.

"Hey!"

"Sorry. I'm tired."

"Yeah, well, we're both tired!"

Gordon pushed back his chair as he stood, catching it before it toppled over. He threw his pen on the counter before heading to get something to drink and, more importantly, some space to breathe. The peace was short lived, of course, because Kenji followed him to the back room.

"Gordon."

Gordon closed his eyes and took a deep breath, knowing it was time to address the enormous elephant that had set up residence between them. But he wasn't ready to part with the tiny flicker of hope he'd been keeping alive by avoiding everything between them—Kenji's kiss, Gordon's confession—and just existing in the weird friendship purgatory they'd found themselves in.

"What?"

"I didn't mean to say that. I mean, obviously I did, but I wasn't thinking about how it would sound."

"Yeah, I know."

"Do you?"

"Yes."

"Really? Because—"

"Yes! Christ, Kenj, drop it."

"No!"

Gordon grumbled, squeezing his body between Kenji and the door frame, forcing himself to ignore the feeling of their bodies sliding against each other. The laptop bag he was searching for was nowhere to be found and he sighed, remembering it was still in the back room.

"Okay. Work it out with yourself, then." He cringed at himself.

"Why are you being such a dick?"

"You apologized, I said fine, you keep pushing it. You're being a dick, not me."

"Well, you won't talk to me!"

"Oh, please. I talk to you every day. You're staying at my house, in case you forgot." Gordon wanted to claw out of his skin and teleport home. He wished he'd never opened his mouth that day, because now everything was awful, and he couldn't seem to stop himself from making it worse.

"Should I stay somewhere else?"

"Don't be stupid," Gordon bit out.

"Well, you know me," Kenji said, sarcasm dripping from his words, but only to hide the hurt.

"Oh, stop it."

"Dammit, Gordon. I don't understand why you're snapping at me, okay? I don't get it, and I can't handle this when I'm already dealing with, um…" Kenji bit his lip and he waved his hand around at nothing, or maybe everything. "I can't lose you too. You're all I have. And I need you to tell me how to make things better. I'm sorry, okay? We can pretend I didn't kiss you. We can just move on."

"Stop calling yourself stupid."

"Stop avoiding this!"

"What do you want me to say?" Gordon asked. It was pointless, because he already knew what Kenji wanted him to say. Kenji had hinted at it seconds ago, and that's why he didn't want to say it. *We can forget it all and just go back to how things were.*

Well, that ship had sailed. There was no way he could go back to how things were, not after tasting Kenji's lips and feeling the lines of his muscles under his fingers. Not after hearing the noise Kenji made when their mouths met, which had been better than he'd ever imagined, and now had to live the rest of his life without hearing again.

"I want you to explain what you meant when you said you're in love with me."

"Come on," Gordon said. "Don't do this."

"I deserve to know."

"Not everything is your business, Kenji!"

Kenji's face scrunched up and he threw his hands in the air. "Well, this certainly is! What kind of stupid ass comment is that?"

That was fair. More than fair, really. It was, without a doubt, the most ridiculous response he could have given Kenji, and when the absurdity of his statement hit him, he couldn't help but laugh. It started small, but before he knew it, Gordon was laughing harder than he had since before Akiko died.

"What the hell is happening?" Kenji said. He was smiling, but tentatively, clearly not convinced it was as funny as Gordon thought it was. "What is so funny?"

"I'm sorry. I just…" Gordon let out one last chuckle before blowing out a breath to relax himself. "You're right. My love for you is very much your business."

Kenji gawked at him. Gordon gave him a weak smile.

"So, you do love me?"

Okay, they were doing this.

"Yeah."

"Currently?"

"Yes."

"And before."

"Yeah, Kenji." Gordon sighed.

"Since when?"

"Like, ten-ish years ago." Gordon hedged his answer, as if he didn't know the exact moment he'd fallen.

"Ten years ago? We *met* ten years ago," Kenji said. He looked genuinely surprised, and Gordon laughed again.

"Remember when I asked you out?" Gordon asked.

"Of course. It was like three months after we met, and you said you had to try, because you knew you'd never meet another guy like me."

"Yeah. I hyped myself up for weeks until I finally did it. And you said no, because I'm not an oat."

"You've never been an oat to me."

"Well, I thought I wanted to be an oat. I was so bummed out, I almost didn't want to see you again. But you were right. I never would have been happy if it had just been casual between us. But I was also right, because I've still never met another guy like you." Gordon shrugged, as if this conversation carried no weight.

He paused, half hoping Kenji would take over and steer the conversation elsewhere, but it didn't happen. He worried he'd lose the temporary courage that had allowed him to engage in this conversation in the first place, so he decided to lay it all out there. He could deal with the consequences later, like he did when he'd asked Kenji out all those years ago. But he knew if he didn't say it now, he might never say it at all.

"Okay, fine. You want to know the truth?"

"Yes. I do," Kenji said.

"I love you, Kenji. Still. Always. It's like… the most basic part of who I am, like you're woven into my DNA. It shapes every aspect of my life, and I don't remember a time in the last ten years when my feelings for you didn't overwhelm me with how powerful they are."

"Oh."

"There's very little in my life that doesn't remind me of you. I can't see an orange leaf in the fall without thinking of that video on carotenoids you made me watch when I had the flu. I can't see a feather without imagining you in your costume, and the hours you spent posing in my mirror when you first got hired at Titan. I can't smell tomatoes on the vine without thinking of the summer you made me garden with you, and I was filled with rage the entire time."

"You hated that summer."

"Yes. I hated it so much. But it didn't matter, because I love you, and I can't turn it off. And I've tried. So many times."

"You tried to turn it off?" Kenji asked, his voice quiet.

"Of course."

"*So many* times?"

"It's been ten years, man. What else was I supposed to do?"

"I don't know." Kenji shrugged weakly.

"You going to Boston was supposed to give me the space I needed to start to move on, but then Akiko died, and I—"

"Wait, you wanted to *move on?*"

Gordon sighed and rubbed his eyes. "Remember that time we were at dinner a few months ago? You were telling me about Rob, and you got irritated at me for repeating everything you said."

Kenji bit his lips between his teeth and tried not to smile. "Yes."

"I get why it annoyed you now."

"I get why you did it."

They stared at each other, both waiting for the other to speak first.

"Are you still trying to move on?" Kenji asked.

"I don't really know how to live my life without you in it."

"The thought of it makes me nauseous."

Gordon nodded slowly. "It gives me heartburn."

"I wondered where the Tums went," Kenji said. Gordon gave him a sad smile.

"Man, I handled this all so poorly."

"There's no handbook on how to tell your best friend you love them. I checked," Kenji said, smiling.

Gordon cringed and looked at the floor, unable to look at Kenji. "If there is, chapter one is probably something like, *wait a few months after your friend's beloved aunt dies before confessing ten years of unrequited love.*"

Kenji laughed, but Gordon couldn't quite read his mood. He was still smiling, but there was an edge of nervousness to it. Gordon could understand that. It must be difficult to figure out how to let your friend down. Again.

"Chapter two could be, *if you messed up step one, maybe you'll get lucky, and your friend will say he loves you too,*" Kenji said, still smiling, which Gordon took as a good sign.

Maybe things would be okay after all. Just clearing the air made it feel like a thousand pounds of weight had been lifted from his shoulders. It's not like he'd never lived his life without Kenji's love.

Gordon chuckled and leaned against the wall, rubbing his hand through his hair. "Yeah. That would be a short book."

"Um," Kenji said, pinching the bridge of his nose. "Okay, maybe chapter three would be something like, *if you're both kind of dumb, don't worry; you can figure it out together, even if it takes ten years.*"

Gordon blinked at Kenji, realization slowly dawning on him. "*Ohhh.*"

Kenji's smile widened. "There you go. And I thought I was the dumb one."

"No. Never."

⁓

KENJI'S HEART was pounding like it might burst out of his chest if he moved too quickly, but he couldn't stop smiling as he stepped towards Gordon's waiting arms. He gripped Kenji's back, pulling their bodies together like he had the first time they kissed. Relief washed over him like he'd been holding a breath too long and was finally able to blow it out. He hadn't realized how much tension he'd been holding until he felt it melting away, dissolved by Gordon's warmth.

Gordon turned his face slightly, their lips grazing past each other, but Kenji was still smiling and giddy, unable to give into the kiss he so desperately wanted.

"Stop! I'm trying to kiss you and you're making it impossible with all your teeth," Gordon said, moving his hands to cup Kenji's jaw on either side, holding his head still. Kenji pinched his lips shut, then finally relaxed them, allowing Gordon to capture them in a kiss.

It felt different this time. Their first kiss had been desperate and confusing, the result of Kenji's inability to handle the number of conflicting emotions he was feeling—grief, anger, and love, all colliding with the feeling of being seen by Gordon in a way he had never known. This kiss was purposeful, and as it deepened, the cobwebs inside Kenji's mind began to clear, shedding new light on the friend he loved so deeply. This newly illuminated Gordon was offering something new and unsung, just waiting for Kenji to explore it. He was ready.

When they broke apart, they stared at each other again. Both were smiling, hesitantly at first, but happy.

"I wonder what Akiko would say right now," Kenji said.

"She would probably say, 'You owe me dinner.'"

Kenji tilted his head. "I don't get it."

Gordon shrugged. "She always told me we'd end up together, and to be patient. But she also told me not to waste my life waiting around for you, whatever that meant. She was confusing when she wanted to be."

"Wait," Kenji said, "she knew?"

"I know you're shocked, Kenji, and it's very sweet, but I'm pretty sure everybody knew. Even Rob knew."

"Rob?!"

"Anyway," Gordon said, squeezing Kenji's arms. "I am really happy. To be clear, I'm *so happy*. Like, I feel like my heart is going to explode happy."

"Okay? Me too."

"But, um…"

"What is it?" Kenji asked, unsure where Gordon was heading with this. He had a feeling Gordon was going to ask him to take things slow—to which Kenji had already prepped a rebuttal. He would say ten years of friendship was plenty slow. They had already wasted so much time dating other people and seeing what else was out there, and none of it ever measured up. Plus, they had lived together off and on at various points and had never had any issues. Gordon liked doing laundry and Kenji liked doing the dishes every night. They both liked vacuuming.

But, as eager as he was, he could admit this was probably scary for Gordon. Maybe scarier than it was for Kenji. Gordon had ten years of hopes and dreams wrapped up in this moment, and new relationships carried a built-in risk of failure. But Kenji was so desperate to experience this with

Gordon that there was nothing he would do to risk their future. So, if Gordon needed slow, Kenji would give him that. Somehow.

"I think I'm pretty much monogamous. If we were together, I wouldn't want to sleep with anyone else. And I don't think I could handle you sleeping with other people. I know that might be a dealbreaker."

Kenji laughed, but immediately slapped his hand over his mouth after seeing Gordon's face, which did not show amusement.

"Well, I know you and Rob were open, and you enjoyed that. But I just don't think it's for me. Not that I've ever tried it, but…"

"I've been in monogamous relationships, Gordon. You know that. I mean, they didn't last that long, but that was really more of a—"

"To be honest," Gordon interrupted, "I usually tune out when you talk to me about the specifics of your relationships. I'm a bad friend."

"No, you're not," Kenji said, his gut twisting with guilt thinking about how many years Gordon had put up with mindless, way-too-detailed chatter about hookups and boyfriends. "I might be, though."

"It's not… it's fine."

"Monogamy isn't a problem for me. Relationship preferences can change, you know? Just depends on what you need."

"Oh," Gordon said. He looked embarrassed, so Kenji squeezed him tight around the middle, pressing his cheek against Gordon's head.

"I could be happy with you for the rest of my life, I think."

"You think?"

Kenji smiled and his heart felt full. "I know."

Gordon squeezed him back, but then wiggled out of Kenji's arms.

"Also, um. I'm wondering if maybe we should... take things slow."

Kenji forced himself not to smile and didn't react beyond a small nod. Inside, though, he was grinning ear to ear, thrilled he'd been right all along. He knew every bit of Gordon, even his insecurities, just like he'd predicted.

"I know you think this is happening now because I'm sad," Kenji said. "And if you were anyone else on Earth, I'd think you were right. But this isn't some reaction to my grief. You and I were destined to end up here, I can feel it. Maybe this is her parting gift to us."

"That's a nice idea."

"You don't want to disrespect her gift, Gordon." Kenji was leaning into him again. He put his hands on Gordon's chest and rubbed the fabric of his shirt between his fingers. "Remember when she gave you that sweater and you never wore it because you said yellow made you look seasick?"

"It looked so bad on me."

"It did. And remember how she made you unravel the whole sweater so she could teach you to knit, then forced you to make two pairs of mittens because she didn't want the sweater to go to waste?"

"Yeah. I still have my pair," Gordon said. He swiped at the stray tear gathering in his eye. "Man, I really miss her."

"Me too. So, let's not throw away this gift she's giving us."

"I'm not. But—"

"Tell you what," Kenji said. "I've got a road trip coming up this weekend. When I get home, I'll take you out on our very first date, and we'll make it official. That's in like... four days."

"That's not very slow."

"It's very slow."

"Anyway," Gordon sighed, lifting his chin to kiss Kenji again. "I am so sorry, but I have to go to the office for a meeting. But I'm glad we talked. I wish we'd done this before."

"Oh. Okay. Well, I guess I'll see you at home?"

Gordon kissed him again, deep and eager. He sighed happily at the feeling of Kenji's tongue sliding against his, but also sighed sadly, knowing they had to cut things short so he could go to the office. But Kenji didn't let go, and his long hair tickled Gordon's neck. He felt goosebumps erupt down his arms and Kenji's hands sliding against them. Somehow, he managed to detach himself, though he wished he could stay there forever.

He cleared his throat. "See you at home."

CHAPTER 19

KENJI AND ANTHONY WERE SPRAWLED ACROSS THEIR RESPECTIVE hotel beds with the first match of the weekend behind them. Kenji could feel the difference in the crowds from what they were a year ago and he was still riding the high of their excitement.

The match left a physical ache in Kenji's body that was equal parts painful and satisfying. He liked being sore after matches. The bruises were like little physical reminders of the effort he'd made to earn the CWA contract someday. Even though Akiko was gone, he wanted to achieve what he'd set out to. Wrestling was about the only thing he'd ever been good at, and he was so close.

That was a relatively new feeling. He'd always enjoyed wrestling and thought it would be a fun career path, but feeling like he was actually good at it was something he hadn't experienced until recently. But with every match, every win, every promise of a title, he knew he was closer than he'd ever thought possible, and he was confident at this point, this is what he wanted. Not the plant store.

The TV in the hotel room was on with the volume low

enough that he and Anthony could chat, but both of them were zoned out, relaxing to the familiar sights and sounds of Jurassic Park.

"Nineties Jeff Goldblum, man."

"Yeah? Is he better than current Jeff Goldblum?" Anthony asked, not looking at Kenji, squinting at the TV.

"He's Jeff Goldblum, Ant. He's never not hot."

"Okay. I'll take your word for it."

"To answer your question, yes. But just barely." Kenji turned on his side, nuzzling his head into the pillow, looking at Anthony. "How about that Laura Dern, huh?"

"Sure. She's nice. Looks good in pink."

"Hmm. How about BD Wong! Everybody loves him."

"Yeah, sure. I like a scientist."

"Maybe the little baby dinosaur in the egg is more your type?"

Anthony chuckled. "Maybe."

Bored by Anthony's refusal to discuss hot people, he rolled over, settling on his back again.

"How's Chloe?" Kenji asked.

"She's fine, I guess. Haven't talked to her much today."

"Oh. Is that normal for you guys?"

"Ah… yeah. Unfortunately," Anthony said, rubbing his forehead. Kenji watched him tap his phone screen and turn it off quickly when there were no notifications.

"I'm sorry."

"It's fine. She sends me kid updates, which is what's most important."

Kenji scrolled through his phone and smiled at a new photo of Peony sent by Gordon. He was eating a carrot shred.

Anthony spoke again. "Marriage is hard, I don't know."

"Is it?"

"It wasn't always. But right now, yeah."

"What's going on with you guys?"

"Nothing. I think that's kind of it. There's like, nothing there."

Kenji sat up, feeling guilty for scrolling on his phone while Anthony opened up. It was so out of character for him, Kenji would have been weirded out if he hadn't looked so serious and dejected.

"You don't love her anymore?" He didn't like the idea of that. Anthony and his wife Chloe had been together for ages. They married young but waited years to have kids. They always seemed like a great couple. Happy and solid, in a boring sort of way.

"I love her. I always will. She's been my best friend since I was a teenager. But no, I don't know that I'm in love with her anymore. Not the way I should be."

"I'm sorry."

"It's okay. I don't think she's in love with me anymore, either."

Kenji's phone lit up with a text from Gordon, and he tried his hardest not to glance down at it, wanting to give Anthony his full attention.

"What do you think you're going to do?"

"Probably nothing until the kids are in school. We're not angry with each other. She could date other people if she wanted to, and I wouldn't be upset."

"Do you want to date other people?"

"Nah."

"Do you miss sex?"

He was quiet for a minute and Kenji was worried he'd stepped over the line. Anthony was strait-laced and reserved and probably didn't appreciate the prodding.

"Sorry. None of my business."

"No, it's not that. I was trying to remember the last time I had sex. We didn't after Chloe got pregnant, and Fox is three months old. You can do the math."

He couldn't, really. It was late and math was hard even on his best days, so he just nodded. Anthony had turned his attention back to the TV, so Kenji used the opportunity to peek at the messages Gordon sent.

> Gordon: I just came up with a great storyline. I'm going to pitch it to Mike, see if I can get you some more work. It starts when Ken Vee betrays Anthony by accepting a bribe that will guarantee their loss in an upcoming title match. Anthony finds out and demands a new partner. Mike says yes, because Anthony is his favorite.

> Kenji: I don't love it so far.

> Gordon: Ant's new partner, let's call him… Grizzly, enters the ring. Their in-ring chemistry is off the charts. They're hot, they're sexy, they're powerful. They win the title and Ken Vee is full of regret. Why did he betray Anthony?! The camera zooms in on his face and the lights glisten on his unshed tears.

> Kenji: Now I like this even less. Does Grizzly have a gimmick, or is he just mean to poor, innocent Ken?

> Gordon: His gimmick is that he's hot and sexy. Even Ken Vee knows that. Pay attention.

> Kenji: omg

Gordon: Now they're backstage. Ken walks in on Grizzly alone in the locker room. He's changing out of his costume, and the sight of him fills Ken with unbridled rage, but also something else... something unfamiliar. He's confused and jacked up from the match, so he approaches Grizzly and slams him into the lockers.

Kenji: Ooh, warming up to it now!

Gordon: Grizzly is okay with it. Ken is weak. He's pathetic. It felt like a mouse shoving him.

Kenji: Okay, can you hurry this up, please? The raptors are about to enter the kitchen in my movie.

Gordon: Ken looks down at his hands and then up at Grizzly, angry that his weak hands didn't hurt him. Grizzly looks at Ken, too, and he says, "Aw. Your hands are like little puppy paws, so soft and clumsy." Ken Vee is outraged. Obviously. And he says, "I can be rougher than that."

Gordon: Grizzly is like, "Show me, pup." And Ken is flustered, like, "who the hell is this Grizzly guy, and why is he calling me pup?" But he can't get any words out. He's so mad but also like, weirdly horny?

Kenji: What the fuck

Gordon: And Grizzly says, "Take my dick out. Show me how rough you can be."

Kenji: I was reading these to Anthony, asshole!

Gordon: :)

"I'm sorry, when did *that* happen?" Anthony asked, laughing at Kenji's embarrassment.

"*That* has never happened before."

"But this is Gordon! When did you get to the point where he sends weird shit like that? Did something happen between you guys?"

"I mean, I guess. But the same asshole who sent me that also told me he wanted to take things slow and he's making me wait for sex like some puritan."

Anthony laughed again, stopping only when his phone rang, which resulted in a string of quiet curse words spilling from his mouth.

"I'm going to take this and go out for a walk. It's about my kid. She's had the stomach flu, and I think Chloe is losing her mind, so this might take a while. I need to call her parents and see if they can help with the baby. Oh, God."

Kenji grimaced. "Good luck, bud."

The door clicked shut behind Anthony and Kenji went into the bathroom to brush his teeth. As he spit the leftover toothpaste, he looked at himself in the mirror and poked at the now visible bruises he'd earned at the match. He wondered what Gordon would say if he saw them. He'd probably get Kenji some ice, even though it was unnecessary. Maybe some ibuprofen.

He climbed back into his bed and pulled the covers up to his chin, surprised at how well the AC unit was working in what was maybe the worst hotel in Millersburg, Oregon, wherever that was.

Warming up and feeling cozy, his mind, predictably, drifted to Gordon. He wished they were together. It felt unfair that he'd just figured out his feelings out and had to leave town immediately.

Gordon: Sorry. Don't be mad at me.

Kenji's phone rang and he answered it immediately.

"Hey!"

"Hey. I didn't wake you, right?"

Kenji pulled the phone away from his face to glance at the clock. "It's not even ten and we were texting five minutes ago."

"You have been known to go to bed early on match days."

"That's true. And I am kind of tired. Did you watch?" Kenji nestled into his pillow and bedding and reached over to turn off the one dim light he and Anthony had on during the movie.

"Of course."

"How'd I look?" Kenji asked.

"Mmm. Pretty good."

"Yeah? What was your favorite part?"

"When the camera fucked up and zoomed in on your butt for like four full seconds."

Kenji cracked up. "What?! Did that really happen?"

"And the lighting was just right. I could see *everything*."

"Okay, I wear like three layers down there, so now I know you're lying."

"Aw."

Kenji heard Gordon shuffling around. "What are you doing?"

"Getting into bed. I have an early meeting tomorrow and have to go into the office. What time do you get home?"

"Probably noon. I have to go straight to Kiko's though, and then I have a match in the evening."

"Oh. That sucks, I wanted to take you to dinner."

"Sorry. I have two days off after that."

"Okay. I miss you," Gordon said. "I know that's dumb. I saw you like three days ago."

"It's not dumb. I miss you, too."

"I wish you were here." Gordon's voice came out breathy and low, which Kenji knew was only because he was tired and getting ready to go to sleep. But he closed his eyes and pretended it was more than that. Like maybe Gordon was thinking about Kenji the way Kenji had been thinking about him.

He decided to try something. Low pressure. No expectations. "Yeah? What would you do if I was?"

Gordon laughed, just a quiet rumble. Not his normal laugh, but sexier somehow. "Grizzly really worked on you, huh?"

"Shut up. Tell me what you'd do to me if I was there."

"Isn't Anthony with you? We talked about this. I don't feel comfortable adding anyone to our sex life."

"He's not here! I would never ask you to—"

"I'm kidding!" Gordon said, laughing again, the real one this time. "I'm kidding."

"Dick."

"Yes, that would be involved."

"You are so bad at this." Kenji said. "I'm going to sleep."

"I'm sorry! Stop. I'll be good."

"I shouldn't have answered the phone. I should have just politely excused myself to the shower to jack off like a normal person before going to bed."

Gordon made a small, choked noise before giving a noncommittal hum.

"Are you okay over there?" Kenji asked, laughing before

softening his voice. "Did the thought of me touching myself make you choke?"

"Yeah," Gordon said. He was back to the breathy sound and Kenji was gone.

"Tell me what you're going to do to me when I get home."

"I... want to do a lot of things to you. But mostly, I want to hold you. Kiss you. So badly it hurts."

Kenji's heart seized. Sure, kissing wasn't necessarily risqué or erotic, though he supposed it could be. What took him by surprise, though, was how earnest Gordon sounded. Like kissing Kenji really was all he needed to be happy in that moment.

Kenji had never loved somebody for as long or as intensely as Gordon had loved him, and he was working to make up for lost time. But something about his immediate answer to that question filled Kenji with a warmth he'd never felt before, and he understood why he said it. Kissing Gordon right now would be worth a thousand of its sexier counterparts.

"I think I'd start with your mouth. Obvious, maybe, but considering how much I've loved the two kisses we've shared so far, I think that will end up being my favorite place to kiss you."

Kenji hummed, content and cozy, letting himself relax to the sound of his best friend's voice.

"But then... you have this little freckle under your right ear. I don't know if you've seen it, because it's slightly hidden. I've wanted to kiss you there as long as I can remember."

"Oh," Kenji said, opening his eyes. He moved his hand down to his dick, already hard. He squeezed it.

"And then I'd move down your neck to your chest and throat. When you wrestle, the lights reflect off the beads of sweat caught in the little divot between your collar bones. Sometimes, if I'm lucky, I'll catch sight of it as it finally spills down your chest. Something about it makes me…" Gordon groaned, and Kenji took a deep breath. "I don't know."

Kenji impulsively raised his hand to the hollow of his neck. "Makes you what?"

"It makes me think about how it would be if you were on your knees for me. When I came on your chest, I'd watch it pool there before it dripped down the rest of your body. I'd lick you there and kiss you. You'd see how good you taste."

"Jesus." Kenji's hand left his chest and went back to his dick, and he moaned into the phone, and he was happy to hear a similar noise come from Gordon.

"Then what would you do, after you kissed me?" he asked. Kenji felt dizzy listening to Gordon. He had no idea this side of him existed and he loved it.

"I'm not done kissing you yet," Gordon said. "I've wanted to kiss and lick your stomach since the first day I saw you. You spilled that espresso on your work shirt and thought taking it off in the café was appropriate. It was not, at all, but you were so unbelievable to look at, I think I would have paid your lost wages if you'd been fired."

Kenji laughed. "Go on."

"That night I went home and barely made it to my room before I took myself out. I imagined you sitting on the counter with your shirt off. I imagined you touching yourself for me while I watched. I didn't even know your name, but I was so desperate for you that I called out *Barista Guy* when I came, and I think it took about twelve seconds. I bet I've come fifty times to that vision of you, most of them were probably within ten days of that night. I was in physical pain for weeks."

Kenji's breath hitched as he listened to Gordon's confession, his voice a low rumble through the phone. The room around him seemed to shrink, the walls closing in on the heat of their conversation.

"Poor baby," Kenji whispered.

"I think once I was done kissing you, I'd give in—I'd make my way down to your cock cock, take it in my mouth, and suck you until you were begging me to stop."

Kenji's hand moved faster on his dick, the thought of Gordon's lips wrapped around it instead of his hand making his head spin.

"Fuck, Gordon," he moaned, his hips bucking into his own hand. "I wish you were here right now."

"Not as much as I do," Gordon replied. The need in his voice was palpable. "I'm imagining you stroking yourself, your hand slick with precum. Are you close, baby?"

"Yes," Kenji gasped, his body coiling tight with impending release. "I'm so close."

"Wait," Gordon said. "I want us to come together."

Kenji bit his lip, surprised that the thought of them coming at the same time, but miles apart, made him feel almost painfully lonely for Gordon. He slowed his movements, and his breaths became short pants holding back his climax.

"Okay," he said, his voice strained.

"Picture me on my knees in front of you. Picture fucking my mouth and coming down my throat."

Gordon had barely finished speaking when Kenji came with a throaty cry. He squeezed his eyes shut and felt his orgasm rip through him, cum covering his hand and belly, up to his chest. He heard Gordon groan on the other end, the knowledge that they were coming together made Kenji's pleasure even more intense.

Kenji relaxed into his pillows, his chest heaving, and he listened to Gordon's breathing on the other end of the phone.

"Oh man," Kenji muttered, still breathing heavily. "How are you doing over there?"

Gordon laughed, the same quiet laugh he gave when the

two of them stayed up too late watching terrible TV. The one that told Kenji Gordon was laying there with his eyes half closed and a sleepy smile on his face. "So good," he mumbled. "I can't wait to do that in person."

Kenji laughed. "Same."

"Man. I really love you."

"I love you, too," Kenji said, his heart squeezing. "Maybe next time we can video call, huh?"

Gordon laughed. "Maybe."

CHAPTER 20

Kenji ran up the stairs, already smiling when as slid his key in the lock, excited to surprise Gordon with his early return. He pushed the door open and dropped his bags, expecting to see Gordon on the couch, working or reading. He'd been working from home more often since Akiko died, which Kenji loved for a lot of reasons, but mostly because Gordon was finally relaxing and allowing himself to unclench about work.

"Gordito?"

He walked into the kitchen and didn't see any signs of Gordon other than a plate, sprinkled with toast crumbs, tossed in the sink. A half empty mug of coffee sat next to it.

Kenji had made an effort to get home early because the shop was closed and Gordon didn't work, and he imagined they'd be able to spend the whole day together. Maybe in *bed*. And Gordon's absence was really hindering his plan.

A piece of paper with its corner tucked under the coffee pot caught Kenji's eye. It was a note from Gordon. *Dropped my phone in the toilet. Gross. Out buying a new one, then I have to go into the office for a few hours. I'm sorry. Home by five. Love you.*

Kenji frowned, sad he'd woken up early for no reason and

feeling kind of bad for making Anthony do the same, especially since Anthony was heading home to a cesspool of bacteria. He would have to remember not to complain to Anthony about any of this.

Gordon kept a visibly tidy home, which was nice, but Kenji knew his secret. Behind each closet door and within every dresser drawer was a collection of random crap he'd saved from years of his life, unorganized and shoved behind random papers and occasionally literal trash. With nothing to do and nowhere to go, Kenji decided to tackle the closet in the office, since that way he'd have Peony to keep him company.

"Okay, Peony, let's see what your dad has stashed away in here. I have a garbage bag, a recycling bag, and a box for things to keep. Let me know if I'm wrong about any of it."

Peony didn't respond, but he nodded his head. Kenji would take it, even though Gordon said that was a sign he was mad, or something.

An hour into his project, Kenji was beginning to question his own intelligence. He was totally capable of cleaning and tidying, but he'd underestimated just how much Gordon had managed to pack into this closet. He'd managed to fill an entire paper bag with recycling, and half a garbage bag with stuff he was certain Gordon wouldn't miss. When he reached in and grabbed a red box, he smiled, somehow remembering the shoes that came in it and the day they'd had when Gordon picked them out.

He lifted the lid of the box and looked at the pile of photos and mementos inside. Photos of Gordon and Kenji at various parties and events over the years and candid shots of himself Kenji had never seen. A pile of sticky notes Kenji used to leave notes on when they'd lived together years ago. The mood ring Kenji gave Gordon after he won it at an arcade, the one Gordon said was broken because it always said he was stressed, and he didn't want to be reminded. A tea bag wrapper from the first time Gordon came to Kenji's house to have dinner.

Kenji smiled down at the items, a mix of fondness and annoyance welling up inside him, mad at himself all over again for missing what had been right in front of him for years.

The sound of the front door opening caught his attention, and he was surprised Gordon was already home. Or maybe it was already late. He wasn't sure. His stomach rumbled with hunger, though, so maybe he really had been in there for several hours.

He stood and ran to the living room, hugging the box to his chest. Gordon was there, so handsome in the slacks and cardigan he wore to work. Kenji once teased him about it, calling the look his "uniform," and Gordon just shrugged, unbothered.

"When I find something that works, I like to hold onto it," he'd said.

Kenji stood still on one side of the couch, Gordon stared back at him from the other.

"Oh. My shoebox," Gordon said.

Kenji glanced down at his hands, having forgotten he was holding it. "Oh. Yeah, I was organizing the closet and I found it. I'm sorry."

"That's okay. I'm sorry if you think I'm creepy." Gordon gave him a small, nervous smile.

Kenji tossed the box down and walked over to Gordon and wrapped his arms around his neck before kissing him. "Never."

Gordon leaned in and kissed him back and Kenji sighed, so happy to be back with Gordon, excited to see where things were heading. He knew, after their time on the phone, that he wanted this even more than he did before, and he was pretty sure Gordon felt the same. He was even more sure when Gordon lined their bodies up and Kenji could feel the evidence of how badly Gordon wanted it. Wanted him.

"I can't stay long. I have to go back to the office for some afternoon meetings," Gordon said between kisses. "I just wanted to see you and touch you. I've been dying all morning, waiting for you to get home. I'm so glad you're here."

"Me too," Kenji said, breathless, leaning his head back to give Gordon room to find his neck, unbuttoning Gordon's sweater so he could slide his hands up his shirt.

Gordon's fingers dug into Kenji's sides. It was almost painful, but Kenji loved it—he was so surprised and desperate and eager to explore this new side of Gordon.

"Come to the bedroom?" Gordon said, mumbling against his mouth.

Kenji couldn't form words, so he just nodded, his lips never leaving Gordon's mouth and chin and neck, and Gordon pulled him towards the bedroom. They tripped over a shoe, laughing and fumbling for a moment like the first time they kissed, but Kenji didn't let Gordon stop it this time. He launched himself back into Gordon's arms, felt the stubble against his chin, felt their racing hearts inside their chests. His hands combed through Gordon's hair before pulling it, drawing a sweet groan from Gordon's throat.

Kenji forced himself to pull away so they could make actual movement towards the bedroom. He took off, walking as fast as he could without breaking out into a run. He felt Gordon's heat behind him and as he turned the corner, he looked back and saw him, flushed and hungry. They were back on each other seconds later.

"I want—"

"Me too—"

"Take this off," Kenji said, pulling them to the bed.

Gordon was on top of Kenji now, their bodies touching everywhere. He was pressing him into the mattress the way Kenji had wished for the previous night, rutting into him, kissing his neck and chin, nipping at the pulse points of his throat. He was so hard and so was Kenji, and there was no way for them to get enough friction for what he wanted and what he *needed*. Gordon made a growling noise and lifted his head briefly, like he surprised himself, and Kenji laughed.

He pulled Gordon back down and kissed him again, loving the attention Gordon was giving his body but wanting to feel his lips and mouth on his even more. He wanted this to last forever.

But three hard knocks on the front door shattered the moment—Gordon lifted himself up again, staring back at Kenji, almost panicked.

"Are you expec—"

Gordon put his hand over Kenji's mouth to quiet him. "Shh. We're not here." Gordon ground their hips together and leaned down to continue kissing him, and Kenji let his legs fall open further, Gordon's weight sinking into him.

"Gordon!" Whoever was at the door was knocking again. "I see your car, dumbass. Let me in!"

"*Fuck!*" Gordon relaxed his body and pressed his forehead into Kenji's still-clothed shoulder. "Goddammit. I'm sorry. That sounds like Victor."

"Your brother?"

"Yeah. One second. I'll be back."

After taking a moment to adjust himself and reconfigure his clothing, Gordon disappeared into the living room, leaving Kenji alone on the bed. He threw his arm over his eyes and sighed, frustrated and aching.

Maybe Victor being there in their home was a good opportunity for Kenji to meet him for the first time. And maybe kick him out for being a massive asshole.

He stepped lightly towards the living room, not wanting to interrupt their conversation, and okay, he wanted to eavesdrop. He peered around the corner.

"Did you get your new phone yet?" Victor asked.

"Oh, no, not yet. I had to stop by the house first. I'm getting it on my way back to the office."

"You don't have time. Chop, chop." Victor said. He held up his phone. It appeared to have an email pulled up.

"Shit," Gordon said, squinting at the phone. "Okay. Let me, um…"

"Why did you come home, anyway?"

"I had to get something."

"Get what?"

"Don't worry about it. I'll meet you at the office."

Victor scoffed. "Sorry, but I am worried about it. As I've told you before, your reputation at work impacts mine."

"I think your reputation is fine."

"It's just hard to trust you to take care of this merger when you can't even keep your schedule straight."

Gordon sighed. "Okay."

"I gave you that time off when you had to babysit the plant store. I've been giving you flexibility with remote work, which I don't have to do, by the way. Don't make me regret that by making me look stupid in front of Shayna."

"I *won't*. Can you just give me a fucking minute?"

"One minute. But no more, because you're on thin ice as it is."

"*On thin ice?* What are you, a grandpa?"

Kenji stepped on a creaky floorboard and they both looked over at him.

"Sorry." Kenji stepped out from behind the corner. "I didn't mean to interrupt."

"Hello," Victor said, looking perplexed, his eyes flashing to Gordon briefly.

"Hi. I'm Kenji."

Victor's eyes opened wide and both eyebrows raised. Kenji watched as he looked to Gordon, then to Kenji, then back to Gordon. Victor looked at Gordon's tousled hair and the light pink tinge to his cheeks and his eyes moved down to Gordon's cardigan, with its mismatched buttons causing one side to hang lower than the other.

"Kenji," Victor said wryly.

"Yes?"

"This all makes sense now."

"Okay. Ominous," Kenji said.

"Ignore him. I'll meet you at the office in a bit, Victor."

"No can do. I told Shayna we'd be there in half an hour. We're already going to be late at this point, and I'm not getting in trouble because I didn't retrieve you. Especially if the reason you're late is because..." Victor waved in Kenji's direction.

Kenji stepped closer to Gordon, unsure if he would be okay with Victor knowing they were... whatever they were. But Kenji decided he hated Victor, and really liked Gordon, so he placed his hand on his back and felt Gordon lean into it slightly.

"I'm so sorry, Kenj. I have to leave. Now, apparently," Gordon said. "But I'll be back for dinner."

Victor made a noise.

"What?"

"This might take a while. I think they're expecting you to meet with the other team to go over all the merger shit."

"Merger shit?"

"Yeah. Anyway, I won't tell Shayna this is why you've been scattered lately if you hurry up," Victor said, glancing at Kenji.

"I'm not scattered," Gordon said, looking to Kenji. "I'm not."

"I know you're not," Kenji said, his hand still on Gordon's lower back.

Victor laughed. "Right."

"Anyway—"

Kenji huffed and took step towards Victor. "What are you, like, a cartoon villain?"

"I'm sorry?" Victor asked, standing up straighter.

"You barge into Gordon's house, lay into him about how he's damaging your reputation, then act like you're bending over backwards to permit the flexible schedule that's written into your employment contracts. And I know that's a thing, because Gordon told me it was. He also told me he's never taken advantage of it the entire time he's worked for your stupid company."

"It's okay, Kenj," Gordon said.

"No, it's not! And then you say he's been scattered because, what, he hasn't been answering your calls in the middle of the night? I've heard the way you speak to him. I wouldn't answer your calls, either."

"I'm sorry, you don't even know me. And you don't know anything about the business, so your opinion on my behavior is meaningless to me. You're the wrestler, right? The one who thinks he's going to be a big CWA star?"

"Yes, I am. And it's true that I don't know anything about the business, but Gordon does. And I don't know you, but I do know him, and I know what he's been putting up with from you even when he has a million other things going on."

"What Gordon does outside of work is not important to me in this context," Victor said.

"Did you know when my aunt was dying, he moved her into his house so she was never alone more than a few hours at a time? And he paid for a nurse to come once a week because her insurance wouldn't cover it? And he took care of our plant store because he knew it was important to us and he didn't want to see it fall apart. He did all of that while he worked full time because he also didn't want to let you or your stupid company down. But somehow, none of that matters to you. Because you're awful. And he's the best. And you don't deserve a brother *or* an employee so wonderful."

"What matters to me is that Gordon does his job. It's my job to ensure it gets done, not to monitor his feelings."

"His job is getting done! He barely slept for a whole month to make sure he didn't miss a single deadline."

Victor sighed and looked at his phone. "Speaking of deadlines, we gotta go, Gord."

"And stop calling him Gord. He hates that!"

"Oh, please," Victor said. "Gordon would let someone call him 'shithead' if it was they wanted."

Kenji clenched his fists at his sides before looking at Gordon, whose face was blank. It broke his heart. Kenji knew that look. Gordon was swallowing it all down so he didn't rock the boat.

"God. The idea that I ever missed the depth of his selflessness just kills me because it puts me on the same level as you," Kenji said.

Victor raised an eyebrow. "Excuse me?"

"You're questioning his commitment to his job while admitting he wants to give everything to everybody. The two are mutually exclusive." He turned to Gordon and whispered, "Did I use that right?"

Gordon smiled softly and nodded, then made a seesaw motion with his hand.

"I'm beginning to think you're the reason Gordon and I have had more than one conversation about his… priorities."

"Leave him out of it, Victor."

"Get out of my house," Kenji said, waving his hand at Victor, hoping he didn't know the house was not at all his.

"This is Gordon's house."

Gordon looked to Kenji, who was bristled and pink, and said, "Yes, but he lives here."

Victor closed his eyes. "I don't have time for this. Gord, meet me in the car," Victor said. He looked at Kenji and smirked. "Ken."

Gordon and Kenji stood staring at the door as Victor closed it behind him.

"Ken?" Kenji finally said.

"He gives everyone stupid nicknames, even if you ask him to stop. Despite what he said, I have asked him to stop calling me Gord. He's the entire reason I hate it."

"I'm so sorry you have to deal with him," Kenji said. "Quit your job. I'll take care of you."

Gordon laughed. "I'm not sure that's a great idea on your salary. It'll be okay. He's just stressed about this merger."

"That doesn't make it okay."

"Thank you," Gordon said, then kissed Kenji and pulled him into a hug.

"For yelling at your brother? That was its own reward. You deserve so much more than me yelling at your brother."

"I love you. But I'm used to him. Don't let him ruin your day."

"It isn't okay just because you're used to him."

Gordon smiled sadly at Kenji and shrugged.

"You know, it's too bad Victor ruined the name Gord. Gourd would be a cute nickname. Like, gourds. You know, the little pumpkin things?"

"I know what a gourd is."

"Okay."

"I'm sorry I have to leave. I'll see you tonight?"

"Of course. I'll be here. You can, um… email me. If you get bored," Kenji said.

Gordon smiled at him. "Bye, weirdo."

Kenji was disappointed Gordon left, of course. He'd been looking forward to seeing him and had really, *really* enjoyed their brief time together. And things got even worse when he walked back down the hall and passed the office, where the disaster he'd created stared back at him. He threw his head back and groaned, knowing he'd have to clean it up before Gordon got home.

But first, he trailed back into the bedroom and got under the covers, pulling Gordon's pillow to his face. It smelled clean, like laundry detergent, but with a Gordon twist. The almond hair oil he used sometimes mixed with cologne and just the faintest hint of soil. He must have been at Kiko's earlier in the day. Kenji closed his eyes and breathed it in, then leaned into the aching need he'd been left with. Fueled with the rage he felt for anyone who ever wronged Gordon, he finished what they'd started.

CHAPTER 21

"I THINK I'M GOING TO SELL THE HOUSE," KENJI SAID ONE morning over breakfast.

Akiko's house had been Kenji's home base since he was a teenager, even when he finally lived on his own, but he had no sentimental attachment to it. Maybe because he'd moved in when he was sixteen after his parents divorced, or because he purposely avoided loving it because he was afraid it'd be gone without notice at some point. There was plenty *in* the house he cared about, but the house itself wasn't his, and he didn't need it to be.

Plus, selling it would net him enough to pay off the loan, and then he would have wiggle room to hire a few employees and focus even more on wrestling.

"Oh?" Gordon asked, mid chew. "Would you buy something else?"

"I was kind of hoping maybe I could... live here for a while. I mean, I'd pay rent, of course. But it's been going okay the last few weeks, right? Us living together?"

"Yeah, of course," Gordon said, sitting up straighter. "You

can live here until… whenever. Or until you find something else. Just put the money away for your future, or something."

Kenji smiled at him, relieved. He hadn't expected Gordon to hate the idea or anything, but he still wasn't sure how quickly Gordon wanted things to go between them.

"When do professional wrestlers retire, anyway?"

"Probably depends how many injuries they've had," Kenji said. "So, for me, like, ninety, probably. I'm that good."

"Uh huh," Gordon said. "Well, let me know if I can help with anything house related. Maybe we can go over this weekend to start looking at what you can part with. If you're ready."

"I'm ready. But, oh, I need your help with something else. If you have time this week, can you go through her financial documents and help me find out where to pay off the loan? She never let me see that stuff, so I'm totally lost. I want to use the money from the house to pay it off."

Gordon took a bite of toast while Kenji was talking, nodding absently at first, but then he choked out a cough. His eyes watered and his face pinkened, and Kenji watched him try to take a breath before reaching out for his coffee to wash down the remaining food. He managed one sip before he coughed again.

"Whoa. You good?" Kenji asked from a half standing position. "Do you need water?"

"I'm fine," Gordon rasped. "It's this billion-seed bread you buy. I choked on a sunflower seed. Or, no, wait. What's this one?"

"Pumpkin seed."

"It's green."

"They're green when they don't have the husk."

"*Husk?* Ugh."

"The husk is removed!"

"Still…" Gordon rubbed his hand across his chest. "I could have died."

"Excuse me for wanting us to get more fiber!"

"I just think there are better fiber options. Vegetables, for example."

Kenji rolled his eyes. "Okay, Chef Ramsay."

"Fruit."

"It's good bread!"

"Psyllium husk," Gordon said. "Just a scoop. There's some in the cabinet."

"Stop!" Kenji laughed. "Leave my bread alone."

"There isn't enough fiber in the whole loaf to make it worth eating this cardboard you've convinced yourself is bread. If I didn't know better, I'd think you wanted me to choke. You've had your eye on Peony for years."

"Well, maybe," Kenji said, smiling into his coffee.

"It's fine. There are worse ways to go than too much toast." Gordon cleared his throat and wiped his mouth.

"Anyway, if you're done making fun of me, can you help me with the loan? I don't even know how much she owed."

Gordon stood up abruptly, ignoring Kenji's question. He grabbed his plate, stacking it on top of Kenji's, crushing his uneaten eggs before taking both plates to the kitchen and throwing them haphazardly into the dishwasher.

Kenji stared at the empty table in front of him. "Um, I wasn't done."

"Oh, sorry. I'll put more bread in the toaster."

"It's okay… just the loan stuff, weirdo."

"I'll see what I can find."

"Thank you."

Gordon mumbled something about needing to check on

Peony and left the room, leaving Kenji with his too-many thoughts and a half-finished morning project. He pushed the jumbled mess of moving, purging, and selling Akiko's house from his mind and scrolled through a list of potential rental options he'd found for the annual end-of-summer Pacific Coast pro-wrestling meetup.

The meetup involved at least ten indie wrestling promotions from across the Pacific Northwest getting together for several days' worth of chaos. It was a big deal. A wrestler's success at the meetup could earn them additional matches during the year if the promo owners showed interest. Any additional ring time meant more visibility for CWA. He hoped this event, plus the training camp he mostly completed in Boston, would be his ticket to a new contract. With Akiko gone and the loan going away, he was able to push the store from his mind and was ready to dive in.

During the last couple events, he'd stayed with the guys from Titan in a block of rooms in a hotel, somewhere cheap and far from the beach. But this year's meetup would serve an additional purpose.

Akiko's ashes had been returned to him and currently sat in a small urn on Gordon's mantel, ever-present during their evening TV binges, Peony's free-roams, and Kenji's quiet, reflective meditations. He had placed a small vase with a single white chrysanthemum next to it, knowing it would wither and die within a few days. Gordon had been stopping by the florist in his office building a couple of times a week to refresh it, never mentioning it.

He and Akiko didn't really have any other family, none that they cared to interact with anyway, and he wasn't planning a wake, so it just made sense for him to take her with him to the meetup. He hoped she didn't find it crass and glanced at the urn from the corner of his eye in apology.

"Gomen, obachan," he whispered to her. "But you loved efficiency!"

He was interrupted by Gordon entering the kitchen, fully dressed for a day at the office.

"Do you have a meeting?" Kenji asked, surprised to see him dressed in slacks and a nice shirt so early.

"Oh, no, I just think it's time to start going in again."

Kenji did his best not to show his disappointment, but it was hard. So far, Gordon had come to the store most days Kenji worked there, and went in alone on the few days Kenji had been out of town. He'd gone into the office a couple of times for big meetings, but he mostly stayed with Kenji. And it's not like Kenji had expected him to do it forever, but it had become a comforting routine, and on some days, that was all that kept him going.

"Is that okay? You look upset."

"No, yeah, it's fine! Of course. You have to get back to your routine." Kenji nodded. "I'll be fine at the store by myself."

"Okay. If you're not, though, let me know. Okay? I'll meet you there. Any time."

"Hey, before you go, I know I told you I'm not having a service for Akiko, right?"

"Yeah?"

"I want to bring her with me to the PCWM this weekend and sprinkle her in the ocean. It's what she wanted. Is there any way you can come with me? I know you've already taken a lot of time off to deal with this, and me, and everything. And I get it if you can't."

"Kenji," Gordon said, moving towards the table with gentle urgency before sitting down next to him. "Of course, I will. I would never make you do that alone."

"Oh," Kenji said, blowing a breath out. "Yeah, obviously. I don't know I was so nervous to ask you."

"Well, things were weird for a while…"

Kenji nodded. "Yeah." He reached out and lifted Gordon's chin, forcing him to look up. "But they're good now, right?"

"Very."

CHAPTER 22

GORDON STOOD AT THE BACK OF THE ARENA WITH HIS ARMS crossed, leaning against the wall. He could barely see the ring, which was fine for now, but Kenji was going on next and he wanted to be able to watch. The venues booked for the matches at this event were a lot smaller than the Titan arena, obviously, so Gordon had opted to stand rather than being stuck on a folding chair between people he didn't know. But it meant he couldn't relax, so he had a lot of time to fidget and shift his weight and think way too much.

The past week had been torture. He and Kenji were like two ships passing in the night, Gordon with his stupid office job keeping him out of the house until six, Kenji spending time at the arena every day after closing up Kiko's. They kind of saw each other at night, in bed, but Kenji always passed out immediately upon climbing under the covers, exhausted from his extra training and practice sessions, and Gordon had to wake up early to get to the office.

They hadn't been able to finish what they'd started the day they were interrupted by Victor, and at this point, Gordon was back to being nervous about progressing things between them.

But the sexual tension between them was so thick it felt like an extra person in the room, and whenever they touched it made Gordon feel like he was made of electricity, but with no outlet.

Even if he ignored the filthy texts Kenji sent Gordon at work, he knew Kenji was feeling it too. He'd been dropping hints about this weekend and finally having some time together, which gave Gordon plenty to think about. But then Kenji always feel guilty shortly after mentioning it, thinking he should be focused on saying his final goodbyes to Akiko, and Gordon spent his time comforting him.

The lights in the venue dimmed slightly and Gordon heard the beginning of Kenji's entrance song. He laughed, like he always did, and looked around for somewhere better to stand. He ended up near a few guys he didn't know or recognize, and figured they were locals or from somewhere other than Portland.

Kenji stripped off his vest and threw it into the audience. It hit one of the men in front of Gordon and the guy laughed before leaning over to his friend.

"Hey, I fucked that guy up in Portland!"

Gordon's stomach rolled hearing it. Not because he was jealous; he wasn't, really. He knew Kenji had kept himself busy for years, and most of the people he slept with had been people he'd met through Titan. But he didn't want to hear a guy talking about it. Especially not that guy, who was soft but broad shouldered, taller and bigger than Kenji.

Not that Kenji had a type—*warm blooded with a hard dick* were the main criteria, according to Kenji.

But still, seeing that man, knowing those hands had touched Kenji places he still hadn't, it twisted something in his guts.

Doing his best to ignore him, Gordon shifted his attention back to the ring and forced himself to focus. Kenji was currently pacing along the ropes, jaw tight and face twisted, while his opponent, a guy named Blake, stalked around the outside. Blake moved to the middle of the aisle and they heckled each other, engaging the audience. Kenji leaned back on the rope to gain momentum before launching himself across the ring. He sprinted towards the ropes and leapt through the middle in a suicide dive—a move that ended with one wrestler diving into another, carefully choreographed to avoid injury, but that carried a decent amount of risk.

Gordon grimaced as he watched it unfold. He could see it happening before Kenji landed, knowing one or both of them was going to be hurt. Not seriously, they'd all sustained worse injuries, but he hated watching it. Kenji twisted his body at the last second and botched the landing, Blake put his hands up at the wrong time, and the two collided slightly too close to the guard rail. As Kenji toppled onto him, Blake's wrist got pinned under his body.

Blake did a great job selling it, both the pain and the landing, and fortunately for both of them, the match had been written to end shortly after. Kenji climbed back in the ring with a sheepish look on his face, then he clotheslined Blake, pinning him after he fell. Kenji won the match, but Gordon could see the disappointment on his face as he shot Blake apologetic glances before leaving the ring.

∿

"Isn't summer supposed to be a nice time of year to come here?" Gordon asked. They had both lived in Oregon their entire lives, so Kenji wasn't sure why he seemed shocked by the weather.

"It's still the coast, dude."

"I guess."

It was windy, because it was always windy at the coast. But it was also cloudy and wet, not the weather Kenji had been hoping for when he imagined parting with Akiko's ashes.

"It's okay," Gordon said. "It'll be good. She loved it here, rainy or not."

"She did."

They waded into the choppy water with their pants rolled up to their knees, which was pointless. The waves pummeled them aggressively, soaking them both to their hips and bellies. Kenji was grateful for the few extra inches he had on Gordon because that was a few more inches he felt relatively comfortable.

"Looks like you pissed yourself," Kenji said.

"Fuck off." Gordon shoved Kenji before his eyes flew open as he glanced down to the urn. "Shit, I'm sorry."

"It's fine. She would probably think it was funny if I fucked this up. Or if you did."

Gordon smiled at him. "Ready?"

"Sure. I guess. No, not really." Kenji shrugged. "I don't know."

"Yeah."

Kenji's hands opened the urn easily, but as much as he felt like he should, he couldn't look in.

"Is it disrespectful if I can't look? I don't want to see… her. Like that."

"It's okay to do whatever you need to do."

As Kenji tipped the urn, the ashes blew away from them in a cloudy mist and drifted towards the water, joining the frothy shoreline before being pulled away by the tide. It was over a lot faster than he expected. It felt empty.

"I don't really have anything profound to say. Just that I love you, and I miss you." Kenji looked to Gordon, squinting one eye against the light rain and wind. "You don't have to say anything, but you can."

"Um," Gordon said, gathering his thoughts. He didn't face Kenji when he started talking. "Sometimes… I wish I was religious. Because the idea that I am never going to see her again is just too much to bear. If I believed in an afterlife, I could hold onto the idea that I'd see her again someday. I'd just count down the days until it happened, then I'd go meet up with her and tell her everything I did during my life. And she would say, 'I know, I was there,' or, 'I know, I saw you drop Jayden's pacifier and put it back in his mouth *again* without telling anyone.'"

Kenji laughed. "She hated when you did that."

"Yeah," Gordon said with a faint smile. "And… while I grieve the fact that I'll never see her again, I do feel comforted parting with her here in the ocean."

Kenji nodded. "Me too."

"Someday, when my ashes have their own journey across the Pacific—"

"After I die, of course."

"No. I will be dying first."

"We'll see."

"Anyway," Gordon continued, "when my ashes have their own journey across the Pacific, all the molecules of my body will spread out with the tides. They'll mingle with the krill, pass by a blue whale, settle on the sea floor next to a starfish. They'll just keep going until they reach a uniform concentration across all the world's waters. And when that happens, we'll be together again. For as long as the planet exists, we'll be part of it, and we'll be together. And maybe, if we're lucky, we'll form something really special."

Kenji took a deep breath. "Oh. I really like that idea."

"Me too."

They stood together and watched the waves for a while. Gordon pointed out various sea birds flying above the waves, but the roar of the ocean was so loud it was hard for him to hear. Kenji bent down to rinse the urn, and it slipped from his hands, launching towards the beach on a powerful wave.

"Shit," he said, running after it.

Gordon ran too, but he tripped when his pant leg unrolled and the resistance from the water pulled him down. He landed on his belly and a small wave passed over him.

"Holy fuck!" Gordon screamed. "This water is so cold!"

Kenji started laughing because Gordon screamed like a girl, and it really was freezing. He managed to snag the urn before it was pulled back in the ocean, but any plans they had to stand and watch the water were over.

"Christ," Gordon said, dripping everywhere, the fabric of his shirt plastered to his soft stomach. Kenji could see the indent of his belly button and the soft roll of his side. It made him feel warm, despite his half-wet body and the windy weather.

"Let's go back to the house," Kenji said. "I'll make you something warm to drink."

~

GORDON STEPPED INTO THE SHOWER, wet sand still caked on his skin, and stood under the warm water long enough that he forgot the stinging pain from the temperature of ocean. When he stepped out, he wiped the condensation from the mirror and looked at himself.

He was comfortable with his body most of the time. It wasn't *great* or anything, but it was acceptable, and he'd decided long ago that it wasn't something he was going to spend time worrying about.

But when he'd made that decision, he hadn't considered that he might one day be naked with someone who looked like Kenji. It was ridiculous, if he was honest. And sure, he knew Kenji worked out for a living, but it still made him nervous to imagine what it might be like to look down and see his fuzzy, soft, pale belly next to Kenji's hairless, spray tanned, defined abs.

He poked at his belly in the mirror, then his pecs, then pulled at his neck skin to get rid of his moderate double chin. When he turned to the side and saw his flat ass and poor posture, he grimaced. The freshly showered hair on top of his head was lying flat, which wasn't helping his general look, so he ran his towel over it to try to even out the size of his head.

"What is taking you so long?" he heard Kenji yell. "I want to eat!"

Gordon nodded at himself in the mirror to hype himself up, then stepped out of the bathroom with a towel around his waist. It was pulled up higher than he might normally have it, covering his belly button. Kenji was cozied up on the couch, also freshly showered, wearing pajamas under a robe. His legs were invisible under a fuzzy throw blanket he'd found when they'd first arrived at the rental.

The suitcases were on the other side of the couch, which meant Gordon was going to have to cross the room and dig in his suitcase… in a towel.

"Shield your eyes," he said.

"What?"

Gordon walked by him, tightening his hold on the towel, taking short strides to prevent gapping. "Nothing, just need to get some clothes. Don't look at me."

"Oh, my God! Are you feeling shy?"

"No!" Gordon finally made it to the suitcase. He'd managed to avoid Kenji's gaze the whole time.

"Yes, you are! You're being shy about your body! The same body I've seen seven billion times."

"I am not being shy! I just think it's weird to walk across the room half naked. What if they have cameras?"

Kenji waggled his eyebrows and Gordon felt his cheeks heat.

"Stop it," Gordon mumbled, trying, and failing, to stop a smile.

"I'm just saying." Kenji shrugged. "Maybe I'll ask for a copy of the tape."

Gordon's cheeks were now fully pink, so he turned his back to Kenji to stare at the wall while he changed. His high school locker room experience, a combination of extreme insecurity and obnoxious teenage ribbing, had gifted Gordon with the ability to dress quickly and efficiently, all under the security of a towel. By the time he turned back around, he was still pulling on his shirt but fully dressed from the waist down.

"Oh, boooo!" Kenji shouted, his hands cupped around his mouth.

Gordon couldn't stop his laugh that time as he sank down onto the couch beside Kenji, close enough to feel some of his warmth, but not enough to touch. Kenji sighed dramatically before scooting over, sitting in a way that plastered them together, from shoulder to thigh. The blanket moved to cover both of their laps.

"You're being weird," Kenji said.

"I'm not being weird."

"You're being a little weird."

"Well, I'm..." Gordon rubbed his chin with his hand and turned to Kenji. "This is weird for me!"

"Sitting next to me? Watching a movie? Basking in my glory? You do all those things frequently."

Gordon narrowed his eyes at him. "No, dumbass. *This!*

Whatever this is," he said, waving his hand between them. "I mean, it's not bad. It's just… big."

"Sharing a blanket with a man for the first time? Aw, that is big."

"Okay, you know what?" Gordon said, attempting to stand up. He decided he was thirsty. Or hungry.

"Stop!" Kenji said, laughing. He kneeled on the couch and pulled Gordon down from behind his knees with some sort of weird grapple that landed Gordon flat on his back with his head on a throw pillow. Kenji wasted no time in straddling him, leaning down so their faces were close to each other. "Stop."

Gordon's heart thumped in his chest.

"If you want me to stop, I will," Kenji said. "I don't want to make you uncomfortable. But I really want this. I want to touch you and make you feel good. Please, Gordon. I've been so patient for you. And *you*…"

"I know," Gordon said, breathy and quiet. He wanted to make Kenji feel good, too. Maybe more than anything he'd ever wanted. For years, he'd imagined the moment they finally ended up here. Ten years of fantasies setting expectations that both excited and terrified him and now a week of extended foreplay that was causing him physical pain. It was time, he knew that.

It was just… the idea of disappointing Kenji was terrifying. There would be no going back once they did this. They'd be stepping into something unknown and life changing, and part of him wanted to keep things the way they were, to stay in the safety of what he already knew.

But with Kenji on top of him, their faces close enough to touch, Kenji's hands pressing into his chest with enough pressure to feel like a territorial mark, Gordon couldn't think of a single reason to wait that made any sense at all.

"Do you want me?"

"Okay," Gordon said.

"Okay?" Kenji laughed. "Okay what? Do you want me to stop? Because if not, I'm going to kiss you in a minute."

"I don't want you to stop."

"Good."

"Good," Gordon said, barely a whisper. Kenji's face got a little closer and Gordon could feel his warm breath on his skin. It smelled like the fruity seltzer they'd been drinking. He wondered if Kenji would taste like it, too.

"Good," Kenji said again. He leaned his face closer still, his lips finally brushing against Gordon's. When Gordon lifted his chin slightly to press their mouths together, he felt Kenji relax against him before adjusting his position on Gordon's lap. It was intoxicating, knowing Kenji wanted him this way. He felt himself getting hard and for a second, he hoped Kenji didn't notice, because they'd been kissing for approximately six seconds. But he stopped caring almost instantly when Kenji ground his hips down on him.

Gordon moved his hands down Kenji's back tentatively before slipping them inside Kenji's sweats. He let out an embarrassing whimper when he noticed there was nothing under them, just his hands cupping Kenji's bare skin. He felt Kenji huff out a laugh against his mouth.

"Just got out of the shower and threw these on," Kenji said between kisses.

"That's pretty cool," was all Gordon said, which made Kenji laugh more.

They were both hard now and Kenji adjusted himself again, aligning their erections and pushing his hips forward slightly.

It's not like it was was a new sensation to Gordon. He'd done it a million times, and with many different men.

But something about this time, whether it was the heightened emotions of the day, his accidental six-month bout of celibacy, or the fact that it was Kenji, *his* Kenji… His hands stilled on Kenji's hips, squeezing hard to stop him from moving.

"Wait," Gordon said. "Oh, God, I don't want to come in my pants." He was too turned on to be embarrassed, but coming in his pants might be a bit much.

Kenji laughed. He leaned back and took his shirt off, still on top of Gordon. He stood slowly, peeling his sweats off, completely naked other than his socks.

"Jesus Christ," Gordon muttered, before throwing his arm over his eyes. He felt his own sweats being pulled down, but he'd remembered underwear. He heard Kenji scoff playfully before pulling those off too, leaving Gordon in just a T-shirt.

"That's better," Kenji said. "Do you want to move to the bed?"

"Sure. Yes. Okay."

By the time Gordon made it there, Kenji was already sprawled across it lengthwise, limbs out like a starfish. The view was obscene and made Gordon feel lightheaded. He sat down on the edge of the bed, still working through his nerves, moving slowly and trying to plan his next move. Kenji surprised him by grabbing him in another move that ended with one of Gordon's knees bent, Kenji laying on top of him between his legs, his arm behind Kenji's knee.

"Ow! God, okay! That's enough with the pins," Gordon said, trying to wiggle his leg out from Kenji's hold.

"That's hardly a pin. Do you want me to pin you?" Kenji asked, holding his leg tighter, kissing and sucking his way from Gordon's ear down his throat. "I will."

"Maybe not this time, but… oh."

Kenji groaned and tugged on Gordon's collar. "You're still wearing a shirt."

"Yeah. Is that okay, or—oh, fuck."

Kenji had lifted Gordon's shirt so quickly he hadn't even noticed, and now Kenji's soft lips were on his nipple. An unexpected jolt of pleasure traveled through his gut and down to his dick. He felt it again when Kenji moved to the other side.

"I'd have more room if you'd take it off," Kenji said from his spot on Gordon's chest. "I want to see you."

He could admit he was being ridiculous. Kenji and his body were making it obvious he wasn't lying about wanting this, and if he wanted it that much, he had to be attracted to Gordon. Right? But it was just so hard. He was so afraid of doing something, anything, that would fuck this up. And that could include being soft. And a little flabby.

It was scary having Kenji this way, the culmination of ten years of patience finally paying off. As much as he'd hated loving Kenji from afar, watching him date other men and knowing it was never going to be his turn, it was a lot safer than having him like this temporarily and being in a position where it might end.

But Kenji was a confident man. He could have anybody he wanted, and he was choosing Gordon. Reminding himself of that, he took his shirt off and tossed it on the bed. He reluctantly looked down at Kenji. The smile that awaited him made it all worth it. Gordon closed his eyes and leaned back, giving himself over to the moment. He felt Kenji give him a soft kiss in the middle of his chest and he felt it flow through his body.

He was considering flipping them over and taking control when he felt the warmth of Kenji's body move down his own. Kenji's tongue was on his sack before Gordon had a chance to change positions, and he'd given up on doing anything other than enjoying the moment when he felt Kenji suck him into his mouth.

No words would come out, which was probably for the best, because he wanted to thank Kenji for being brave enough to make this happen. What he really wanted was to thank him for making his dreams come true, but that felt dorky and inappropriate for the moment, so he tried to shut his mind off and enjoy the sensations of… everything.

By the time Kenji moved to Gordon's dick, he was so close to coming he was almost dizzy from it. He reached down and intertwined their fingers, desperate to show Kenji any way he could how much he loved him. Kenji's head bobbed up and down on him and Gordon's hips instinctively thrust gently to meet him in the middle. He hit the back of Kenji's throat unexpectedly, causing him to gag and sputter.

"Shit, I'm so sorry," Gordon said, squeezing Kenji's hand.

"It's okay." Kenji rubbed Gordon's thigh reassuringly before returning to his task. His free hand brushed below Gordon's balls, putting light pressure on his taint. Gordon's hand reached down, first caressing Kenji's hair before grabbing it hard and pulling it with his movements.

Kenji hummed a happy noise before swallowing around Gordon's dick. The feeling of that and Kenji's dick on his leg, hot and hard and leaking was too much.

"I'm already close, Kenji, fuck," he said.

Kenji stopped and moved his way back up Gordon's body, straddling his waist again. Gordon held onto him and moved into a sitting position, leaning against the headboard so Kenji was seated in his lap. He reached down and grabbed their dicks together and Kenji thrust into his hand as they kissed slowly and deliberately. Gordon had finally moved beyond the frantic chaos he felt every time they touched, and he just held

Kenji's body close. He felt like he was on the verge of tears, which was mortifying.

"I can't believe we're finally doing this," Kenji said. "Sorry. That's not sexy."

Gordon huffed out a small laugh, not willing to move his mouth from Kenji's. He reached over to grab the lube and condom he'd shoved under his pillow.

"I think it is."

"You planned ahead!"

"I didn't want to chicken out," Gordon said. He opened the lube and poured some into his hand, warming it between his fingers before reaching behind Kenji and brushing his hole with his fingertips.

"Oh," Kenji said, pushing himself down on Gordon's fingers before rising up again. "I'm glad you didn't."

They stayed that way, kissing softly and holding each other, Gordon's strong hands working Kenji, getting him ready. He breathed a sigh of relief when Kenji leaned over to grab the condom from where it lay next to Gordon's thigh. He couldn't remember ever feeling this level of need for anyone and wasn't sure how much longer he would last with Kenji in his lap.

When the head of Gordon's cock pressed against Kenji's hole, they both held their breath. He didn't know what Kenji was thinking, but for Gordon, it was like the whole world stopped. He took a deep breath to compose himself. Kenji started off slow, and Gordon was grateful to exist in the moment. But Kenji started riding him fast and hard, and he was grateful for that, too.

"Oh, fuck, Kenji." He dropped his head back, hitting the headboard, but he didn't even feel it. All he felt was ecstasy, Kenji's hard cock dragging against his stomach, a trail of moisture left behind. He put more lube on his fingers and gripped Kenji's cock tightly. They both moaned and grunted, the sounds of Kenji's thighs hitting Gordon's, and the slick sound of the lube was all either of them could hear. Gordon had no idea how long it had been, but he had a sudden need to come. He started working Kenji faster, hoping he'd get him there first, and he did.

"Shit, Gordon," Kenji said, his rhythm growing choppy and stilted.

"Come on, baby," Gordon said, nipping Kenji's jaw.

Kenji's body tensed and Gordon watched the muscles on his body strain and flex. There were some he didn't know existed, like the stripy ones on his rib cage. He ran his fingers down Kenji's sides to feel them as his body went still.

"Fuck!"

Gordon felt a splash of cum cover his belly, up to his neck. Seeing Kenji's face and feeling his release combined with the feeling of Kenji's body contracting on his dick pushed him over the edge and Gordon came seconds later as they both breathed each other in.

Kenji lifted himself off Gordon's lap and collapsed on the bed next to him and trailed his finger through the hair on Gordon's chest. They both closed their eyes and just existed together, not speaking.

Eventually, Gordon felt exposed and self-conscious. After disposing of the condom in the small trash can next to the bed, he reached for his shirt, which was wedged under his leg. He'd only put one arm through it before Kenji grabbed it from him and threw it on the floor.

"No," he whined.

"What? I'm not allowed to wear shirts now?"

"You are. But not if it's because you're feeling weird because of me."

"It's not that," Gordon said, a bit unbelievably, even to his own ears.

"I like your body, Gordon. Okay? It's sexy. I like this hair. And I like that you're comfortable and huggable and strong."

"Okay."

Kenji sat up with his back against the headboard, looking at Gordon, his gaze soft. He grabbed a tissue from the bedside table and wiped Gordon's chin and neck of his mess. "If you want to know the truth, I like everything about you."

Gordon shifted, reaching out with his toe to grab his shirt before putting it over his head and tugging down the hem before finally looking at Kenji. "I just don't know what to do with that shit."

"What shit?"

"You saying stuff like that to me."

"Well, get used to it, dumbass," Kenji said. He gave Gordon several long, slow kisses before rolling off the bed. "I'm hungry. Find somewhere to eat. I'll be out in a few."

Gordon watched Kenji stride across the room, throw Gordon's remaining clothes to the bed, and disappear into the bathroom. It was only then that he let free the enormous grin that had been trying to escape for the last twenty minutes.

CHAPTER 23

KENJI WAS PRETTY SURE THAT ON THE LIST OF WORST MOMENTS OF his life, the first two were obvious, and the third was quickly becoming the moment Gordon had asked him to help install the new cabinets he'd purchased for his kitchen. Kenji hated home projects more than most things in life, but Gordon *loved* them, so when Gordon mentioned this project, Kenji said he wanted to help.

But he just didn't understand why Gordon bought new cabinets, considering the old ones worked perfectly fine. Even more confusing was Gordon deciding their rare, shared day of freedom would be best spent installing the stupid things. But he was helping with a forced smile on his face, because what else was he going to do?

"You need to hold it higher," Gordon said. "I can't reach in there and screw it to the wall if you don't hold it straight."

"I'm trying! You're the one leaning on me!"

Gordon grumbled in his ear and stepped onto the small ladder he'd brought in. Kenji was straining under the weight of the cabinet combined with Gordon's elbow crushing him, so he spread his legs slightly to brace himself.

"Ow! Less elbow!"

"Oh, my God. Stop whining, we're almost done."

"With one of four," Kenji mumbled.

"Do you want me to do this without you?" Gordon asked.

"Yes! That is what I've been trying to communicate to you, and you figured it out. We really are connected on a deeper level, aren't we?"

"That was a rhetorical question. Please just hold that straight and we'll take a break after this one."

Kenji held it—perfectly straight—and Gordon finally finished screwing it into the studs behind the wall. He stood back with his hands on his hips and tilted his head.

"Oh, God. What now?" Kenji asked. He wiped the sweat from his brow and grabbed a beer from the fridge. "Do you want a seltzer?"

"Sure," Gordon said, rubbing his chin. "I don't like the color I chose."

Kenji took a deep breath and continued facing away from Gordon, afraid if he turned around before Gordon completed his thought, he'd be forced to help paint.

"I guess it's okay, actually. I might just need different curtains to lighten things up."

Kenji cheered internally and handed Gordon his seltzer.

"Yes, I think it looks great. Can we go take a break? Let's go watch the Hour of Wreckoning I recorded. We can place bets on who wins. My vote goes to Jared Looza," Kenji said, shoving Gordon into the living room.

They settled in, Kenji with his feet in Gordon's lap. He felt truly happy for the first time in a while. The fog of grief was lifting, allowing him the pleasure of good days again.

It wasn't even like the most confusing aspects of his life had changed—he still didn't know when, or if, he'd get a contract with CWA, and he still didn't know what to do about the plant store. But with Gordon on his side, things just felt easier. Even if he never *made it* and he had to run the Kiko's for the rest of his life, coming home to Gordon every day would make it manageable.

"What are you thinking about over there?" Gordon asked, digging his thumb into the arch of Kenji's socked foot.

"You," he said, sighing with pleasure. "I'm just happy today. Minus the cabinets."

"It's important for us to do that together. I think I read once that installing things with your partner without murdering each other is the number one indicator of successful long-term relationship."

"Really?"

"No." Gordon smiled at him. "But we still like each other. That seems promising."

"Well, don't get ahead of yourself. We have three more to go and I have very little patience left."

Gordon laughed and Kenji poked his belly with his foot.

"Seriously, though. I just feel very peaceful today. No work, no stress, nothing I need to actively worry about," Kenji said. He felt Gordon squeeze his foot.

"It is."

"I could never fully relax around Rob."

"No?" Gordon turned slightly to look at Kenji.

"No. He was impossible to keep up with. And I don't usually feel that way. But he was always off schmoozing, but I never got to know the details of anything he was up to. Even when I went to that event with him, he explained it to me, but I didn't really understand. I felt stupid, and he seemed okay with that. I'm rambling. My point is, I trust you entirely. You make it so easy."

"You make it easy, too," Gordon said, patting Kenji's ankle. "And I'm glad you realized how much Rob sucked."

"It's weird."

"What is? How much he sucked? I think like five separate people could have told you that. You should have asked."

"Man, I never even told you I ended up taking a rideshare to the airport because he ditched me last minute."

Gordon's hand stilled on Kenji's ankle. "God," he said, shaking his head. "I want to punch him again."

Kenji laughed. "Yeah, same. But no, I just meant how different you guys are, and how long it took me to realize what was right under my nose. I'm embarrassed about how much of my own behavior I see reflected in some of his. It took me so long to put it all together. I took advantage of you. Your generosity and kindness. I feel awful when I think about how I've hurt you over the years."

"You haven't," Gordon said, stroking Kenji's ankle.

"I have. I know I have. And I'm so sorry."

Gordon rolled his head to look at Kenji. "It's okay."

"It's not, though."

"You can make it up to me by helping me install cabinets."

Kenji smiled. "Okay. For you, I'd install thirty cabinets."

"Just four. Three now!"

Kenji laughed again, spilling the beer he'd been balancing on his stomach. It soaked into his shirt and the crotch of his pants, some of it even spilling onto the couch and floor.

"Aw, shoot," he said, glancing up to Gordon.

"Oh! One sec." Gordon left to grab a kitchen towel, and when he came back, Kenji was in the middle of removing his beer-soaked shirt and pants.

"Ooh," Gordon said, his eyes bright. He walked towards Kenji and wrapped his arms around his waist. "You should spill beer more often."

Kenji, enveloped by Gordon's arms, leaned forward and kissed him, moving from Gordon's mouth to his jaw, then kissing his way down Gordon's neck, placing feather light kisses at the top of his collar bones. He gave one a quick suck, knowing it would make Gordon squeak. He moved his hands up Gordon's chest before wrapping them around the back of his neck, threading his hands through his wavy hair. He smiled when he heard Gordon whimper.

Gordon pulled back suddenly and narrowed his eyes. "Why are you smiling like that?"

"What?"

"You're smiling. Nothing funny happened, and we have done this enough at this point that you don't do, like, giddy smiles anymore," Gordon said, waving his hand at Kenji's mouth.

"I don't know what you're talking about."

"Oh, my God! You tricked me!"

"I did not!"

"You poured beer on my couch on purpose so you could get naked and distract me!"

Kenji thought for a moment before frowning. "It's *our* couch, Gordon. I didn't know you still thought of this as *your* house."

"Stop it. Go get dressed, we're putting up the rest of the cabinets now. You ruined it for everyone, I'll never believe you need a break again."

"That's harsh, Gordon. I'm over here pouring my heart out to you, and this is how you treat me?"

"The only thing you poured was your beer. On my couch. Go get dressed." Gordon bent down to soak up the spilled beer, but Kenji could see him smiling.

"Fine. But you owe me dinner when we're done."

CHAPTER 24

"Look what I brought home!"

Gordon looked up from his spot on the couch. His face was washed out by the glow of his laptop, or maybe he was just tired. He'd been working so much, at Kiko's and his regular job.

Guilt ate at Kenji seeing Gordon like that, and his smile faded a bit. But Gordon's face lit up when he spotted the bouquet of dandelions Kenji held, and he breathed a bit easier as he crossed to the front of the couch and sat down, holding the flowers in front of Gordon's face.

"They don't smell like anything," Gordon said.

"Not really, no."

"But they're ready?" Gordon asked. He closed his laptop and tossed it on the ottoman before poking at the bouquet. "They're really kind of pretty if you don't think of them as weeds."

"I know."

Their eyes met briefly, and the weight of the moment seemed to hit them at the same time. The dandelions Kenji held were the same ones Akiko had helped planted for Peony.

Even without discussing it, they'd both cared for them to be closer to her after her death. The flowers had fulfilled their end of the deal, to grow fat leaves and flowers for Peony, and both Gordon and Kenji seemed to have the same sense of finality about it all.

"We could replant one and let it go to seed. That one still has its roots. We could harvest them and keep the line going every year," Gordon said. "Then she'd always be around."

Kenji loved him so much, and he loved the symbolism Gordon was going for, but it wasn't necessary. "It's a dandelion, not some heirloom species of corn that would die out without human intervention."

"I know, but if it would make you feel better…"

"It's okay. Imagine if she was watching us harvest and store dandelion seeds year after year. She'd yell at us to just go outside and pick some."

Gordon gave him a quick kiss. "Okay. It was just an idea."

"I know. And it was a nice idea. And I love you, and I missed you today."

"Me too. Hey, look!" Gordon said, pointing to a little red ladybug on the leaf of the largest dandelion.

"Oh! Shit. That's Akiko 2."

"Um."

"She's been living at the shop, and I named her Akiko 2. I know it's her, because look, her left antenna is bent." Kenji smiled down at her but wasn't thrilled she'd hitched a ride. Now he had to figure out how to get her back to the shop without losing her.

"Oh. Hi, Akiko 2." Gordon squinted to look at her.

"She can tell you didn't mean that. But that's okay. Now, you go get Peony, I'll go get Tupperware for Akiko 2. Don't bump her or scare her. Actually, don't touch the dandelions at all. I don't want her to fly away." He set the dandelions on the cushion of the couch, careful not to jostle them. "Stay there, Akiko 2."

"Kenj," Gordon said. Kenji didn't respond, too busy hustling into the kitchen to find Tupperware for the ladybug. "Kenji."

"Found one!" He returned to the living room to find Gordon missing temporarily before he came back, staring at him, holding Peony. He was staring tenderly, at least. But he looked worried and had a small frown that didn't sit right. "What?"

"She's a bug," he said. "You know that, right?"

"What the fuck?" Kenji snapped. "I know she's a bug. I'm not an idiot."

"Okay. I'm sorry."

Peony's three legs were hanging over Gordon's forearm and his stunted tail whipped around gently, probably noticing the dandelions. When Gordon set him down on the couch cushions, Kenji dropped to his knees to stop him from going towards the leaves.

"Dude! I told you I was going to put the ladybug in Tupperware."

"Oh, shit, I'm sorry."

The two of them reached out at the same time, Gordon reaching for Peony, Kenji reaching for the flowers. Their hands bumped into each other above Peony, startling him and causing him to run to the other end of the couch. His path passed directly over the dandelion bundle, crumpling the paper and frightening him even further.

"Shit," Kenji said. He picked up the dandelions and sorted through the leaves, searching for Akiko 2, but he couldn't find her. "Where is she?"

"Hold on," Gordon said, trying to grab Peony.

"Where did she go?" Kenji said, panicked and unknowingly crushing the crinkled stem of a dandelion. He sorted through the leaves, checking every crease and fold for Akiko 2. His eyes darted back to the couch, inspecting the cushions. "She was right here! On the leaves of this big one, and she's just… gone."

Gordon shuffled up next to him on the floor, lifting a throw pillow and sticking his hands between the couch cushions. "She has wings, she probably flew away. She's just—"

"Don't," Kenji said, cutting him off. "Don't say she's just a bug. I know she's a fucking bug."

"I was going to say she was just doing her bug thing and flew away somewhere. I know you know she's a bug. I promise."

"I know she's not really in there, okay? It's just been nice having her around. She likes all the same plants and everything. My friend once said when your loved one visits you in a dream, it's like their soul telling you they're okay. She hasn't visited me, yet, but… this felt like that."

Gordon smiled at him like he was comforting a kid who lost his sandwich to a seagull. Like he truly believed Kenji was stupid enough to think his dead aunt was inside a ladybug.

"I wasn't trying to—"

"What *were* you trying to do, then?" Kenji asked, tears brimming his eyes. "It feels like you're trying to make me feel stupid for enjoying the company of a bug who reminds me of my dead aunt."

Gordon blinked at him. "I—"

"I'm losing *everything* that reminds me of her. I'm selling her house. I don't have enough room to bring all her stuff here. I'm too busy at work to spend much time at the store, and worse than that is that I don't even want to be there anymore. I want to be busy at Titan, and I want a CWA contract, and admitting that feels like an insult to everything she worked for." Kenji sniffed and wiped his eyes with the hem of his shirt. "I'm losing so much of her against my will, but I'm also making this decision to sever the only major connection we have left. It feels horrible and I don't know what to do. I convinced myself Akiko 2 was a sign from her telling me it was okay. And now she's gone, and… does that mean it's not?" Kenji's heart physically hurt, and it was beating so fast he thought he might pass out.

"Hey," Gordon said, crouching down next to him. "Hey, take a breath. You're all splotchy."

"I just miss her so much. I wasn't ready to say goodbye to her."

"I know."

"And now my bug is gone, too."

Kenji shifted so he was seated on the floor with his legs folded in half. He put his head on his knees and his face crumpled before he let the tears fall. With his hands pressed against his eyes, he cleared his throat to stop the sobs, but it was futile. He felt Gordon's arms pull him close, and everything he'd been holding inside was finally set free.

KENJI HAD RECOVERED from his breakdown earlier in the evening, Peony had finally gone back into his enclosure, fat and happy and full of dandelion greens, and after forcing him to eat some dinner, Gordon had even managed to get Kenji to sit on the couch and watch a movie with him.

"Thank you," Kenji said.

"For what?"

"Just… everything. Loving me even though I'm always a mess these days."

"I'm a mess, too. Hey, we could be a tag team," Gordon

said. His face lit up and Kenji waited for whatever he was about to say. "The Dumpster Duo."

"Garbage gang."

"Clutter crew?"

"Eh. I think we peaked with Dumpster Duo. I'd rather wrestle you straight up, anyway," he said, nuzzling into Gordon's neck.

"Please don't throw me again," Gordon groaned. "I'm still recovering from last time. I think I pulled something."

"You love it." Kenji bit Gordon's neck gently, eliciting a sweet moan from his lips. "And that."

"Yeah," he said, dropping his head against the back of the couch. "That's a little nicer than the other stuff."

Kenji continued kissing him, nibbling the shell of his ear, licking down his neck. Gordon's eyes had closed, and Kenji used the opportunity to climb onto Gordon's lap. He felt two hands slide down the back of his shorts and he sighed into Gordon's mouth, but things didn't progress beyond that. Kenji relaxed against him and leaned his head on his shoulder.

The two of them were dozing off together, Gordon's steady breathing lulling him closer to sleep. He was seconds away from finally giving in when he felt Gordon shift slightly. He opened one eye and glanced at Gordon, who was looking back at him.

"Kenj?" Gordon whispered

"Yeah?" he whispered back.

Gordon kept his voice low, and Kenji moved his head to be able to hear him better. "Why did Dom try to bench press you at that barbeque?"

Kenji burst into laughter before closing his eyes entirely. "I don't know."

Gordon's laugh rumbled in his chest and Kenji fell asleep.

CHAPTER 25

THEY WOKE UP AFTER SLEEPING FOR AN HOUR, BOTH FEELING lighter. Gordon made them dinner, with Kenji supervising for nutrition reasons, and they'd settled in on the couch to watch a movie. Kenji was scrolling on his phone, figuring out what to watch next, when he turned to Gordon.

"Hey, can you figure out the loan stuff tonight?" he asked.

The question caught Gordon off guard. He hadn't thought about the loan recently with everything else going on, and he kind of thought Kenji had forgotten about it. He'd hoped so, anyway.

"Uh, yeah. Sure."

"Like, now, maybe? Can you just figure it out on your phone? I know have access to all her documents on there, don't you?"

"I do."

Kenji turned his head and narrowed his eyes at him. "Okay?"

"Do you want a snack?" Gordon asked, getting off the couch. "I saw ice cream in there."

"No, I'm pretty full from dinner. Plus, I'm cutting right now, which we talked about when we made dinner like, two hours ago."

"Right. I forgot."

"Why are you being weird? Don't you want me to pay it off? We could hire more help with the extra money."

"We're handling it okay, aren't we?" Gordon asked. He knew they weren't. Both of them were miserable and over-worked after months of splitting their time between their day jobs and the store, and the teenagers Gordon met through Curt could only work in the afternoons. Kenji was having an even harder time than Gordon, since he mostly worked in the evenings and was shipped out of town every other weekend.

"You can't keep helping out as much as you have been," Kenji said. "You told me yourself you can't focus when you work at the store, and you've been working late every day."

"Hmm. That has less to do with the job, and more to do with me wanting to kiss you all the time instead of working."

Kenji rolled his eyes. "I'm serious. I don't want your actual job to suffer just for the store."

"My job is fine. It's just boring." That wasn't entirely true, and Victor had started griping about how much Gordon continued to work from the store, but he wasn't going to worry Kenji with it.

"Okay, forget the job. We'd be able to do date nights at places with zero plant-life. Like a real restaurant. Or even a club."

"I'm not super into clubs. So many people touching me."

"Okay, that was just an example. Focus. Please log on and figure out how much I owe or give me the login and I'll do it while you get ice cream. The money from the house should hit my account by the twenty first."

"One sec," Gordon said. He headed into the kitchen to get ice cream he didn't even want to eat. Kenji stayed on the couch but leaned over to glare at him through the door frame.

"Okay, what is going on? You're making me nervous. Is it like four million dollars or something? Am I going to have to sell the store?"

"No, no, nothing like that." Gordon's mouth was dry and he made a hacking noise. "I need some water."

"Oh, my God. Now you're just pissing me off. Come back in here, please."

Gordon had known this moment would come eventually. After Akiko died, he'd started thinking about it more and more often, the weight of it heavy and constant, the inevitable fallout inching closer.

What had started as an action with noble intent had spiraled into something that would feel like a betrayal. And... it was. Gordon had laid awake countless nights trying to find a way to explain his motivations in a way that wouldn't expose him, but he never managed to. Now he could only hope that with time, Kenji would see things from his perspective. And maybe find a way to forgive him.

"Okay, um," Gordon said, sitting down on the couch next to Kenji, who was inching away from Gordon, obviously nervous about what he had to say. "I have to be honest with you about something, and I just want to say first—"

"Just tell me! What the fuck."

"I paid off the loan." His voice was shaky, but he did his best to steady it. "It was back in May. Akiko and I talked about it, and she said she wanted to sell the store, and I told her it would be better if I just paid it off because then the store would belong to you free and clear after she died. She agreed, so I paid it."

Kenji just stared at him. "What?"

"She's been putting the extra funds into an account, I guess imagining you'd use it as a nest egg or something."

"You paid off the loan?" Kenji's voice was similarly shaky, but from anger, not fear. "And she knew?"

"Yeah. Kenji, I am so sorry."

"How could you do that? You went behind my back and made a huge decision about a store that you don't own, that was never going to be yours, and thought I would... what, be happy about it?"

"No. I knew you wouldn't be happy, but she was so worried," Gordon said, a little surprised by the venom Kenji spat. Of course, he knew he didn't own the store, but he had been there more than Kenji for the last two years. He'd carried it on his own for the two months before Akiko died. Kenji didn't even know how to log into the systems without resetting his passwords every time. Surely, Gordon's efforts had to mean *something*.

"So, you knew I wouldn't be happy, which could only be because you knew how important it was to me to do it on my own, but you did it anyway. Why?"

"I know you won't believe me, but I was trying to help. I didn't want her to stress about it. Whenever we talked about it, her only concern was—"

"You guys thought I couldn't do it. That I'd never get the contract and never be able to save enough money to pay it off. You sat around and figured out a way to pay off the loan that didn't rely on me getting the contract."

"No! That's not it at all. Christ, Kenji, I believe in you more than anyone. I wasn't trying to undermine you. I just—"

"You just what? Needed to fix it for me?" He stood up and walked to the fireplace to glare at the photo of Akiko they'd placed there before turning back to Gordon. "This was the one thing I asked you not to do for me, Gordon. The one thing I told you was important for me to do on my own to prove to everyone I am not a total fuck up and I am worth something."

"You're not a total fuck up and you *are* worth something! You're worth everything. That's why I—"

"She died thinking I'd never do it and that you swooped in to rescue me again, like always."

"It's not like that. She didn't think that. I didn't rescue you, I was just trying to make things easier on you both."

"It's not about being easy!" Kenji shouted. "It was never about that. God, Gordon! It was about me proving to my aunt and to myself that I could do it on my own. Just once in my life, to prove to myself that I was good enough. I wasn't good enough for my parents, I failed out of college, I don't even have my own apartment, but I could have done this. I was so close. And even if she's gone now, she would have known, somehow, that I did it."

Gordon looked at him with his face wracked with guilt. He couldn't think of anything to say that he hadn't already said so he just stared, waiting for Kenji to continue.

Kenji scrubbed his hands over his face and dropped them to his sides. "You can say whatever you want about how much you believe in me, but at the end of the day, this is just another situation where Gordon Whitaker had to rescue Kenji Ashida from himself. Right?"

"No, it's not—"

"Just stop," Kenji said, holding up his hand to cut him off. "I don't even have anything else to say to you, and you have nothing I want to hear. You took something from me when you did this, and I can never get it back."

He looked around the room, anywhere that wasn't Gordon's face, and his gaze landed on the gym bag by the door. "I'm heading out for a bit."

Gordon felt unexpected heat rise in his chest, a mix of guilt and frustration. Yes, he had fucked up, but listening to Kenji tear into him stung in a way he wasn't prepared for. It stung and it infuriated him.

"Okay, wait a minute, Kenji," Gordon said.

Kenji's eyebrows raised. "Excuse me?"

"I know I fucked up here, okay? I did, and I feel like shit about it. But I think you're being a little unfair."

"How am I being unfair? You're the one who overstepped."

Gordon's chest heated even more. His jaw clenched, and he took a deep breath so he didn't scream. "Have you already forgotten that I took care of the store by myself while you were gone? I'm the one who kept the lights on, took care of the plants, risked my job. All for the store, which as you've reminded me, I don't own, nor will I ever own," Gordon said. "I did it because I love you, and I love Akiko."

Kenji walked towards the door, his hand reaching for the gym bag hanging from the coat rack. "It doesn't feel like love when you go behind my back."

"Fine. I accept that. But love isn't watching the store fall apart when I can prevent it, either. Paying off that loan allowed Akiko to relax and worry less. You're acting like I swooped in because I don't trust your ability to get it done, but it has nothing to do with that. I did it because she needed help. You both needed help."

"She knew I was working on it," Kenji said quietly.

"Yes, she did. But she was dying, and she wanted this for you."

"Right," Kenji said, rolling his eyes.

"You haven't been here, Kenji. For *months*," Gordon said.

"Yeah, because I was working to get a contract so I could pay off the loan!"

"You can stop pretending the only reason you want the contract is for the loan, Kenji. We all knew this is what you really wanted, and we were happy for you. That's why I wanted to pay it off—I had the ability to help, so I did. Do I regret the way I went about it? Yes. I regret hurting you more than anything. But I don't regret helping her relax for the last few months of her life, and I don't regret helping you balance the store with your career."

"The store was doing fine. She would have told me if it wasn't."

"You've been pretending things were better than they were for years!"

"You told me it wasn't losing money!"

"I also told you there was no wiggle room in her budget. But you know what? None of that matters now. I admit I fucked up. But you don't get to treat me like some villain for one bad decision and ignore everything I've sacrificed over the last two years."

Gordon watched as Kenji's jaw clenched this time. "I didn't ask you to sacrifice anything."

"Well, that's what you do when you love someone, Kenji! You do things that make their lives better!"

Kenji's chest rose with tense, heavy breaths and his hand tightened on his gym bag. "I can't do this right now."

"Where are you going?"

"Where do you think?" Kenji asked, holding up his gym bag.

"Are you coming back?" Gordon asked, his anger fading, turning into nauseating worry.

"God. Yes, Gordon, I'm coming back. Now can I leave?"

"Fine."

Kenji slammed the door, and Gordon heard him stomp across the porch before the sound stopped abruptly, then grew closer. The door flew open.

"And I'm paying you back, end of discussion!"

Kenji slammed the door again and Gordon watched him leave. He stared at him out the window until his car pulled away from the curb, then Gordon glanced at the photo of Akiko above the fireplace.

"Oops," he said, before curling up on the couch with a blanket to wait for Kenji.

CHAPTER 26

EMOTIONAL TURMOIL WAS A GOOD WAY TO ENSURE A SUCCESSFUL workout. Maybe he'd ask Gordon to keep more secrets from him if it meant he was able to lift a little heavier and a little longer. Mitch, the team's physical therapist, was spotting him, cursing under his breath as Kenji racked the weights.

"You're going to hurt yourself, man, slow down," Mitch said. "I have a trip planned and can't be helping you through some wild-ass injury."

"Sorry. I'm done for now anyway. No injuries."

"Good," Mitch said, walking to his folding table. "Good workout, though. I haven't seen you push that hard in a while."

"Yeah." Kenji wiped his face on a towel and considered if he wanted to tell Mitch why he was upset. He decided against it, because everyone at Titan loved Gordon. And he made a shitty, selfish decision, but he was still Gordon. Kenji still loved him.

"You seem off today. I'll just offer this as an extension of a listening ear, if you need it. No pressure."

"I'm okay. Just missing my aunt today, I guess. Nothing big."

"Got it. Have a good night then, Kenji. See you tomorrow."

Kenji waved at him, then turned to wipe down the equipment and caught a glimpse of himself in the mirror. He noticed a faded hickey on his chest and smiled briefly, but it disappeared when he remembered their fight.

"Hey, Kenji!"

Kenji turned around and saw Mike standing in the doorway, his face unreadable.

"Office, please. Whenever you're done."

Kenji nodded silently as his stomach dipped. He figured Mike would pull him in sometime soon. His matches had been suffering since Akiko died, but he thought he had done well enough to keep the momentum he'd built.

He thought back over the last few weeks and cringed at each of the tiny mistakes he'd made and cringed harder at the big mistakes he'd made, like his botched dive at the coast. Blake had been so angry and legitimately injured that Kenji had been tempted to throw the match and lose intentionally just to get out of there. He hadn't, of course, because he wasn't about to deal with Mike after that, but it was the first time he'd ever messed up that badly. But it was possible Mike wanted to talk to him about it anyway.

Kenji finished up in the shower and got dressed before walking down the hallway to Mike's office. He'd done everything he could think of to stall, including stopping by the ring to watch Will and another Titan, Curt, spar for a while, while glancing at Mike's office occasionally to see if he could feel out Mike's mood. When Will and Curt finished and headed to the showers, there was nothing left to do but talk to Mike.

Other than the few mistakes he'd made in recent weeks, he didn't have any tangible reason to think Mike was about to fire him. It was more likely he was going to put his time, energy, and finances into someone else and start sending them out of town more. That would be fair. Kenji had been with Titan for several years now, it wouldn't be a surprise if Mike was done putting in the effort to get Kenji a contract.

If Boston wasn't his future, he still had the store. He still had Gordon.

As hurt as he was, even Kenji could admit Gordon paying off the loan really would make his life easier by opening up the income slotted for payments. He could use it to hire employees so he could focus on the books instead of the day-to-day operations. He could be home for dinner every night. They could even travel together. Creating these opportunities for freedom was the whole reason Gordon did it. Making Akiko and Kenji's lives easier was why he did so many things, and Kenji took it for granted.

But still, Gordon did it knowing it would upset Kenji.

It was all so confusing, and Kenji's brain hurt to the point that confronting whatever issue Mike wanted to discuss was preferable to thinking more about the moral compass of Gordon's actions.

He pushed the office door open and gave a fake smile to Mike, who was grabbing something from the cabinet behind his desk. Kenji chose the seat closest to the door in case he needed to make a hasty escape. He took a deep breath and looked up at Mike, who was sitting on the edge of his desk, grinning, with a bottle of champagne and two plastic champagne flutes.

"Uh, what's up?"

"Congratulations," Mike said. He held up the champagne and glasses.

"For what?" Kenji asked, embarrassed that he'd clearly missed something.

"I heard from my friend Graham at CWA today." Mike walked around the other side of his desk and set the items down before pushing a pile of papers towards Kenji. "They want to buy you out of your Titan contract."

Kenji's brain stuttered, unable to comprehend what Mike was saying. He heard *congratulations* and *CWA* and *buy you out*, but he couldn't piece it together.

"I'm, um…"

Mike sat back in his chair. "Is this not what you wanted?" He looked puzzled, which was fair. It *was* what Kenji wanted and what the two of them had been planning and working towards for years. "I'm confused."

"No, it is! It is. I'm so sorry, I've had a weird few weeks and then Gordon and I got into kind of a fight, and I'm just out of it. But holy shit," Kenji said, grabbing the papers and pulling them to his chest. He looked down at them, and sure enough, it was an offer letter from CWA. He broke into a huge smile and looked up at Mike. "Holy shit."

"Okay, that's more like it. Champagne?" Mike asked, uncorking the bottle. He poured it into the two glasses and handed one to Kenji with a big smile. "I'm so proud of you. So proud. You've worked so hard."

They tapped their plastic cups against each other and the champagne fizzed over the top onto Kenji's offer letter. He screamed, trying to wipe off the spill, but it was too late to save it.

"Oh, God, what did I do?" Kenji asked.

Mike blinked at him, bewildered by his behavior. "I printed that out of my email, Kenji. Relax."

"Oh. Right, yeah. Of course." He lifted the champagne to his mouth with a shaky hand, draining the entire thing.

"More? Seems like you need it."

Kenji pushed his cup across the desk and nodded.

"You have some time. They don't want to debut you until the Jingle Ring, which is a few months away."

"Oh, okay. That's probably good. I need to... do a lot of things before I can get out there."

"Of course. No rush. But, um," Mike started, but then hesitated.

"What?"

"Well, I'm going to be reallocating the funds I've been putting into your extra matches to Curt and Will. I'm sorry, it's not personal. Obviously. But..." Mike shrugged and tapped the damp contract offer.

"Oh! Yeah, no, of course. That makes a lot of sense. That's probably good, actually. I need the extra time to figure out Kiko's and everything."

And he had to figure out what to do about Gordon, whose life was in Portland. They had never discussed moving elsewhere, and even when Kenji had fantasized about getting a CWA contract, Gordon had never implied he would want to go with him.

"You'll still have local matches."

"Perfect. Thank you, seriously. I am so appreciative of everything you've done for me."

"You did it all. I'm just really proud of you. You're going to do great. I can't wait to tell the rest of the guys."

"Yeah! They'll be so pumped. I hope," he said, laughing. "But can you wait a few days? I have some stuff I have to figure out. I want to run the offer by my attorney, too."

"Of course. Just let me know."

INSTEAD OF GOING HOME, Kenji drove up to a viewpoint that overlooked the city to tell Akiko his news. He'd always imagined how he'd tell her someday, like buying a big cake with

CWA's logo on it or buying her a bunch of Boston ferns and waiting patiently until it clicked in her mind. Sitting in his car, looking over the city she spent most of her life in, saying the words aloud with no one to hear them was not on his list of preferred announcements. But that was his reality, so that's what he did.

"I know you were unsure when I first told you this was my plan to help you with the store," he said. "And I know you were unsure when I told you to trust me, and that I was actually pretty good. But I did it! And I guess… I'm moving to Boston. I think. God, I don't know what to do. I wish you were here so I could ask you."

Akiko didn't answer, obviously. Kenji waited, thinking maybe he'd see a shooting star or UFO, or maybe hear a plane he could say was his aunt cheering him on. But nothing like that happened. It was anticlimactic, which shouldn't have surprised him, since he was talking to a dead person.

The surprise of how brief and empty it felt hurt in an unexpected way—the sudden realization that for the rest of his life, any time he achieved something or got excited about something, his only option would be telling the empty air around him, hoping it would reach her. And if that was the case, how could he be excited about anything ever again?

Deep down, he knew that wasn't realistic. He didn't have Akiko, but he had Gordon. Gordon, who was probably at home, panicking and pacing grooves into the floor, thinking Kenji wouldn't come home. The same Gordon who had made a shitty decision but did it to help Akiko in her final months of life. The Gordon who took care of everything for two years while Kenji worked to progress his career.

Because that was the truth. Kenji could claim he didn't ask Gordon to sacrifice anything, but that wasn't entirely true. Kenji lived his life knowing Gordon would mediate the fallout from whatever decisions Kenji made, and he did it because making Kenji happy made him happy.

When he pulled up to the house twenty minutes later, Kenji glanced up at the windows, hoping he could see Gordon's silhouette. The lights were on in the living room and bedroom, so he must have been awake, but he wasn't visible through the curtains.

When he told Gordon about CWA tonight, he'd be telling his best friend. The one person in the world who would know how much it meant to him to have made it. It should have been exciting, but it felt muted by their argument and Akiko's absence. The memory of their fight hung around him like a fog, and he was still so hurt he couldn't see through it. But he also knew he hurt Gordon, and maybe had been for so much longer than he ever could have imagined.

He wished he hadn't found out about the contract tonight. It felt like such a waste.

As he walked up the steps to the door, it opened unexpectedly. Gordon was there, sad, worried, and unsure of how to handle Kenji's presence.

"Hi," he said. He stepped to the side and let Kenji walk in, plenty of room between them.

Kenji toed off his shoes and dropped his gym bag by the door.

"Hey."

"I am so sorry for what I did. I've been sitting here for two hours reliving our fight and I just... I shouldn't have gone behind your back. I know how much it meant to you to pay the loan yourself, and you're right, I took that from you. I feel awful."

"I know." Kenji grabbed his hand and squeezed before heading to get changed.

Gordon followed him to the bedroom. Kenji sighed and sat

on the edge of his bed. That wasn't hidden enough, so he laid on his side and put a pillow over his head when he heard Gordon mumble something.

"What?" he said, muffled from beneath the pillow. He felt the mattress dip on the other side of the bed under the weight of Gordon's body.

"Please, talk to me. Yell at me or something."

"I don't want to yell at you."

"What?"

"I don't want to yell at you. I want to… I don't know."

"I can't hear you with the pillow." Gordon lifted the pillow from Kenji's face and must have seen Kenji's puffy eyes because he gasped softly. "God, I'm so sorry. I wish I knew how to fix this."

"It's not that. I went for a drive and talked to Akiko for a while. It just got me all in my feelings."

"Oh."

"I'm sad and hurt, but I still love you, Gordon. But I'm so embarrassed, knowing she asked you for this. She really didn't believe in me."

"Of course she did. She believed in you, but she also just loved you. And she was tired. But when we talked about it, the only thing she cared about was that your life was easier, so you could focus on wrestling and not the store."

Kenji nodded, and Gordon shifted with slow, careful movements until he was on his back next to him. His fingers reached out and touched Kenji's forearm.

"I'm sorry, too," Kenji said.

"For what?"

"Being a fucking asshole, for one. I'd be so lost without you, and I'm so sorry I made you feel like you weren't part of the shop and an equal part of our lives, like your help and sacrifices didn't mean anything. They meant *everything*. I wish

I had been better at acknowledging that, and I'll never make that mistake again." Kenji's fingers crept up to Gordon's and latched on.

"It's okay."

"It's not, really. Even when I got home, you apologized to me again, after I'd been so shitty to you."

"Well, you deserv—"

"Stop. I love you, okay? I'm sorry. Just accept that. Or don't, that's your decision. But don't argue with me. I want you to know that I am sorry, and that I appreciate everything you do for me. But also, I'm exhausted. Do you mind if we just sleep?"

"No, of course not."

CHAPTER 27

THEY WOKE UP NEXT TO EACH OTHER IN KENJI'S ROOM, ON TOP OF the covers, both in the previous day's clothes. When Gordon opened his eyes, he looked over to find Kenji silently staring at the ceiling.

"Hey."

"Good morning."

"What are you looking at?" Gordon asked, following Kenji's line of sight.

"Whenever I stayed here before, I'd always count the texture bumps inside that little water stain."

"Oh."

"I always get up to like sixty-two or sixty-three before my eyes start crossing and I can't identify them individually anymore."

"Hmm." Gordon tried counting them, but by the time he got to eleven his eyes hurt.

Kenji reached over and grabbed Gordon's hand, squeezing it. "I love you."

"I love you too."

"I got a contract buyout offer from CWA."

Gordon let go of Kenji's hand and lifted himself up on his elbows, his head swiveling to look at Kenji. "What?!"

"Mike told me last night. That's why I got home so late."

Gordon jumped off the bed and ran to Kenji's side. "Kenji! This is fucking incredible! Holy shit!"

But Kenji wasn't reacting the way he thought he would. He hadn't even smiled yet, and Gordon was awash in guilt thinking he'd broken Kenji's spirit.

"Aren't you excited?" Gordon asked.

"Yeah, I mean… yes. I am. But I don't know."

Gordon knelt by the side of the bed and turned Kenji's face so they were looking at each other. "What don't you know?"

"I just can't get excited about it."

"Because of what I did?"

"Not entirely."

"Then what is it? I promise, I'm not trying to fix this." Gordon said, grabbing Kenji's hand again. "I just want to listen."

"Last night, I had this realization. This is the most pivotal moment of my career, you know? It's almost every Titan's dream. I should be bouncing off the walls, but instead, I'm just empty. I want to tell her so badly. I want her to be proud of me."

"She is proud of you."

Kenji scoffed, then sniffled. "She's dead."

Gordon's heart ached with the weight Kenji's pain. But he was right, of course. "Yeah, she is. But that doesn't matter. I still tell her everything, and listening to her voice in my head helps. For example, she told me not to call you every five minutes last night when I thought you were leaving me forever."

Kenji's lips twisted into a tiny smile. "She would have told you to get a grip."

Gordon laughed a little. "She probably wished she could cause a lightning storm that struck my phone, and my phone only."

"I thought I saw a small flash over our neighborhood when I was sitting on Mt. Tabor last night."

"Listen, Kenji, I won't pretend I know what it's like to have something like this happen and not be able to tell the person you want to tell. But… I'm really fucking proud of you. You did it, just like you said you would."

"Yeah. I did."

Kenji finally smiled, and Gordon couldn't help but smile back even as his own emotions were in turmoil. A CWA contract had been Kenji's dream for years and watching him achieve it was beyond anything Gordon had felt for him before, but… this meant he would be moving to Boston.

"Do you want to go get breakfast?" Gordon asked, unsure what else to say.

"Yes, I do."

Gordon stood up and brushed some lint from his pants before he pulled Kenji off the bed and gave him a kiss, quick and soft. That was going to be it before he went to find fresh clothes, but Kenji pulled him back and wrapped his arms around his neck, kissing him harder, not letting go. Both of them had morning breath and it was really kind of gross, but he couldn't bring himself to care because Kenji was still here, and still loved him, even after what he'd done. So, he leaned into it and trailed his hands down Kenji's body, grabbing him and pulling them into each other, dumbfounded again at how he'd been so lucky to end up here.

Before things heated up further, Kenji pulled away and scrunched up his face. "Man. We both taste awful."

"Yeah." Gordon grimaced. "Sorry about that."

"Let's brush our teeth and *then* get breakfast."

. . .

IT HAD RAINED OVERNIGHT and the sidewalks were still damp, so the walk to Gordon's favorite brunch spot meant avoiding puddles and worms. He held onto Kenji and kept their bodies close, using the smaller sidewalk footprint as an excuse. Kenji didn't buy it, but he also didn't complain.

Neither did Gordon, until they turned the corner and saw a line of patrons spilling out of the restaurant.

"Ugh, why does everyone in the city need brunch right now?" Gordon asked.

"I mean, we're here too. We're part of the problem."

"Yeah, but we live nearby. These people definitely drove over here. I can tell."

Kenji looked at the people gathered by the entrance and squinted at them. "How can you tell? The lack of rain jackets?"

Gordon stifled a smile and gave him a kiss on the cheek. "You are so sweet. I love you so much."

Kenji smiled back at him, but then looked back to the people, as if he was still trying to figure out how Gordon knew.

By the time they were seated, Kenji was on his third cup of coffee and had spent the thirty minutes they'd waited in line talking about Kiko's and the plans he had for its future. Gordon hadn't heard him so excited about the store in a while, and while initially he'd been interested in Kenji's ideas, he started to worry that Kenji was stuck on the store and hadn't mentioned CWA or Boston at all.

"I'm going to get pancakes," Kenji said. He patted his stomach. "Cheat day."

"Didn't you have a cheat day like two days ago?"

"Cheat days. With an S."

Gordon laughed. "I'm not judging. You could have a cheat life and I'd think that was great."

"Cheat week, here I come."

Gordon tilted his head and looked at Kenji. He opened his mouth to speak, but the server stopped by to take their order. When they finally left, Gordon leaned forward on the table, resting his forearms there, reaching out for Kenji's hand.

"Hey," he said.

"Hey!"

"Um, you've been talking about Kiko's a lot today, and all the future plans you have."

"Yes. I have a lot of ideas. Ooh, what if we expanded to outdoor plants?"

"Well, first we'd have to have room outdoors."

"We could do seeds."

"Yeah, we could, but…"

Kenji poured more sugar into his recently refreshed coffee and stirred it, not looking at Gordon.

"I can't help but notice you haven't said anything about Boston at all, though," Gordon said, tapping Kenji's hand with his finger, trying to coax him into looking at him.

"So?"

"Well, don't you want to talk about it? Talk about where you're going to live and when your debut is? I want to hear everything."

"I don't know anything yet."

"Okay."

He didn't want to push Kenji into talking about it, but he could feel the presence of whatever was bothering him. Kenji's thoughts were calm and weirdly focused, which meant he was avoiding something.

Maybe after breakfast, when Kenji was full of pancakes and coffee, he'd be willing to open up.

The sun evaporated all the puddles while they ate, and their walk home was pleasant and warm. Gordon braced himself before asking Kenji, again, if he wanted to talk about Boston.

"So, um," he started. He chickened out. "Are you going to the gym later?"

"Nah."

"Really?"

"Don't feel like it. Do you want to go into Kiko's with me? We could talk autumnal decorations," Kenji said. "I'm thinking... *leaves.*"

"We're not open today."

"Yeah, so we can get a lot done!"

"Kenji."

Kenji kept walking and took the steps to Gordon's house two at a time, leaving Gordon behind on the walkway.

"Kenji!"

"What?"

"Can you just wait? Why are you being weird about Boston?"

Kenji didn't respond, just turned around and threw the screen door open before going inside. Gordon lingered on the walkway, unsure how to approach him, or if he even should.

Obviously, something was wrong, but repeating the mistakes he'd made by constantly trying to rescue Kenji wasn't something he could afford to do again. Especially if the reason Kenji was unwilling to talk was even partly because of their argument the night before.

He decided to give Kenji space for the moment. There was work waiting for him, like always, so once he got inside the house, he grabbed his work bag and went into his office. He left the door open as a quiet invitation, just in case Kenji decided to wander by.

After wrapping up a few emails, Gordon was deciding whether to start on a new project at work or doom scroll on his phone to eat up time. Neither sounded particularly appealing. He heard a soft knock on the door and turned around to find Kenji leaning on the doorway, looking dispirited and sad.

"Hey," Gordon said.

"Hi."

"I wasn't sure if I should come find you."

"That's okay. I needed to think."

"Yeah? What did you think about?" Gordon asked, hoping his tone was casual enough to keep him from disappearing again.

Kenji walked into Gordon's office and sat on the chair next to the window. He put his foot on the windowsill and poked at the blinds with his toe.

"You need to dust these more often."

"Okay. I will."

"I don't want the store anymore," Kenji said, staring at his toes, his face emotionless and blank.

"You don't want it? Like at all?"

"Yeah. I want to sell it."

"What about all those plans you were making at brunch?"

"I don't actually want to do any of those things."

"Okay. I'm confused."

"Akiko worked until the day she died because she wanted me to inherit the store. We discussed her selling it over the years and she always said no, because it was supposed to be mine someday. What kind of person am I if I turn around and sell it as soon as she's dead? How could I live with myself?"

Gordon didn't know what to say. He could offer platitudes, of course. Tell him Akiko wouldn't want him to do anything he didn't want to, or that his happiness was what was most important to her. But even if they were true, he knew Kenji wouldn't want to hear it.

"You're a person whose life has changed paths. It happens."

"I guess."

"Let's find a buyer, then."

"What?"

"You can sell it. Use the money to start your life in Boston."

Kenji just sighed.

"Or not. You could hire employees?"

"I don't want to run a store from across the country. I just don't... want it."

Gordon leaned back in his chair and looked at Kenji, whose face was resting against the back of the chair, and he was still staring out the window, refusing to look in Gordon's direction.

"So, sell it. She would be mad at you if you kept the store and it turned to shit because you were being precious about its ownership."

Kenji huffed out a laugh through his nose. "Yeah, that's true."

"There's someone out there whose life's dream is to own a plant store. Probably. I mean, not me, and if I never step foot in one again, it'll be too soon. But some people really like that shit," Gordon said. He nudged Kenji's knee with his foot to make him smile.

"That's true. The store does deserve an owner who loves it," Kenji said.

"Like a dog."

"Yeah. Or an iguana."

"Obviously. So, we look for a buyer. Okay?"

"Okay. Thank you for convincing me I'm not awful."

"But wait. You said Boston was an 'option.'"

"It is," Kenji said, finally showing some emotion on his

face. Unfortunately, it was a single raised eyebrow that said, "Gordon is kind of an idiot."

Gordon rolled his eyes. "It's not an option. It's your future. You're not seriously considering staying in Portland, are you?"

"I mean, not really. I want to go to Boston. But what about us?"

"What *about* us? You realize I've waited ten years for this, right? I think I can handle visits to Boston for a year or two until you have a little more freedom," Gordon lied. He probably couldn't, really.

"Ugh, I hate that idea," Kenji said, frowning. "I can't believe we're finally here and I'm leaving."

Gordon nodded. "It will suck."

That was an understatement. There was no way Gordon would ruin this for Kenji by being whiny and unsupportive now that Kenji was finally talking about it, but inside, he was trying to stop the pieces of his heart from crumbling into dust.

"Can't you just come with me?"

Gordon laughed, unsure if Kenji was serious. Of course, Gordon wanted to move with him. Even before they were together, Gordon couldn't handle the idea of Kenji moving to Boston and leaving him in Portland.

In fact, whenever Gordon imagined this moment over the years, Kenji would tell him about the contract while confessing his undying love, then ask him to move to Boston to start their new life together. But in his more rational fantasies, those grounded in even the slightest bit of reality, he knew that wouldn't be an option because of Akiko and the store.

But, with Akiko gone, and the store moving to the hands of someone else, there was no reason he had to stay here. All his ties to the city were gone, other than the job he hated.

"I'm serious," Kenji said, taking his foot off the windowsill. He leaned towards Gordon and grabbed his hand. "I know you have a job and house here, but they have that stuff in Boston."

"Maybe Victor will let me work remotely," Gordon said, his heart picking up a bit.

"Maybe," Kenji said, his nose scrunching up. "But it is Victor."

"Well, I could quit my job."

Kenji choked out a laugh. "Sure."

"I could! I hate working for Victor."

"Gordon. You'd have a panic attack if you quit your job and moved to Boston with nothing lined up."

"No! I wouldn't. Well, I might, but I have some savings. You'll be working. I can be your house… boyfriend."

Kenji put his hand to Gordon's forehead.

"What are you doing?"

"You don't seem feverish…"

"Stop! I'm serious. I have savings. I have a good resume. Stop trying to talk me out of this," Gordon said, his cheeks heating up. "I've decided—right now. I'm quitting."

"I'll believe it when I see it, buddy," Kenji said.

"Look! I'll text Victor right now."

"Uh huh."

Gordon pulled his phone out and pulled up his text thread with Victor. He cleared his throat and began narrating the text he was typing. "Victor… please consider this my two weeks' notice. While my experience with this company has been mostly positive, my manager sucks, and nobody likes him, especially not me. Best, Gordon."

Kenji gaped at him. "Gordon! Are you serious?"

"No. Of course not. I did text him to set up a meeting, though. Maybe he'll let me work remotely, but if not, oh well. On to the next," Gordon said, though he felt a little sweaty.

"Who are you?!"

"Shut up." Gordon's lips turned up into the smallest smile and Kenji laughed again.

"I'm sorry it took me ten years to realize our relationship would have been even better if we were sleeping together."

Gordon stood up and grabbed Kenji's hand, pulling him to his feet before giving him a quick kiss. "You should be. You have a lot of time to make up for."

Kenji pulled Gordon in for a kiss before backing him up and pinning him against the wall. "Let's get to it."

CHAPTER 28

"I swear to God, Gordon, if you ask me one more time if you should bring a specific shirt you haven't worn in over five years, I will drag you to the arena in Boston, throw you in the ring, and pay Dom a hundred dollars to sit on you."

Gordon smiled a too-big smile at Kenji. "Okay, if you must."

"No! In a non-sexy way. A crushing way," he said, wishing he'd never showed Gordon any photos of his new coworkers. The ones where Dom's white shirt had stuck to his body after he jumped into the pool at the barbeque had been of particular interest to Gordon.

"I'm sorry! I just don't know what to get rid of!"

Kenji grabbed the shirt Gordon was talking about and held it up. "You've literally never mentioned liking this band, and right now, I am looking at you through a hole in the armpit."

"It could be a good sleep shirt."

Kenji made a noise that landed somewhere between a sigh and a scream. "Okay, you know what? I love you, and that's why I have to leave the room right now."

Gordon laughed from his pile of clothes on the floor and shoved more of them into a garbage bag, which was how he was choosing to pack his clothing for the move—another reason Kenji needed to leave the room immediately. He hoped wherever they ended up in Boston had separate closets for each of them.

The whole thing was starting to feel real and his time at Titan was winding down, which had him on edge. Mike was letting him out of his contract early so he could focus on selling Kiko's and finding somewhere to land in Boston, but he still felt like he was spiraling with an endless list of tasks that would never get completed in time. Watching Gordon help by packing his toiletries in the same box as his wrestling memorabilia was enough to make him want to tear his hair out.

He'd been wrapping glassware in the kitchen for a while, which had become meditative and quite enjoyable, when Gordon came out, phone in hand.

"Put that down and go find something to wear," he said.

"Wear where?" Kenji asked, then laughed. "Wear where."

"I called the movers and asked if they can pack, too, so we don't have to do any of this. And now I want to take you to dinner before your party."

"Oh, thank God. If I had to watch you put more stuff into garbage bags, I think I would have climbed in one myself."

"Okay, you know what? Go get dressed, or I will ask them specifically to pack all of your stuff, including the plants, in garbage bags."

Kenji gave Gordon a kiss and took off to his room to find an outfit.

∾

WHEN THEY FINALLY PULLED UP TO the arena, they were more than fashionably late, which was not Gordon's fault at all. Kenji had asked to stop by the gas station to get a lottery ticket after passing a billboard on the freeway showing the enormous jackpot, and then he remembered all the succulents he'd started for the Titan staff were back at Kiko's. The party was already in full force by the time they got to the doors, which was not Gordon's ideal way to enter a party. But, he reminded himself, it was all for Kenji.

Gordon opened the door and led Kenji in, the sounds of music and laughter and yelling growing louder as they walked down the hall towards the mass of people they saw in the main room. They could see people messing around in the ring, which was lit up by colorful spotlights, and a handful of kids running top speed into the grappling dummies they kept around. They were all familiar faces, all people Gordon had met at various Titan-related activities over the last few years, and he felt a surprise pang of sadness—he was really going to miss them.

"Oh, my God," Kenji breathed, his eyes wide with delight.

Gordon glanced at Kenji and his heart skipped a beat seeing how happy he was. He deserved every bit of this celebration. There was no one who put in more effort to achieving their dreams.

He nodded at Niall and Anthony across the arena, then looked to Kenji again. He was staring at the banner hanging above the ring, laughing. He followed Kenji's line of sight and what he saw was ridiculous, but as he glanced back to a very proud Will, he realized it was not at all surprising. The banner read GOODBYE GORDON in enormous letters, and a much smaller banner beneath it read congrats ken.

"Gordon is here!" Will's voice echoed through the room and startled Gordon. "Hey, Gordo!"

"This is so fucking stupid," Gordon said.

"I love this so much," Kenji said. "We're taking that home."

"Hey guys."

"Will. Nice banner," Gordon said.

"Thank you, it was not cheap, but you're worth it, buddy."

Gordon laughed. "Thank you."

"Yeah, and check it out," Will said, pointing towards a group of kids gathered around a guy wearing a fancy balloon hat. "He'll make you anything you want. A crown, a sword, a wiener dog on a leash…"

"You got a balloon guy?"

"There are kids here!"

"I'm going to go get a hat and mingle. Be back soon," Kenji said, walking off towards Mike and his wife.

"When does he leave?" Will asked, watching Kenji walk away.

"Tomorrow morning."

Tomorrow was so soon. Not that it mattered, because Gordon would be joining him in a few weeks when the keys to Kiko's were handed over. His sister's friend was renting his house, so that was set. But still, he hated being away from Kenji at all, especially now that Mike had kept him local since he got the news about his contract.

"This sucks."

Gordon shrugged one shoulder, not wanting to dwell on how sad he was. "It does. But it's good, too. Kenji is excited."

"Yeah, I bet." Will looked at him sadly. "Do you think you'll ever move back?"

"I don't know. I guess it depends on what CWA asks of him."

"That makes sense."

"We'll see you out there some day, I bet!"

Will punched him in the arm playfully. "I don't think so,

man. I'm not cut out for that life. I'm happy out here. Plus, I really like your sister…"

"That's great, man. I've heard you're okay, too," he said.

"Uh oh. What's going on over there, I wonder?" Will said. He put an olive in his mouth and chewed slowly, probably trying to eavesdrop. Gordon couldn't blame him.

"I'm not sure. I know a couple of those kids, though. They helped out at Kiko's when Kenji was in Boston. They're good eggs."

Will laughed. "I love it. They look like good eggs! Look at them in their little party outfits."

"Whoa, Curt looks mad."

"Yeah, he does. You should go find out what he's mad about."

"Me?"

"Yes, then come back and tell me what happened."

~

"Mike, hey!" Kenji finally found Mike and his wife, Linda, after he'd stopped to request a purple and red balloon crown and loaded up a plate of food at the buffet table.

"Kenji, how's it going? Are you ready to make me proud?"

"Well, kind of. I'm nervous. But I'm excited, yes."

"It's going to be great. Linda here was just telling me about a cat she saw today at work. His name was Ken Vee Jr."

"What?!" Kenji laughed. "That is the best!"

"He was very pretty. Long white hair, long tail, big green eyes," Linda said.

"Just like me."

Linda smiled at him and Mike punched his arm, almost causing him to drop his plate.

"I'm going to miss everyone so much, this sucks."

"We'll miss you, too."

Kenji looked across the room and squinted. "What's going on with Curt? He looks mad."

"Curt is always mad."

Kenji laughed. "Yeah. That's true."

"But whoa, yeah, he does look mad. I'll be right back," Mike said before walking towards Curt and the group of teenagers, Linda trailing behind him.

Gordon approached Kenji, cringing as Mike and Curt's voices carried through the room.

"What the hell happened?" Kenji asked.

"Curt's teenagers broke a bunch of pyro equipment. I think they wanted to sell it, but they broke it when they tried to shove it in their bags."

"Oh. Shit."

"I don't envy Curt," Gordon said.

Will approached them with Anthony and his wife in tow, and all five of them pretended not to listen to the argument behind them, which was hard, because Mike was loud.

"Gordon told me what happened," Kenji said to Anthony. "Word travels fast."

"Apparently!" Anthony said.

"Congratulations, Kenji. I know Anthony is really going to miss you," Chloe said, rubbing Kenji's arm gently.

"I'm going to miss him a lot," Kenji said, his mouth turning into a small frown.

Anthony reached out and squeezed Kenji's shoulder. "Maybe I'll see you out there some time."

"Hey, Gordon, this is my wife, Chloe."

"Hi. It's nice to meet you finally."

"It's nice to finally meet you, too, after so many years of this guy talking about you two," she said, nudging Anthony.

Gordon grimaced. "All good things, I hope."

"Mostly," she said, smiling. "Although, I did once overhear Kenji on the phone complaining to Ant that you're always on him about wasting seltzer. I think that's the worst of it, though."

"I told him he could use it to water the plants, and he didn't believe me! And I asked him, who do you think would know better? Me, or you? And he didn't have an answer for that," Kenji said.

"He did that to me, too! We were doing the dishes after a party, and he wouldn't stop scrubbing them before putting them in the dishwasher. I told him he didn't have to pre-wash them, and he didn't believe me, even after I brought up the instruction manual on my phone," Will said.

"Okay, guys, that's—"

"Hey, I have one, too! Remember when Gordon told me to put heat on that bruised rib I had, and I told him Mitch specifically told me not to use heat in the first forty-eight hours and Gordon was unsure about that?" Anthony asked.

Kenji gasped. "I do remember that! Gordon, being loudly wrong about weird, unimportant stuff is like… your thing."

"My *thing*?"

"Yeah," Anthony nodded. "It totally is."

"Are you guys talking about Gordon being loudly wrong about stuff?" Mike said, making his way back to the group.

"Okay, Kenji and I are leaving now." Gordon shoved Kenji away from the group and Kenji laughed.

"Aw, I should have told them about how you said you can't store soy sauce on the fridge door."

"The temperature fluctuates!"

"It's salt!"

"Anyway," Gordon said, sighing, "why don't you start making your rounds."

Kenji exchanged hugs and fist bumps with his colleagues. Gordon hung back slightly, offering handshakes and nods to a few of them, offering a steady presence to an emotional Kenji. There were promises to keep in touch, though Kenji knew that was unlikely to happen, which made his chest tighten. He received a few teary goodbyes and he did his best to power through without breaking down. After saying goodbye to everyone he saw, sometimes more than once, he watched Gordon hug his sister.

GORDON AND KENJI ended up on top of Mt. Tabor again in the same spot Kenji sat when he told Akiko about his contract.

"Is this okay?" Kenji asked. "I just don't want to go home yet."

"Of course. Whatever you want."

Kenji dropped his head against the headrest. "I can't believe I'll never be inside Kiko's again."

"That's not necessarily true. We can visit when we come back to Portland," Gordon said. "And the buyers seem great. I bet they'll make it even better."

"You know what I mean, though."

"Yeah. It's bittersweet." Gordon reached over and held Kenji's hand. "Good, though. Right?"

"Yeah. It is."

Gordon turned around and grabbed something from the back seat and set it on the center console.

"What's this?" Kenji asked.

"Well, we won't be together on Akiko's birthday next week, so I thought we could celebrate now."

Kenji opened the small box and found a tiny strawberry cake inside. He stared at it and felt his throat tighten and tears well up in his eyes, but he blinked them away. It was Akiko's favorite cake, and even though she claimed she didn't care about birthdays, Kenji always brought her one at the store.

"You didn't have to do this," he said.

"I know. I wanted to, though."

CHAPTER 29

The airport was crowded and overwhelming, as airports tend to be, but this time felt a little more suffocating. Gordon was walking Kenji inside even though he'd told him it was unnecessary, but he was secretly glad, not sure he was capable of handling it on his own. He'd told Gordon he would just wait until they were able to fly out together, but Gordon said he'd wanted Kenji to fly out and get his bearings before he was there to distract him.

It was two and a half weeks. Kenji was being a huge baby, but he couldn't help it. He was nervous about leaving Portland. Everything he'd ever known was there, and the last memories of his aunt were staying there, and there was no way to make more in Boston.

"Want to get a snack before you board?"

"No, I'm too nervous. I don't like to eat when I fly."

"You're not going to arrive in Boston for like nine hours!" Gordon said, incredulous. "You're going to starve."

"Hmm." He eyed the coffee kiosk nearby. "Maybe just a bagel."

They made their way to the kiosk and Kenji ordered a

bagel with nothing on it, not even toasted. Gordon wrinkled his nose.

"Not even toasted?"

"I'm nervous about the flight! Leave me alone. It's not my fault this is the first time you've seen me in an airport."

"It kind of is. Remember when I offered to take you to Seoul when I went on that business trip like two years ago?"

"I had a road trip!"

"It was one night in Vancouver, Washington. You slept at home."

"Whatever!" Kenji looked down at his sad, unadorned bagel and sighed. "It will be fine. I will be fine."

Gordon put his arm around Kenji and squeezed. "You will be fine. You'll be there before you know it."

"I hope so."

"You're over thinking this. Come sit."

They sat at a nearby café table and Gordon leaned his chin on one hand, staring at Kenji with a dopey smile on his face. Kenji took a small bite of his bagel and chewed slowly.

"Get your fill now, buddy. This face is outta here in about twenty minutes." He was trying to make himself laugh, but it didn't work.

"You look so content, eating that dry lump of wheat. I'm going to miss your terrible bread choices for the next few weeks."

"Are you?"

"No. But I know you'll have some waiting for me when I get home."

"Home, huh?" Kenji asked, finally giving Gordon a small smile.

"Well, yeah. It'll be home if you're there." Gordon shrugged and smiled back. He said it so simply, like it was so obvious.

Kenji looked at him for a moment and felt a quick pang of jealousy at Gordon's lack of uncertainty. His words buoyed him, though, and knowing Gordon would be there in a few weeks lessened some of the fear he had around their move.

"Yeah. I guess you're right. Home is where the heart is, and whatnot."

"And whatnot? Who the fuck says that?" Gordon laughed.

"I do!"

"I've never heard you say whatnot in ten years."

"I've definitely said whatnot many times over the last ten years." Kenji kicked him under the table before his eyes caught the departure board and he noticed the time. The first leg of his flight was departing in an hour, so he needed to get through security. "I have to go, I think."

"Alright. Hey. You'll be just fine, Kenj."

"I know." Kenji smiled at him. He felt like it was true that time.

"And please, when you land in Boston, eat something with protein in it." Gordon placed his hands on Kenji's shoulders and leaned forward, forcing Kenji to look in his eyes. "I cannot handle you calling me in a rage about not being able to find your sunglasses, even though it will be ten o'clock at night and you will have absolutely no use for them."

"Hanger is a real thing that affects millions of Americans, Gordon! You choose me, you choose all of me."

"Okay, you know what, I'm putting this twenty-dollar bill in here in case you lose your wallet or something." He shoved his hand into Kenji's pocket and pinched his thigh, making him yelp.

"We are in public!"

"Sorry," Gordon said, grinning.

"I'll call you when I land."

"Okay."

"I love you so much."

"I love you. Call me."

Gordon dropped a quick kiss on his cheek. Kenji headed for the security line, the rest of their lives laid out just a few steps ahead.

EPILOGUE

"WHERE THE HELL do they expect us to keep all of this?" Gordon was sitting in the middle of a pile of elaborate feather boas and fake fur boot wraps Kenji had brought home from work a few months earlier. He held one up and waved it at Kenji. "This one is like, forty pounds."

"It's not forty pounds," Kenji said, grabbing it from his hands before rubbing his face on it. "I don't know. Storage unit?"

"Is there some reason we have to keep them?"

"I can't get rid of them!" Kenji whined. "I have such fond memories of all of them."

"Okay. I'll look into a storage unit, I guess. Or, hey, why don't you send them to Titan?"

Kenji glared at him.

"Okay, sorry. Storage unit, got it."

Kenji had spent the last two years paying back the cost of the loan, which had been non-negotiable for him, but he secretly appreciated Gordon's willingness to accept smaller payments over time. They'd put the money in an account to use for a down payment on a townhouse, which was an upgrade from their current apartment, but still not very big. It had led to some arguments about what was worth keeping and what wasn't.

"Sorry we can't all store our things in garbage bags in the storage room, Gordon."

"I didn't store them in garbage bags! I consciously placed them in there so I could easily transport them to our new home. And now they are packed up in boxes. As you can see, all around us. Everywhere."

Kenji kissed the top of Gordon's head.

"I'll keep doing this, I guess," Gordon said, rubbing his hands over the faux fur. "It can all be stored, right?"

"Yes. Except for that furry purple vest. I'm keeping that for later." Kenji winked.

Gordon laughed and taped a box. "Okay. I'm looking forward to whatever you have planned. I think."

"Do you want to go for a hike?"

"Right now?" Gordon asked, looking around the room at the many boxes surrounding him. "I'm busy doing… this."

"I know. But I'm bored."

"Okay."

THEY ENDED up just outside of Boston at a relatively flat nature preserve, one they'd explored more than once, and that Kenji really seemed to like. He took off ahead of Gordon, who enjoyed the view of the water, the trees, the trails, and Kenji's tiny shorts that resurfaced very summer.

They sat on a bench overlooking the bay and Kenji took out the snacks he brought, offering some to Gordon.

"We should do this more often."

"We hike a lot."

"We could go more, though," Kenji said. "The water is nice."

"Okay. Whatever you want."

"Can iguanas walk on leashes?"

"I'm sure they can. Peony never has, though." Gordon looked at Kenji seriously. "We're not bringing him."

"Fine."

They sat together quietly, watching the gentle ripples in the water hitting the shore.

"I wonder if Akiko has made it this far," Gordon said. He assumed it would take longer than that but being near the water brought him some peace anyway.

"I hope so." Kenji waved at the water.

A while later, Kenji stood and raised his arms above his head, stretching his back before moving to his hamstrings.

"What are you doing?"

"I'll race you back."

"I'm not racing you."

"We'll see."

Gordon shook his head and stood, walking a normal pace in the direction of the car. Kenji took off running, disappearing behind some trees. Gordon paused for a moment, then stumbled exaggeratedly, yelling for Kenji to come back.

"Oh, my God! What happened?" Kenji said, running back to Gordon's side.

"I think I twisted my ankle on that rock," Gordon said, breathing heavily and grabbing his leg. "It really hurts."

"Can you stand?" Kenji reached down to lift Gordon into a standing position.

"I can stand, but I don't think I can walk."

"Shit, Gordon… I don't think I have any service out here," Kenji said, looking at his phone and holding it in the air.

"How far are we from the car? Like a mile?"

"I think so. What if I give you a piggyback ride?"

Gordon let out a breath and nodded. "Yeah, you might have to."

Kenji bent down slightly, hooking his hands behind Gordon's knees. Gordon put his arms over Kenji's shoulders and around his neck.

"You okay?"

"Pfft. You're like a backpack. No problem. Plus, now I don't have to go to the gym."

Gordon laughed and rested his head against Kenji's shoulder, holding on so he didn't slip out of Kenji's grip. As they approached the car twenty minutes later, Kenji was breathing so heavily Gordon almost felt guilty.

"Almost there," he wheezed. "I can see the car."

"You can put me down now. I think I can make it the rest of the way."

"Are you sure?" Kenji asked, letting Gordon slip out of his grip slowly. He turned around and held Gordon's waist. "Can you walk?"

Gordon smiled at him and took off running to the car.

"What the fuck? You asshole!"

He looked over his shoulder one last time, catching sight of Kenji's pink cheeks and tired smile, then climbed into the car and waited for his ride.

The End

ONE MORE THING

Indie wrestling promotions in many parts of the US (and world) are LGBTQ+ friendly and awesome, and I encourage you to check out your local events! And if you're ever in Portland, I'll go with you.

I donate a portion of my royalties every month to LGBTQ+ wrestlers and LGBTQ+ focused promos. If you have suggestions on who should receive a donation, please send me an email or a note on social media so I can include them!

valsimonswrites@gmail.com

ACKNOWLEDGMENTS

To Deb, Gordon's number one cheerleader and the person who all but gave birth to him, I hope you love him. Don't tell me if you don't, though.

To my beta readers Jenny, Danielle, Ellie, and Julia, thank you for the time and energy you put into reading the beta draft of this. It feels like a new book in some ways, and I'm sorry for what I put you through with Kenji v1.0. Whoops. (Except the seltzer thing—Kenji and I cannot apologize for our carbonation preferences.)

To my sensitivity readers Zeus and N, thank you for your expertise and lived experiences, allowing me to ask questions, and creating more authentic characters in Kenji, Akiko, and Gordon.

To my Discord writing buddies, thank you for your endless patience while I complained, hours and hours of sprints, holding my hand while I edited sex scenes with one eye closed (I'm working on it), and one lively discussion about whether or not Kenji and Gordon experienced a third act breakup. I still say no.

To Rebecca, because in some ways, these are all for you. Or us. Or something. :)

And to my family and parents, always. I miss you, dad.

ABOUT THE AUTHOR

Val is a romance enthusiast whose journey began with a broken ankle, eight weeks of bed rest, and a surprisingly prolific backlog of X-Files fan fiction (thank you, authors). Craving stories that didn't revolve around Mulder and Scully, she eventually turned to books. She spent years devouring stories that ended in happily-ever-afters before she decided to write the books she longed to read but couldn't find.

She was born and raised in Portland, Oregon, and just kept living there.

This is the second book in the Titans Wrestling series. The first book, Headlocks and Heartbreak, can be found on Amazon or through her social media accounts.